# He'd disappeared from her life for years,

and then reappeared like magic. Seeming so much like the Mitch she'd loved with all the depth of her romantic girl's heart—yet a stranger. A man with edges of danger that excited her…secrets that scared the living daylights out of her. And an untamed sexuality she suspected she'd only glimpsed so far.

How could a man like Mitch, always on the fringes of risk, want *her?* At first, yeah, for the family he'd never had; she'd understood that even as she hated it. But now? Dare she believe him when he said he wanted her—only her? He seemed to be burning alive for her, but, as she'd found out over the past few weeks, nothing with Mitch was what it seemed.

And finding out the lies beneath the secrets would break her heart.

Dear Reader,

This month we have something really special on tap for you. *The Cinderella Mission*, by Catherine Mann, is the first of three FAMILY SECRETS titles, all of them prequels to our upcoming anthology *Broken Silence* and then a twelve book stand-alone FAMILY SECRETS continuity. These books are cutting edge, combining dark doings, mysterious experiments and overwhelming passion into a mix you won't be able to resist. Next month, the story continues with Linda Castillo's *The Phoenix Encounter*.

Of course, this being Intimate Moments, the excitement doesn't stop there. Award winner Justine Davis offers up another of her REDSTONE, INCORPORATED tales, *One of These Nights*. A scientist who's as handsome as he is brilliant finds himself glad to welcome his sexy bodyguard—and looking forward to exploring just what her job description means. *Wilder Days* (leading to wilder nights?) is the newest from reader favorite Linda Winstead Jones. It will have you turning the pages so fast, you'll lose track of time. Ingrid Weaver begins a new military miniseries, EAGLE SQUADRON, with *Eye of the Beholder*. There will be at least two follow-ups, so keep *your* eyes open so you don't miss them. Evelyn Vaughn, whose miniseries THE CIRCLE was a standout in our former Shadows line, makes her Intimate Moments debut with *Buried Secrets*, a paranormal tale that's as passionate as it is spooky. And Aussie writer Melissa James is back with *Who Do You Trust?* This is a deeply emotional "friends become lovers" reunion romance, one that will captivate you from start to finish.

Enjoy! And come back next month for more of the best and most exciting romance around—right here in Silhouette Intimate Moments.

Leslie J. Wainger
Executive Senior Editor

Please address questions and book requests to:
Silhouette Reader Service
U.S.: 3010 Walden Ave., P.O. Box 1325, Buffalo, NY 14269
Canadian: P.O. Box 609, Fort Erie, Ont. L2A 5X3

# Who Do You Trust?
## MELISSA JAMES

Silhouette®

INTIMATE MOMENTS™

Published by Silhouette Books

America's Publisher of Contemporary Romance

**SILHOUETTE BOOKS**

ISBN 0-373-27276-6

WHO DO YOU TRUST?

Copyright © 2003 by Lisa Chaplin

This edition published by arrangement with Harlequin Books S.A.

® and TM are trademarks of Harlequin Books S.A., used under license.
Trademarks indicated with ® are registered in the United States Patent
and Trademark Office, the Canadian Trade Marks Office and in other
countries.

Visit Silhouette at www.eHarlequin.com

**Printed in U.S.A.**

**Books by Melissa James**

Silhouette Intimate Moments

*Her Galahad* #1182

---

## MELISSA JAMES

is a mother of three living in a beach suburb in county New South Wales. A former nurse, waitress, store assistant, perfume and chocolate (yum!) demonstrator among other things, she believes in taking on new jobs for the fun experience. She'll try almost anything at least once to see what it feels like—a fact that scares her family on regular occasions. She fell into writing by accident when her husband brought home an article stating how much a famous romance author earned, and she thought, "I can do that!" Years later, she found her niche at Silhouette Intimate Moments. Currently writing a pilot/spy series set in the South Pacific, she can be found most mornings walking and swimming at her local beach with her husband, or every afternoon running around to her kids' sporting hobbies, while dreaming of flying, scuba diving, belaying down a cave or over a cliff—anywhere her characters are at the time!

## Acknowledgments

I wish to give thanks to my editor, Gail Chasan, for liking this book and thinking up its title, and to Gillian Hanna, for loving this book and giving pertinent suggestions, and also to Susan Litman for the same. Thank you, ladies. Deep thanks once again to Andrea Johnston and Maryanne Cappelluti, my dear friends and trusted critique partners, who always tell me what I need to hear. And to my daughter Jaime, whose ideas on what a hero should be helped bring Mitch's background and character to life. Finally, thanks to Deri Banez and Manuel Hanares, for sharing their knowledge of the Tagalog language with me.

And a very special thanks for this story must go to those who helped inspire it: to the refugees of the world, those suffering through war, so many helped, so many others merely unheard cries of protest amid the problems in more affluent countries.

## Dedication

To my very own Lissa. This book is for you. I love you. We will never forget. Your loving Aunty and adopted "Mum."

# *Prologue*

*Ka-Nin-Put Village, Tumah-ra Island, Arafura Sea*

McCluskey pulled back on the throttle to lose altitude: eight thousand feet and falling.

*Don't go beneath ten thousand feet before the official UN nod to go, Skydancer. Strict government orders, McCluskey. The militia shoots first and won't ask questions later.*

Anson had known the orders were impossible when he gave them, which was why he'd sent him to this war-ravaged island. Mitch McCluskey, code name: Skydancer. Also known as the rule breaker.

His cover was perfect, bona fide work with the Vincent Foundation, doing food drops to war-torn towns and villages the world over. He handed out bags of grain and long-life milk, throwing extras at the militia to stop them from shooting pregnant women and hungry kids, snatching food to tame their aggressive corps. He had great footage—if you could stomach watching it—of Tumah-ran men torching buildings in their hometowns, shooting old people, dragging girls and young women away with them. Boys as young as ten destroying their neighbors' homes and tearing friends' families apart for the sake of the warped politics they'd been force-fed—in reality, for control of the oil-rich shelf below the coral reefs surrounding the little island, an untamed paradise until the hated strike of black gold.

Then he'd returned to Darwin and traded the official DC-10 for his own Maule bush plane, on recon work for the Nighthawks, a select bunch of expert international troubleshooters. Answerable only to Nick Anson, an ex-CIA hotshot who'd made it his business to stop military takeovers in small nations from becoming bloodbaths. Only the cream of the top brass had even heard of Nighthawks. The heads of governments of the world only used them when they had to make public denials of involvement. If the rebel flyboys, ex-Navy SEALs and one-time Special Services or Green Berets were captured in hostile territory, they were on their own.

He wasn't gonna get squat on film this high up, with this dark, turbulent band of monsoon cloud beneath him. He had to drop lower. After Bosnia and East Timor, the world wouldn't invade another disputed territory unless there was compelling evidence of human rights abuse by the ruling junta.

Which was today's job description. Survey the hot-spot island, make a lightning check of the land for incinerated pits or half-hidden, telltale pockmarks, and bring back footage to give the government—and the media, if those in power didn't want to know. Give the disaster-hungry rumormongers the irrefutable proof of what the world didn't want to know about.

Mass graves of the militia's victims.

Like the ones he'd found and filmed in thick forest close to the Albanian border. The ones that still gave him nightmares. The dead faces still wearing looks of terror—begging for help that never came. Pleading for their lives as they were mercilessly gunned down, old and young, women and babies—

But not the young girls. They had a worse fate.

Damn, I'm getting too old for this.

He lowered the plane by the nose through clashing, roiling clouds, until the altimeter hit four thousand feet. No weapon possessed by Tumah-ra's cheap, gung-ho militia boys could bring him down from this high; but just one photo of an Australian plane here would destroy any chance of a peacekeeping force in Tumah-ra. The recent spy charges against the two Aussie CARE workers in Bosnia left the bloody taste of suspicion in the minds of paranoid dictators. The militia, the real rulers of Tumah-ra now, would jump on their current puppet boys in government to get rid of all international interference, and more innocent people would die.

So go in fast, get the shots and fly out faster.

But the weather and Tumah-ra's roughneck terrain shot his ambitions to hell. Lightning flicked around him. Rain pummeled the wings. Wind slapped the plane in the face, jerking it back, up and to the side. Clashing storms between hills, half-torn jungle and the sudden rise of slumbering volcanoes turned the flight into a crazy game of dodge-ball hide-and-seek.

What was the bloody use of killing himself, staying at this altitude? He had to drop right down, even if the local crazies started taking potshots at him—and they would if they saw his gray kangaroo mascot on the tail. After East Timor, Aussies were about as welcome in rebel-run Tumah-ra as a dose of black plague.

Let 'em try to kill him. He wasn't about to die now. This was his last Nighthawk mission.

With a little smile, he pressed his fingers to his lips and touched the picture taped to the panel. A nearly three-year-old photo of his precious Matt and Luke, the last time he'd seen them. "I'm coming for you, kids. Hang in there. I'm coming home."

Rain pounded on the wings. A clap of thunder hit right over the plane. Down and forward he pitched like a bat out of hell—and another volcano loomed in front of him. "Damn!" He pulled back on the throttle and circled the clouds—and he all but ran into a long hill standing above the streaming jungle like a dank bald head, at an altitude a slingshot could pick off. If some half-baked sniper in the jungle aimed at his fuel tank—

But he had to take the risk. For on the eastern end of the hill, half-hidden by a canopy of trees outside the thatched-hut village of Ka-Nin-Put, he found it: the best footage op he would ever get. He pulled on his special goggles, similar to night-vision lenses, so he could see clearly. "Oh, my sweet godfather," he breathed.

It was worth a Pulitzer Prize. The UN would have to send in a peacekeeping force after seeing it. He didn't want to take the shot—wouldn't if he had his way—but he had no choice. Circling the hill for the best angle he got a clear view, aimed out the powerful, high-tech digital camera built into the underwing, and started taking footage that the world would soon see.

A child standing on the edge of a gaping hole: a rough manmade crater half-filled with broken bodies.

She couldn't be more than four. Her dress was ragged, filthy, hanging from a malnourished body covered in sores and scratches. Mud poured in from the torn lip of the crater as the torrential downpour dissolved the earth around her. She stood still, wailing the same words over and over— probably cries for the dead parents who lay in that hole beneath her.

Within minutes she would fall in and join the body count.

Where to land? Damn it, why didn't Anson get him a Harrier, or at least a chopper? A jet or bird could V/STOL—do a vertical short landing and takeoff in almost any weather conditions—in seconds. Even in this tough bush plane, his chances of landing safely were almost zip in this downpour. If the ground collapsed, he'd take the kid out instead of saving her.

"Holy Hannah, this is suicide!" But he looped the hill in a mad circle for the approach, like a kamikaze on a death mission.

The hill was a strange, bare swathe about a mile long and two hundred feet wide. If the plane were bigger, he'd never be able to land or turn for takeoff. In this rain the only way to do it was to land at the other end and make a run for her, hoping like hell the militia were hiding somewhere out of the insane weather.

He patted the console. "C'mon, Bertha, we can do it!" He released the throttle, eased the wheel forward, pulled out the landing gear and flew straight over the child, touching ground a scant twenty-five feet from her. The wheels skidded on the sodden ground. He had only one chance at this. "Work! Come on, Bertha, *work!*" He pulled back on the throttle, easing the brakes to stop the plane fishtailing.

The trees rushed to meet him. He needed turning space—oh, God, Matt and Luke, his precious boys—he couldn't die now, not when he finally had the chance to have his kids with him again—

Then a tire tripped on a lump of rock; Bertha slowed with shocking suddenness, and Mitch hit the brakes too hard in reaction. His body slammed against the wheel; he heard a crack in his lower chest, then felt stabbing, searing pain.

*Forget the pain. No time to think!* He scanned the land. Fifty feet turning space, max. He locked the brakes, grabbed his assault rifle, a coil of rope and ran.

With every step more ground dissolved beneath his feet. Holes and jagged cracks appeared. He fell, got up and stumbled on, dragging in ragged breaths of agony.

As she saw him, a big-built man in fatigue greens—damn Anson for insisting on the khaki fatigues and dark face paint for jungle cover like the militiamen!—coming at her with a rifle, the child cried, "Ima! Tatay!" and scrambled away. The lip of the crater imploded with the impact, and she toppled into the hole in a shower of mud and rocks.

Throwing the rifle back, Mitch dived toward her, landing on the fast-decaying lip. He threw the rope to the wailing child, cowering near a pile of bodies. Dear God, what if this happened to his boys? Had Matt and Luke cried out for help on a forsaken Sydney street after they'd found their mother's lifeless body? Who had been there for them? "Take it, little darlin'!"

Big, almond-shaped eyes looked up at him. Her hands reached out to the rope, then fell. A river of mud showered over her head; she started to sink beneath its weight. "Please, darlin', let me help you!" he cried desperately.

She just stared. Her teeth chattered under the onslaught of cold mud and constant rain. The ground shifted beneath him. He had seconds to gain her trust before they both died. Damn, why hadn't he learned to speak more than the most basic Tagalog for this mission? But then, those who'd done this to her spoke her native language—they were her own people. "Australia," he called down, thudding his throbbing, burning chest. "Me. Australian."

She blinked, slipped further. Her head tilted sideways.

"I know I don't look it; my face and hands are painted, and I've got brown skin, anyway, God knows from who. But I'm not one of them!" He knew his babbling was downright stupid, since she couldn't speak English; but he said it again. "I'm not one of *them*. I'm *Australian!*" He controlled his voice to as soothing a pitch as she could hear. Yelling wouldn't make her understand him better if she'd never heard the word; it would only remind her of the half-assed genocidal jerks who'd taken her family from her.

The child stared unblinking; then her hand moved to her lips, mimicking eating, a questioning look in those lovely dark eyes.

"Yes, darlin', that's it. The people who fed you last week!" Cudgeling his brain, he could think of only one way to convince her. He sang, "'Australians all let us rejoice, for we are young and free.'"

She slowly smiled, and started humming the national anthem the Vincent Foundation workers had taught her.

Mitch shook the rope. "C'mon, darlin'. Let's get outta here."

She looked down into the hole. "Ima. Tatay." A sad little chant; a baby's farewell. Then, thank God, she grabbed the rope.

He half slipped into the hole pulling up even her slight weight. Wrapping the rope around his waist, he crawled back along the crumbling earth, taking her with him inch by excruciating inch. The rain poured down, and the mud kept sliding on top of her, half drowning her tiny body. "Don't let go of the rope, little darlin'. Hang on!"

A sudden scream; Mitch toppled backward with the lack of weight on the rope, and he knew he was out of miracles.

Three times, handhold by foothold, he inched back, giving her the rope, moving back. He couldn't even lean forward far enough to show her how to loop the rope over her wrist; his weight would collapse the hole on her.

The fourth time, when he'd all but given up hope, a tiny head appeared above the rim; then her shoulders; then, like giving birth, she slid from the gaping maw headfirst into his hands.

He grabbed her, snatched up the rifle and ran for the plane, stumbling through holes, sliding in mud, holding her safely in his arms, taking the falls on his knees and back.

Three hundred feet to go—two hundred—one-fifty—

A jagged streak of lightning touched ground between him and the Maule.

*Oh, my God, not now—Matt, Luke, my beautiful boys, I'm so sorry!* So damned stupid, taking risks with his life now! But what choice had he? How could he leave this suffering child to die?

But the fork of lightning hit water, riding on the stream away from him. "Thank you, God," he breathed, knowing

how close they'd both come to being a charred heap of ash
and cinders. He stumbled into the Maule, put the child in
the passenger seat and buckled her up. She cringed and
whimpered, shivering violently. "It's okay, little darlin'!"
He threw a thermal blanket over her, tucking it in tight.
"That'll keep you warm till we get above this freak-show
weather." He rummaged in his backpack, found a half-
eaten Snickers and handed it to her. She stared in amazed
delight, then shoveled it into her mouth as if afraid he'd
snatch it back. Once she'd swallowed it, she gave him a
timid smile. "Go for it, little darlin'. There's plenty more
where that came from. C'mon, let's sing." Though he
dredged his brain for what few songs he'd learned in his
stark childhood, only one came to mind. "D'you know this
one? 'Doh, a deer, a female deer…'"

There was only one way to get skyward in this hellhole
of lightning, mud and water. The grave. The pit of death,
which probably held the kid's own family, was their only
chance at life. If he could get enough speed up, he could
use the hole and the falling slope of the hill as a pathetic
sort of launching pad. Like a glider, they might just take
off. Or not.

Only a psychopath would attempt this liftoff…or Mitch
McCluskey. He grinned to himself. They won't believe it,
not even at work. *Crazy Skydancer does it again.*

The rain pounded down. The lightning kept streaking in
jagged paths all around them. The sound of crashing thunder filled the cockpit. The child screamed, covering her
ears. Mitch gritted his teeth and propelled the Maule forward, trying to avoid pits and puddles. The needle moved
like a slug around the speedo, but he couldn't afford to go
faster in case he buried them in mud. Twenty-five knots.
Forty. Forty-five…halfway down the crumbling runway…
62…64…68. Water swirled around the plane in flying
fountains from beneath the spinning wheels—but thank
God, they kept moving, not digging in deeper in a self-
made hole.

Moving. Still moving—

"Come on, Bertha, we need 79. We can get there!" He patted the console again in grim encouragement as they hit the three-quarter point. Seventy knots. "Come on, baby, we can do it…73…74…"

A fickle swirling wind hit the plane in front, propelling the craft up. Mitch pulled the throttle and wheel back, sweat running with rain down his face. "Go, baby. *Go!*"

The plane lifted a bare three feet from the hole, but in the grab of a sudden twister, they jerked skyward. He lost control of the instruments, and they were flung and tossed like salad with the freak winds. *Please, God, don't let us die! Don't let me die when I'm going home to Matt and Luke. Not when I finally have a chance to see Lissa again. Please, Bertha, just don't roll!*

All he could do was hang on and wait.

The wind released its captive; the Maule wing-dived groundward. Mitch hit half throttle, sailing with the wind until he found an updraft. He leveled off and climbed above the storm, thanking God for his Air Force training, and for the bizarre twist of fate that had stopped the craft from rolling.

He flicked a glance at his tiny charge, wondering at her calm quiet during their life-and-death situation. Cuddled in the thermal blanket, worn-out with cold and shock, she'd fallen asleep. Her chocolate-and-mud-smeared face rested against the door, her matted hair stuck to the handle. "Sleep well, little darlin'. You're safe now." He caressed the slimy bob of hair. He turned the craft southwest toward Darwin.

He'd done it. The baby girl who'd seen death too young was safe now. So what if he had to face the music over the child's illegal entry into Australia? That was small potatoes compared with the crazy hell his life had been the past few years since he'd lost the boys.

The nightmares that chilled his soul had finally gone.

Matt and Luke were alive and safe—and they were with Lissa.

Soon, very soon, he would be, too. He'd have his sons with him again, where they belonged—and he'd see Lissa for the first time in twelve years. Delicate, haunting, gray-eyed Lissa with hair like a waterfall of shining honey, an unspeakably gorgeous mouth and a smile as beautiful as the home and hearth he'd never had. He'd ached to see her every single day of the past twelve years. To touch her. Craving the peace of soul he'd only known when he was with her. She was the only woman he'd ever wanted or thought of as becoming his wife. The only woman who'd ever held his heart in her hands. But she was another man's wife—and not just any man's wife. She was Tim's wife. Tim, his one-time best friend, who could offer Lissa every-thing: a home, a family, a real name. All the things he'd never had and would never have.

So somehow, some way, he had to take Matt and Luke and go, walk away from the only woman he'd ever loved—again.

# Chapter 1

*New South Wales, Australia*

"Somehow I thought I'd find you out here." A shadow fell over Melissa Carroll as she knelt in the damp earth, hand hoeing the fallow patch of ground, ready to lay the next planting of vegetable seeds. "G'day, Lissa."

Lissa shivered in half-thrilled trepidation. *Mitch...*

After twelve years just the sound of his voice roused so much turbulent emotion in her she felt weak, sick, filled with fears and hopes and dreams forever unspoken.

What if he'd only come to take Matt and Luke away—the boys she had known only five months, but now loved as her own?

What if that was all he wanted? What if he just thanked her and walked back out of her life, disappearing again, taking her darling boys with him?

But the deepest terror of all was Mitch himself. Terror that, after all these years, he could still weave the old Merlin-like power over her soul. Already she could feel the pull. The power of one quiet, complex man, drawing her to him against her will. The boy had wrapped her heart in a darkly glowing, spellbound fascination, holding her in a thrall so deep she'd never truly found her way out. Now that he was a full-grown man, the thought of what he could do to her—heart, body and soul—appalled her.

A fear justified by one look at him. No, he hadn't changed. It was still there: the unspoken intensity of soul, the hint of unleashed power, the invisible hunger—for what, she'd never known—and the old, sweet love, exclusive love, a best friend's devotion to her alone. It wasn't the sort of love she would once have given her life to have had, but it was close, oh, so close....

With one look, without even a touch, she was chained again, shackled to him with a wanting she couldn't conquer or deny. It had nothing to do with his looks, though he was so beautiful to look at he almost blinded her. Tall and strong, with deep, fathomless chocolate eyes, dark-olive skin and careless black curls. Though Mitch knew none of his forefathers, they must have been a big, bronzed race. He was so tall he dwarfed most men, big built and tightly muscled. From the first moment she'd seen him working their neighbor's farm seventeen years before, he'd robbed her of breath with his stormy male beauty. From the moment they'd met, he'd haunted her with the shadows of unspoken secrets in his eyes, half-shuttered windows to a turbulent soul.

Boy to girl, man to woman, nothing changed. Even now, after half a lifetime apart, he still took her breath away, still made her hunger for more. Always haunting her, even long after he was gone: invisible whispers to her soul by day, her restless warrior walking with her by night in the dark grace of sensual dreams unending and unfulfilled.

And now he was here. Achingly familiar yet so long gone. Almost within reach, yet so far away; too much and never enough. And still she ached for him.

He spoke again, his voice warm with laughter. ''You

can't be that shocked to see me. You knew I'd come. Don't you have any words of welcome for me?''

She gulped a second time and forced her frozen vocal cords to work. ''Yeah—you took your sweet time getting home, McCluskey. That must've been some mission the Air Force gave you to keep you away twelve years.'' She pushed her hat back, squinting up at him in the heat of the late-summer sun. He was smiling down at her. The affection in his eyes warmed and yet hurt her somewhere deep inside, for he was still closed off from her, by just being Mitch. Mitch, the dark, dreaming rebel, whom she'd always known would have so much more to his life than this sleepy little west-of-the-mountains backwater had to give...far more than a plain farmer's daughter had inside her to give. But, oh, it never stopped her dreams....

She'd dreamed of seeing him again, hungered for him through the long, burning years of a loneliness born of never being alone—the internal isolation that so many people filled with the faces of strangers. She'd never been able to do it, aching for one face only; yet now that he was here at last, she wanted him to go. Go and leave her in peace, without the tumultuous upheaval in her heart and soul caused by just knowing he stood near her.

''Sorry, Liss—the brass sent me out again right after East Timor. I gave notice as soon as I could. I'm on three months' leave at the moment until I set myself up in a business. I figured Matt and Luke would need me full-time for a while.''

Just his voice, lush like rumpled dark silk, filled her with daydreams of sensuous hot nights in satin sheets—dreams she could never fulfil in real life. Which was why she always let the kids answer the phone Sunday nights when he would call from East Timor to talk to them. And when he asked to speak to her, she'd keep it to a minimum. Just talking brought to life desires and needs she'd fought long and hard to banish.

He held out a hand to her. She allowed him to lift her

to her feet, feeling somehow small and feminine in her dirty paint-marked shorts and tank top. Even through her gardening glove she could feel the heat burning inside him that he always kept guarded from her. Just one touch and she trembled. Her pulse pounded so hard she could feel her throat quiver…and for the first time in twelve years she remembered she was a woman. "I see you've still got your patch of earth to till, Farmer Annie."

She grinned at him from beneath the shade of her hat, trying for normality. "Can you imagine me without it?"

"Nope. Never. Through the years, when I've imagined meeting you again, it was always out here. It was where we always got together—your land or Old Man Taggart's, didn't matter. It was our place, and it was us." The gentle smile softened his strong, masculine face, sending warm shivers down her spine. "It's been a long time, Lissa. Too long."

"Twelve years."

"You barely look any older. And the farm…" He looked around the Miller family's side of the fence, its drenched greenness dreaming in the soft silver haze of a warm February sun. "It's like time froze here. It's all the same. Serene and beautiful."

"Changes happen everywhere, Mitch." She pulled off her dirt-encrusted gardening gloves, checking her hands to make sure they weren't shaking. "Even in sleepy little towns like Breckerville it happens—like under a microscope, beneath the surface where you can't see it…"

*Stop babbling, Lissa.*

He smiled at her in tender reassurance, as if sensing her internal monologue. "Some things have changed if Lissa Miller doesn't give a friend a hug."

"It's Carroll now, remember?" she whispered, knowing he didn't need the reminder but needing to give it. Needing to recall the reasons why she shouldn't touch him, start up the old merry-go-round of anguished yearnings and unrequited love.

"You'll always be Lissa Miller to me." With a small, tilted smile and darkened eyes, he opened his arms to her. "Come here."

Aching, terrified—unable to resist, or deny him—she walked into his arms.

He held her close, just as he did years ago, in the days of their innocence, resting his chin on her hair. "It's been so long since I held you. Too long. I never stopped missing you, Lissa."

She held him close against her, filled with warmth and beauty and long-forbidden desire, just from his holding her. Loving it and hating it. Needing to push him away, yet never wanting to let go. Wanting more. Always wanting more when it came to Mitch. Loving him too much, wanting him too much, knowing it had never been that way for him. Dreams and fantasies of pushing her hands beneath his shirt, finding that glorious summer-heated maleness beneath— "You could have come to visit," she whispered.

"You know why I didn't."

The scene at her wedding.

She suppressed a shudder. Tim Carroll, her brand-new husband, in the grip of the sudden and shocking aggression that comes from being roaring drunk for the first time. Throwing Mitch, his best man and longtime closest friend, out of the reception hall and out of their lives. Okay, so Mitch had been a little drunk, too. More than a little. So he'd watched her every move that night, in a tense, brooding stance that made her shiver...but not with fear. And so what if he'd chosen to speak about the beautiful bride instead of the bridesmaids, and how much he loved her? It was no secret how close Mitch was to the girl next door who'd married his best friend. It was anyone's guess why Tim suddenly got to his feet in the middle of the speech and threw Mitch out.

Everyone knew Mitch's story: the bounced foster kid taken in by a dour, old, widowed farmer, who only tolerated him for manual labor. Mitch never had any family of his own, no one to love him or care for him until he'd come to Breckerville. Which was why Tim's act, in the middle of his own wedding, in front of all their friends, seemed so cruel and inexplicable. The mystery of Mitch McCluskey's dramatic and permanent exit from town was still an occasional topic for speculation and gossip.

As was Tim's less flamboyant exit from town. Less visual, but no less dramatic.

Lissa wished she *didn't* know the reason for Tim's lashing out at his best friend. And she'd never tell Mitch—not about the wedding nor about why Tim left her. How could she tell him that Tim, her husband— No, it was impossible.

Just as anything but friendship between them was impossible, now and forever. If she'd ever worked up the courage to tell him how she'd felt before she married Tim…but marriage to Tim had changed everything—her innocence, her belief in love…her belief in herself. It was all gone.

"How are the boys?" Mitch asked now, as if he knew she wanted the subject changed.

She relaxed against him, then pulled away. *Don't think. Don't feel.* "They're wonderful. They turned nine a month ago."

"I wish I'd been here." He tipped her chin up, searching her face with a tender gaze. "Thank you for taking them in after the police notified me they'd finally found them. They didn't go into the foster system, thanks to you. You don't know what it means to me." He bit down a smile, taking her face in his hands. "Dumb remark. You know better than anyone what it means to me." He leaned forward, softly brushing her mouth with his. "Thank you, my beautiful, generous-hearted Lissa, for everything you've done. For them. For me. Thank you. Thank you."

She couldn't control the quiver that ran through her at the words, at the touch. He'd called her beautiful…

And for the first time his mouth had touched hers.

Once, only once before had he come close, and, as things

had always been between them, it was too little and years too late.

In the kitchen of her parents' house. He'd given her a locket for her seventeenth birthday—a year after she'd started dating Tim, his best friend. A candy-pink enamel-and-gold heart-shaped locket, a cheap, bargain-store replica of the one Gilbert gave to Anne of Green Gables. Unable to believe he'd remembered, let alone respected her little dream, her sweet, foolish dream that she'd find her own Gilbert and receive her own locket of love. He'd used what little money he had to fulfil it. She'd thrown her arms around him and reached up to kiss his cheek. He turned his face to hers, whispering huskily, ''Lissa, don't you know I—'' He'd searched her eyes for an intense moment, and she knew that all the yearning in her heart for his kiss must be clear to see, shining like a beacon in the night. Slowly he'd lowered his mouth to hers as she waited, breathless and hungry for the touch....

Then Tim's laughing voice sounded outside the room, and they sprang apart like guilty lovers. Neither of them could bring themselves to hurt Tim, his best mate and her boyfriend.

Oh, how she'd wished, in the long, cold years after her birthday night, that she'd had that kiss before it was too late. But too late had come and gone years ago. She'd lost her innocence too young. She'd learned cynicism too well. Even if by some miracle Mitch wanted her—and why would he?—she knew exactly what she was. Not enough for any man.

With a smile she knew trembled, she backed off. ''Still full of blarney, McCluskey? You must have had a touch of Irish in you.'' She swept a hand over her grubby gardening attire, the battered straw hat perched atop her simple pony-tail. ''I've lived in this face and body thirty-one years. I know what I am.''

His gaze never wavered. ''I can't speak pretty words, Lissa. I only speak what I know.'' Stepping forward, he tipped her face up with a finger. "You were a sweet, pretty girl when I knew you before. Now you're a beautiful woman, with a heart as gentle and lovely as your face."

She trembled even at his simplest touch; the tiny flare of forbidden heat came alive, warming her shivering soul, making her stupid dreamer's heart wonder if maybe, finally—

*Fool!* She had to break contact. Now.

She stepped back so fast she almost fell into the aubergines. "You can't know what I'm like now. You haven't seen me in twelve years. Times change, people change. I'm not the girl you knew."

Again Mitch allowed her withdrawal, his gaze following her, dark and brooding; yet his words held the simplicity of faith. "You took my boys in when they were in trouble. You went to Sydney for them, brought them home and kept them safe here when I couldn't leave East Timor. That's the Lissa I knew I could trust with my sons—and you came through. For them. For me. And that makes you more beautiful to me than any supermodel could be."

"Yep. The perennial nice girl next door. That's me," she said blithely, hiding the strain of bitterness beneath the words. "Everyone's best friend and little sister, who always comes to the rescue. Good old reliable Lissa."

A short silence, as if he weighed his words. Then he spoke, his deep, rumpled voice speaking his unique brand of blunt truth. "You've always been a 'nice girl,' you did live next door, and yes, I've relied on you—but from the moment we met, I've *never* thought of you as my sister, Lissa. Not once. Not ever."

She couldn't breathe. Her gaze felt pinned by his, trapped by the power of words she'd never dreamed of hearing from Mitch McCluskey, the beautiful, dark-hearted rebel who was always going to fly away from this hick town. "How...how did you think of me?" Then she swung toward the house, her face burning. "No. Don't answer that.

Would you like coffee? The boys will be home from school in about twenty minutes, and Jenny—''

''Are you frightened of me?''

The question halted her midstride. Slowly she turned back to him, trembling, needing, ashamed. She didn't want to say it, but she'd never lied to Mitch; she'd only kept secrets.

She met his gaze, hers filled with unflinching honesty. ''Terrified,'' she said softly.

His hands, reaching out to her arms, dropped. ''I hoped it was only him who'd wanted me to go that day. I'd hoped you at least still trusted me.''

''I do!'' she cried. ''I do, Mitch…but I—'' She floundered, biting her lip. Haunted by past pain, hemmed in by secrets, by the fear and self-hate that walked beside and inside her, night and day. ''It's just that I— Oh, I can't explain…but it's not you,'' she finished lamely.

''I see.'' His face twisted. ''That's why you keep moving away from me like I'm a monster.''

The pain in his eyes found an echo in her soul. *Mitch, oh, Mitch, I wish it didn't have to be like this!*

She owed him the truth. She knew what his life had been before they met, how few people he cared for or trusted since living through the foster system. But he trusted her.

''I learned a long time ago not to believe in everything Tim said or did,'' she said, giving him what truth she could. ''I never wanted him to say those things to you. I didn't want you to go out of our lives like that. I'm glad you're here now. The boys have missed you so much.''

''Thanks for that.'' He nodded, as if thinking of something else. ''What time does Tim come home from work?'' His voice was slow, thoughtful.

''I—'' She blinked. ''*What* did you say?''

His brow lifted. ''It's a simple question, Lissa. What time does your husband come home from work?''

Without warning everything shifted focus. She felt dizzy,

disoriented, as though she'd stepped back in time to a strange new world where only one truth made sense.

*Mitch didn't know.*

Blinking to clear her mind of the unexpected turmoil, she tried to speak, but it came out a harsh croak. "Tim left me six years ago."

Mitch staggered back, as if she'd decked him. *"What?"*

She shrugged, seeing no need to repeat herself.

"You're divorced?" He watched her with an intense gaze, as if trying to make sense of a simple fact. Waiting for her to deny what he'd just heard. "You're free?"

Lissa flinched. Oh, how she hated the word *divorce*. It was a word unheard of in the Miller family—until Tim walked out, left her for— "Yes."

Obviously, he'd seen her expression. He'd been looking at her with all his brooding intensity. "Do you ever see him now?"

"Of course," she answered, relieved at the change in subject. "He comes to see Jenny, our daughter. She's five."

"Did he leave you for someone else?" The question was as grim as the look in his eyes.

She dragged in a breath. At least she could answer that question honestly. "Yes."

"He left when you were pregnant with his child."

Unable to look at him, she nodded. If he knew the truth—

"Damn it. I'm going to kill him."

She blurted without thinking, "How is it any different from you? It's exactly what you did to Matt and Luke's mother—except you didn't even bother to marry her before you did your runner!" She clapped a hand to her mouth, horrified by the burst of anger she hadn't even seen coming, destructive fury born of twisted jealousy. "I-I'm sorry, Mitch. It's none of my business."

Another short, uncomfortable silence, the words he didn't say hanging in the air between them. "I could do with a coffee, if that's all right."

"O-of course." She led the way into the old weather-board farmhouse, shaking so bad she could barely use her hands to hang her hat and gloves on a hook on the veran-dah.

Mitch walked in without waiting for an invitation—but then, he knew he didn't need one. The Miller farm had been his only real home in all his life. Her parents had become like his own, and he, their son.

For a little while. Until Tim stepped in and she'd ruined it all by giving in to a girl's temptation to have a boy-friend—any boyfriend. Fool!

"The place has changed a bit." He surveyed the big, open country kitchen, soft and mellow, honey and gold toned beneath the flooding sunshine of the skylight. "It was darker before."

"When my parents retired three years ago I bought them out. I sold four hundred acres to the Brownells, keeping just the fifty around the house to grow fruit and vegetables. Mum and Dad live in a cottage by the ocean. They're in Europe at the moment; Dad wanted to see the Formula One. Anyway, since it's my place now, I did up the parts I didn't like. I felt oppressed by the dark floor and bench tops." She filled the filter with coffee.

"I like natural floorboards. I did something similar to my place in Bondi before I sold it. It was too gloomy."

"Where do you live now?"

A second's hesitation, then he said slowly, "I live here."

The jug of water slipped in her hands, spilling over the bench. *"Here?"*

"Yes, here in Breckerville. I'm buying a place. Let me help you." He stepped forward, grabbing a towel to dry the mess.

He'd always been like that. Always wanting to help her, always close to her. Just never close enough. Always the best friend she'd ever had, never the lover she craved.

Tears of helpless confusion filled her eyes. "I can do it." She snatched the towel from him, hiding her face.

Again she felt his gaze on her, sensing her quiet despair. Gentle as a whispering breeze he touched her cheek, turning her face to his. "Don't be sorry about what you said, Lissa. Don't ever be scared to speak your mind to me."

Unable to stop herself, she drank in the dark, rebellious face whose memory still walked the land outside her window, whose essence still haunted her dreams inside the windows of her soul. "But I am sorry," she whispered, lowering her gaze.

Though she couldn't see him, she could feel the warmth of his gaze on her. "Liss, you know how I feel about my father walking out on my mother when she was pregnant with me, her dumping me at the church steps because she had nowhere to go. Can you honestly see me walking out on a woman having my kids, like I didn't care that she, or they, might have the life I had before I met you?"

Shamed, appalled by her unthinking judgment, she whispered, "Tim did."

"No, baby," he answered gently. "No man who knows you at all would ever think you could abandon your child, like my mother did to me. But he hurt you. You loved him, trusted him, and he hurt you. He left you when you needed him the most."

His voice was so warm, so tender. He cared for her, and she was answering him with half-truths. But how could she tell him the truth about her marriage? "Yes. Yes, he did." Well, that much was truth. Tim had left her, the *only* time she'd needed him.

"Where does he live now?"

Hearing the note of grim promise, she felt seventeen again. Mitch had always pounded Tim when he thought his friend wasn't treating her right. "Not for my sake, Mitch," she said with a shy, half-hidden smile. "He's Jenny's father."

Quietly he asked, "Why didn't you tell me any of this when I asked you to take the boys? My God, if I'd known you were alone, running this farm, a single mother—"

"Which is why I didn't tell you. Matt and Luke needed a home and a family, after what happened with Kerin." She refilled the jug and set the coffee going. "So I hear you made lieutenant in the Air Force, fly-boy McCluskey."

"Squadron leader, actually. I would have made it my career, but the boys need me home more than the life can give."

She glanced at him as she poured the coffee, afraid to ask the obvious question. "So what are your plans? Are you still going to work with planes?"

He leaned against the counter, watching her as if refreshing his eyes with her face—just her face. "I'm setting up a country-based courier business here. I have two planes, as well as a Maule bush plane I keep for fun, and I do aid drops for the Vincent Foundation every once in a while."

She grinned. "Don't tell me, I'm-Gonna-Save-the-World-Rebel McCluskey. You do all the runs for kids in crisis, and you've risked your neck to save a few."

Mitch laughed at the perception of old friendship. Oh, yeah, she still knew him all right—better than any other woman ever had, or would. He could no more turn down a kid in need of help than he could live without flying— but she, so protected and innocent, would never understand his new, hidden work.

Just as well she didn't know he'd left the Air Force for the Nighthawks almost two years ago; that his usual job description entailed flying over and into the world's war zones to smuggle out captives and civilians unwittingly locked inside the unstated boundaries of heated battle. As for his adventure in Tumah-ra, and its potential repercussions with little Hana, if he couldn't—no. There was no way he'd tell her; he didn't want to shock her.

But lying to Lissa had never been an option.

He grinned and said, "Guilty as charged."

She grinned in response, and the sweet warmth of it fired his soul, as well as more intimate places. "You haven't changed a bit. Still the world's softest touch for a kid in need.'' She bit her lip and shoved him his coffee mug over the counter.

He didn't touch it, barely noticed it. He knew he was staring at her, but he couldn't stop. She'd changed from the fragile, hauntingly lovely woman-child who'd married his best mate at nineteen. She'd filled out, matured. She held herself with a quaint, unconscious dignity, standing aloof from the hedonistic angst of the world. But she still had the incredible mouth that made men thank God He made women—and she wore the same unique scent of sunshine and earth and grass and a touch of something wilder, sweeter beneath. Just like Lissa herself—a heady mixture of natural, glowing sensuality and sweet, untouchable purity. Lines touched her face, marks of the woman's rite of passage: the strength and beauty of pain of childbirth and motherhood, the stress of unspoken sorrow and abandonment.

God, she was beyond beautiful now, but in a way that almost hurt him to look. She was a fairy-tale heroine straight from the mind of the brothers Grimm: a shackled maiden lost in the forest. A figurehead carving they put on the bow of old ships, like the *Flying Dutchman*. Forever sailing on, standing at the front of a boat flying unstoppably through a world and time she had no control over. Beautiful and cold, so untouchably cold. In those eyes of sweet country mist, shadows ran rampant. Shades of fear. Specters of isolation and emptiness. As they did in her heart. The ghosts of the past owned her soul.

But she was free of Tim—which was a greater miracle than any he'd hoped for—and he'd take her any way he could have her.

And he *would* have her. He'd fight for her with everything he had in him, every ounce of strength and skill he'd learned. He'd fight clean if he could, dirty if he had to. This time no man was coming between them.

He had to force himself to answer her teasing in the same light vein. ''So I'm obsessed with saving kids? Says she who took my kids in for the past five months, no questions asked.''

She stilled, looking anywhere but at him. ''Are you going to take the boys away from me?''

He stared at her, shocked by the question, by the way her sweet eyes wouldn't meet his. Damn it, he should have known it would come to this; but he hadn't thought it through, thinking she was Tim's wife. ''You don't want them to go.'' It wasn't a question. ''Lissa, surely you know I'd—''

''We love them, Mitch,'' she blurted, staring hard at the creamy-tiled wall with hand-painted diamond tiles interspersing the plain squares. ''They've become my sons, Jenny's big brothers. They had their troubles when they came. I expected it after the way Kerin died. But it's settling down. They're happy here…they have a home and family. They need family stability, Mitch, and they love us, Jenny and me—'' She turned to him, pleading in the depths of her pretty eyes. ''Please don't take them away from me.''

Quick as a flash, he made up his mind. ''I knew they'd love you, Lissa, and I knew you'd love them. I counted on it. Which is why I came back here to live.''

She kept her gaze on him, eyes wide, pupils dilated. Filled with half-scared questions only he had answers to.

''Matt and Luke need a mother,'' he said quietly, formulating his plans with the lightning speed of a man trained to think on his feet, or in the cockpit. ''One who'll be more loving, more stable than Kerin could ever have been. And no woman could be more loving, more stable than you. I know that from experience.'' He watched the soft rose flush fill her cheeks, and ached with the need her fresh, country-girl beauty always set off in him. The need to hold her, run his hands through that shining honey-gold waterfall of hair, touch her silky, golden-brown skin. Shed her clothes and kiss every secret part of her until she was glowing in her earthy sensuality and crying out in pleasure for him—

Oh, how he ached to make her his. But the only emotion she'd shown at all so far was for his kids.

When he spoke again, his voice was harsh with the strain of his never-ending craving for her. "I've had constant nightmares since Kerin took off with the kids from school—horrifying visions they'd end up in places I've been. But when you said you'd take them, the fear died. I knew you'd love my kids as your own. I trusted you to keep them safe. I can't take them away from here, from the only real family and mother they've known."

Lissa sagged, gripping the counter for support, white-faced and shaking. Her knuckles were transparent to the bone. "I've been so scared you'd take them from me," she whispered. "I think I'd want to die if I lost them now."

Oh, bloody hell. He should have seen this coming, should have known his girl wouldn't just care for Matt and Luke, or love them simply—simple just wasn't in her nature. She'd taken his sons right into her heart, and she'd hold on to the love with all the tenacious, desperate strength her delicate frame belied. Just as she'd once done with him. And while he'd half-counted on that, it made telling her his plans a whole hell of a lot harder.

But then, nothing was ever simple between him and Lissa. Ever. Not even the unspoken burning in his gut for her.

Especially not that.

He drew in a breath. "But I can't just leave them behind. They're my sons, and I love them." He touched her arm to keep contact with her warmth; he felt so cold with fear, his teeth almost chattered. "You know me, Lissa. You know how I've always wanted to be part of a family. I've come home to find my family."

Her eyes fixed on his face, filled with trepidation. Anguish. And, though he hunted as deeply as he dared, he couldn't see a trace of the longing that filled him for her, body, heart and soul. "What are you saying?"

He dragged in a breath. "I'm saying I'm home to stay.

I want a family—and that includes you and Jenny. If you'll have me.'' He took her hands in his, feeling like a drowning man holding on to a lifeline—and he finally said the words he'd been holding in since the girl he loved started dating his best friend fifteen years before. ''Marry me, Lissa.''

# Chapter 2

"Wh-what?"

It wasn't exactly the answer Mitch hoped for. Nor was the look on her face. Surprised, yes. Stunned, maybe. Joyful, beyond his dreams. But the one look he hadn't expected from her was that of a fawn he'd just shot.

Stricken. Bewildered. Betrayed.

So much for dreams and half-hidden hopes. He'd done it again. What a fool. What a heel. The world's biggest jerk. Come home after twelve years, make conversation for five minutes and what did he do? Propose to her! He shouldn't have blurted it out like that. He should have taken it slow, courted her with care; but no, he'd gone at her like a bull at a gate, let the dam break—and all he'd accomplished was to shock and confuse her.

He had no option but to go on with it now. He had to try to repair the damage he'd caused. "Think about it, Lissa. It's the perfect solution for us all."

She whitened and her eyes went dark like a lamp shattered by stones, bloodless and cold and broken. *"No."* She tugged until he released her hands; she stumbled away from him, her breaths harsh and heaving, like she was trying not to throw up. "Don't say it again," she finally muttered. "Not ever!"

"Lissa—"

"I said *no*." She flung up a hand between them. It was small and delicate, like Lissa herself—yet because it shook so hard, it was as effective a barrier as bricks and mortar, halting his advance. She turned her back on him, picking up her mug, sloshing coffee on the counter as she took unsteady swigs. "The kids will be home from school soon." She spoke as if nothing had happened. "Matt and Luke will be so happy to see you—but expect hostility from Jenny. She loves her brothers. We're a family." The implication was clear: *And we don't need you.*

Mitch dragged in a breath, seeing his life's dream besides flying planes crumbling before his eyes. To him Lissa always had, always would, represent everything good and right and decent in the world. All that was beautiful and precious in his eyes lived and breathed here in Breckerville, on a sleepy verdant farm and in a pair of gentle gray eyes, a mouth made to love his body and a heart that had never known what boundaries were.

Except in this, obviously.

God, oh, God, he'd lost her. She didn't love him. Didn't want him. Not even to keep his kids—kids she obviously *did* love. "Won't you even think about it?"

"I don't *want* to think about it. I don't want a 'perfect solution' to a problem I didn't know I had!" Spitting the words out like epithets, she swiveled around to face him, her face filled with burning wrath. "You've been gone over twelve years, and in all that time, I never get a thing. No word, no call, no letter. I didn't know if you were alive or dead until you needed my help with Matt and Luke. Now you waltz home after almost half a lifetime away and tell me *you* want to get married, just like that." She snapped her fingers, her eyes flashing. "I'm not a dog you can call to heel, Mitch McCluskey."

He bit the inside of his mouth. Somewhere along the line, his gentle Lissa had grown feisty. She'd squared up to him like Mike Tyson in a prematch slanging bout. What the hell had he said to make her quiver with fury like that? "I'm sorry." He stumbled over the long-unused word, jerking a hand through his hair, and cursed when it caught in his tangled curls. "I hated leaving you. I've missed you like crazy the whole time I've been gone. Not a day's passed when I didn't think about you, want to see you, call or write—but Tim made his feelings pretty final."

"But *I* didn't," she snarled, startling him with the vivid passion in her face. "You just left me—left us both behind. You knew how much Tim cared about you. Surely you knew he'd regret what he'd done when he was sober? And he did, Mitch—but we both thought you'd come back. And how do you think *I* felt, waiting day after day for a call or letter to know you were safe? I had to call the Air Force a year later to make sure you were alive!" She whirled on him again, a delicate china tigress, even her sheathed and painted claws ripping his heart to shreds. "I *loved* you, damn it. You knew I'd worry myself sick about you, and you never once bothered to let me know you were alive and all right!"

"I knew. You and Tim were the only two people on God's earth I was sure cared about me." He turned aside, looking out the window to the vista of shimmering, sun-drenched fields he'd loved from first sight, seventeen years before. Breckerville and Lissa. The only sense of belonging he'd ever had; the only place he ever felt at home, at peace, where the tempests roaring inside him calmed like the waters of the Jordan at a word from the Messiah. "But when he did that to me right in front of the whole town, and you didn't stop him, I didn't know what to think. Sure I was out of line with the speech about you. I was stupid, jealous of what you two had, and more than a bit drunk, I'll admit it—but I'd forgiven him far worse. Did he ever tell you why?''

Her voice came to him, strained. Hiding secrets. Hers or Tim's? ''I think that's something he'll have to tell you himself.''

So she was still loyal to Tim, even after all he'd done to her. He held the sigh in. The path he'd finally hoped clear was far from smooth. *Mitch the dreamer strikes again— shot down as usual by the Red Baron of reality.* ''Where does he live now?''

''Sydney. Ashfield. He owns and runs a gym near the city with a partner. He comes up here every second weekend to see Jenny. Sometimes during the week, too, depending on his schedule. He's become a father figure to the boys in the past five months. He takes the kids to football games, plays with them, helps them with school projects. Things like that.''

He turned to her, but she'd averted her face. She was talking too much. Lissa always did that when she was scared, or hiding something. ''Does he stay here?''

''Yes.'' She fiddled with the cloth on the counter. Waiting for the question. He knew it. He sensed the pot boiling inside her, the potent stew of dread and anger, daring him to speak.

Like a fool, he plunged on. He couldn't stop the gut-deep jealousy eating at him, clawing with the sharp-edged talons of Iago's cunning. ''In your bedroom?'' he rasped.

Like a flash she turned on him. ''And who's been in your bed lately, Mitch? Who's filled your lonely nights the past twelve years? How many times have you sunk to doing things you hate so you're not alone, even for a few hours?''

He'd expected her to shove the question back in his face, but not with such raw intensity. Oh, yeah, she'd walked his path, if from the other side of the fence. He understood that loneliness. The darkness of nights filled with aching. The sunrises and sunsets over concrete and stone, standing alone in a city of four million people, that city not where you ached to be, none of those people the one you hungered to be with. Even when he was on a mission, even when he'd saved someone's life, it only patched over the gap for a few hours, before the gut-gnawing voracious need for home and family and Lissa. Dear God, how he'd ached for her; a devouring need to sink inside her, lose his pain in her smile, her arms and welcoming body forever left the wound open again, savage and unhealed and bleeding.

He'd learned long ago how to live alone. Taking another woman to his bed or hers—even women who knew the score—had only ever intensified the loneliness, the anguished yearning. An hour, a minute of mind-numbing forgetfulness nowhere near compensated for weeks of self-hate, using a woman as a replacement for the only woman he'd ever truly wanted.

Kerin's fall from grace completed the lesson forever. He'd used her in his unhealed grief for Lissa, taken Kerin's eager smile and giving sexuality as a shallow replacement for real love, and discovered too late the abyss of unbalanced emotion that lay beneath. But by then, she was pregnant with his children, and leaving her wasn't an option.

But now Kerin was gone, Lissa was free—and his heart and body, primed and hard all day, thudded till the pounding need roared in his ears, reminding him they'd been starved way too long.

In his whole life he'd never known love the way Lissa used to give love to him. She sneaked him food when Old Man Taggart left him hungry again. She helped him with his homework, even did it for him when he didn't have time. She sat and talked to him by the pond that joined their farms when the sun went down—the loneliest time for him, when families gathered around the tables to be with their kids—often giving up her own family time to be with him. She'd listened to him as he talked about his hopes and dreams for the future, and confided hers to him. Sweet Lissa Miller of the popular crowd at school really cared about unknown, unimportant Mitch McCluskey. She worried about him, fussed over him, poured her heart and soul's care over him until he'd swum in it, drowned in it, lived and breathed the love filling him. Even when she started dating Tim—*damn* Tim for asking her to their formal first!—Mitch never felt less than special, less than loved by her, even when he'd been jealous enough to murder Tim when he touched her, kissed her.

Even now the memory had the power to make him burn.

How could he feel so much, hurt so much, and she not know it?

Deep inside, he'd always known this sort of love only came to a man once in a lifetime. He'd learned long ago that to have another woman in his arms and bed was nothing more than an empty cheat, fool's gold, a poor substitute for what he wanted. To have and to hold the woman he loved, forever. To have, not just her body, but her trust, her joy and pain, to grow old beside her at the place they loved best. To love and be loved in return.

And if he'd been the one to marry Lissa he'd never have walked out, never left her. He'd have loved her forever, kept that innocent joy glowing from her eyes—eyes now filled with the cloudy shadows of suffering and rejection.

Suffering Tim had put there. Shadows he'd have to erase before she'd even consider his proposal.

Why had he ever stood aside for Tim? Why didn't he ever *tell* Lissa how much he wanted to be the one?

Never a time, never a place, he'd always thought. But the simple truth filled him with self-contempt. *Because you were a bloody coward, always terrified she'd say she only loved you like a sister. Too scared you wouldn't be enough for a girl like her.*

He still was. He, who regularly looked death in the face, was too scared to look into the eyes of a delicate, five-foot-four woman and tell her he loved her. If only Tim hadn't walked in on them on her seventeenth birthday—but Tim had. And then he'd had to walk away. Tim had a home, a life, security—a *family* to offer Lissa. He, Mitch, didn't even have a real name to give, just the minister's surname from the church steps his mother had dumped him on as a newborn. He was a hooker's unwanted bastard, pushed from place to place all his life, a worker begrudged even the basics of life, like food or affection. How could he ever think she'd love someone like him, beyond the miracle of her friendship?

"Mum!" At the other end of the house, a door slammed once, twice. "Hey, Mum, you shoulda seen this cool girl-fight—" Matt ran in, saw him, gaped and yelled, *"Daaad!"*

*"Dad?"* Luke came flying in. "Dad! Oh, Dad, you came!"

Within seconds two blurs cannoned into him. He staggered back, laughing. He hitched them up in his arms, feeling the identical little heads snuggle into either side of his neck.

Matt and Luke. His boys. His beautiful, precious sons. So like him, and so alike few could tell them apart—but they were his kids. He would know Matt from Luke any time. "Of course I came, matey. You knew I would, as soon as I got off my tour."

Matt pulled back, looking at the father he closely resembled, with a solemn frown. "Kerin's dead, Dad."

His heart ached for the boys who'd never called their own mother Mum. "I know."

"She topped herself on crack," Luke added.

He shook with the primitive fury he still hadn't conquered, even after her death. *Damn* Kerin for her paltry revenge on him, making the kids suffer! No nine-year-old boy should know what *topping* meant, let alone crack—and little guys of eight should never have to find their mother's body with the empty crack pipe hanging out of her mouth. "I know, mate."

Luke's gaze was anxious. "We didn't want to go with her. We didn't want to steal your stuff, Dad—it was Kerin."

Mitch kissed his son's hair. "I know, mate. I knew it wasn't you." Just Kerin paying for her bloody drugs. Trying to hit out at me any way she could. Needing someone to blame for her life.

"What took you so long to get here, Dad? Mum said you'd be here in a few weeks, an' we waited an' waited—"

So it's Mum already. Oh, yeah, taking the risk of calling Lissa when Nick told him he'd found Matt and Luke had paid off all right. He knew Lissa's gift of healing hearts— he'd been a recipient of the same loving treatment. And now his kids had that same total love, the unconditional support, he'd once had.

Then it hit him: they'd forgotten Kerin already. They told him about her death like an item they'd watched on the news, only anxious to know he didn't blame them for anything Kerin did.

His gaze met Lissa's. She nodded and touched her finger to her lips. *Counselor,* she mouthed.

He'd never wanted to kiss her more than now. The love he'd counted on for so long was there for his sons. She knew what his fear had been, the shadows of old ghosts still stalking him, and she'd led him to the sunlight with a single word. She wasn't fostering Matt and Luke. His boys were loved, an integral part of her family.

His heart whispered in delicate hope, She did it for me.

He couldn't fool himself for long. Lissa, his lovely, open-hearted girl, would have done the same for any child in need. As she'd done for him once—until he blew it.

*Thank you,* he mouthed back.

"Sorry, kids. I couldn't get away from work," he answered Matt's question. "The brass wouldn't let me off until yesterday. I couldn't even quit a day early."

Luke's mouth twisted. "Cityfellas."

Mitch chuckled and ruffled his son's tousled mop of curls. "I see Lissa's been passing on some of her ideas about the city. She used to call me that, until I'd been here a year or two." He grinned at her. As a kid, he'd loved the

way she'd called him Cityfella, poking her tongue out,
wrinkling her nose in cute teasing. There was never any
malice intended, no offence taken. Being a cityfella had
given him the sort of glamorous mystique he'd never had
as a plain unwanted foster kid—and it gave him undivided
attention from the girl whose angel-faerie face haunted his
dreams, night and day.

Lissa's smile was slow in coming, but when it did, her
soft, dove-gray eyes twinkled. She bit her lip, then poked
her tongue out and wrinkled her nose. "You still stink with
it—cityfella." She snorted. "Buying a house at Bondi
Beach. What a yuppie!"

Matt wriggled. "Wanna come see our room, Dad? It's
mega cool. It's got pics of Mick Doohan and Wayne Gard-
ner—"

Luke jumped off Mitch's hip. "And Luke Longley, An-
drew Gaze, Michael Jordan and the Shaq—"

He laughed. "I see you two are as alike as ever."

The boys grinned. "Basketball. Kids' stuff," Matt
snorted. "Who'd wanna waste time playin' with balls, just
runnin' up and down and *dribbling,* when you can burn
rubber at 220 an hour?"

"Bikes are all right, I s'pose," Luke retorted with lofty
condescension, "but I'd drink the grog if I won. Who wants
the good stuff poured all over your head?"

"Hey, mithter, do you like Barbieth?"

Belatedly, Mitch noticed someone was tugging at his
shirt. He looked down to the source of the little, lisping
voice.

Oh, dear God. Living proof of Tim and Lissa's love. A
sweet sprite gazed hopefully at him, a child with Tim's
riotous blond curls and an angel's face. Lissa's face.

"You must be Jenny."

Jenny rolled her eyes, reminiscent of her mother. "Mithter, I *thaid,* do you like Barbieth?"

Oh, yeah, this was Lissa's daughter all right—with her

one-track mind. The boys were sniggering already. "Watch out, or she'll get you into the dollhouse."

Jenny's brow lifted; she stared Matt down, her childish lisp adorable and impatient. "*You* play with me all the time, so don't you talk!" She turned back to Mitch. "You gonna play or not?"

"Jenny."

The quiet word brooked no denial. Jenny sighed dramatically. "Sorry, Mummy. Sorry, Mister. *Please* are you gonna play with me?"

Lissa put a hand on Jenny's pigtail. "Jenny, this is Mitch. He's Matt and Luke's daddy."

"No!" Jenny's sweet, flushed face drained white; those lovely china doll's eyes filled right up with tears and spilled over. "Don't take my bruvers. Don't take Matt and Lukey away from me!"

"Jenny."

The little girl's tiny, flower-like face lifted, drenched with tears. "No, Mummy, no!" she sobbed. "Don't let him take them, Mummy! Make him go away!"

Lissa squatted before the sobbing child as Matt and Luke stood either side of her, patting her in awkward affection. "Mitch is a friend of mine, and Matt and Luke's father. Would you like it if Matt and Luke told your Daddy to go away?"

Jenny sniffed and gulped. "But he's gonna take them away from us, Mummy! Stop him, stop him!"

"No, I'm not, Jenny," Mitch cut in quietly, aching for the child's pain. So much like her mother...

Jenny's eyes grew round. "You're goin' away? Yay!"

But the twins gasped, forgetting Jenny's grief in an instant. "Dad?" Matt's voice quivered.

"D-don't you want us?" Luke whispered.

Oh, damn. This was a delicate minefield he had to walk—especially with Luke—and he wasn't any good at careful balance with words. Or with saving people's feelings.

There was too much at stake here. Either way he could lose. How the hell could he explain the situation—what he wanted for them all—without either betraying Lissa's trust, making the boys resent her, or looking like he wanted to dump Matt and Luke with the first available caregiver?

*Just like Kerin—even after she went to the trouble of stealing them from me.*

"Of course he wants to be with you both," Lissa answered for him, caressing Luke's curly mop of hair with exquisite tenderness. "He wouldn't have come for you if he didn't. He means that he's moved here, to Breckerville, so he can be near us all. And you guys have the choice. You can go with your Dad, or keep living here if you want to, and he'll be—"

Watching her founder, he supplied the first words that came to his mind: "Right next door."

Lissa whirled to face him. "N-next door? You bought Old Man Taggart's place?"

"All two hundred and fifteen acres of it, rotting fences and all." Well, he would by tomorrow. He'd be the master of the place he'd once worked at for nothing. The For Sale sign he'd passed was so rusted and sagging he knew he'd get a bargain—and guaranteed a quick sale. Old Man Taggart must've died ages ago. The house and land were in such a state of disrepair—

He saw the flash of anger in Lissa's gaze before she looked away. "You have it all worked out, don't you?"

He shrugged, hiding the quick spurt of pain. Was she making it hard for him because she resented his manipulating the situation to his advantage, or because she didn't want to know about marrying him? "It seemed like a good idea at the time. And it's not as if I don't know the land, is it? I know every inch of it. Seems fair to get something out of it this time, instead of Old Man Taggart getting it all."

He was right. After all the years of thankless effort he'd put in, Old Man Taggart treating him like a slave instead of an honest worker, it was right he finally reap the rewards from the land he'd always loved to till. Still, Lissa shook with primitive anger at his blatant maneuvering of her life.

Join families. Join the land while we're at it. The perfect solution for everyone…except me.

But the fury melted into heart-deep guilt when she saw the radiant joy in the boys' faces.

"So you're staying here forever, Dad?" Luke cried, his little face blazing with eagerness; "And we don't hafta leave Mum?"

"I'll be right here with you guys from now on, mate. Living and working in Breckerville." Mitch grinned at his son. "I quit the Air Force to be with you—not just a desk job with the force like last time. I'm out for good."

Matt's face lit up and fell at the same time, giving his face a mercurial, humorous appearance. "Don't you fly no more?"

He gave the rich chuckle that still did funny things to her insides. "Me? Not fly? Come on, Matt, can you see that?"

Luke snorted. "Yeah, right, Matt. What a geek. As if Dad could ever stop himself!" He grinned up at Mitch. "So whatcha gonna do now?"

Mitch told his sons his plans to start up a country-based air courier business, but as he did, she saw all the quick glances at her. Gauging her reaction.

Uh-huh. She might be just an ignorant country girl, but even she could read the writing on this wall—it was in dripping fluorescent letters, screaming like the neon sign over the local video arcade. Mitch had them already married in his mind—wedded to his "perfect solution" of making them one family.

One unit. A regiment like the one he'd just left. And she, no doubt, would be on permanent KP/cleaning/child-minding duty.

Sure as eggs, it wouldn't be long before Matt and Luke started giving her the exact same glances Mitch did now.

A mother struggling to make it alone; a man wanting a family; two boys needing stability, a full-time mother as well as a dad. Before a week passed the twins would cotton on to Mitch's plan, falling over themselves trying to help. Hints and innuendoes. Getting Jenny out of the way. Plotting when and how to play Cupid.

Well, it wasn't going to happen. No way, no how. Not now, not ever—no matter how Mitch still affected her senses or how many pretty words he used on her.

Tim had done that, too.

Words were a sweet deception, a manipulation, nothing more. She was tired of being neatly boxed into "perfect solutions" for everyone but her, sick of being used by men who wanted security, stability and a home from her, but didn't want—

History won't repeat—not for this little black duck!

She clapped her hands. "Right. Scoot, everyone. I need to start on dinner," she announced.

Mitch was still watching her, unnerving her with his quiet perception. "I booked a table at Bob's for us all."

Before she could open her mouth, the kids started shrieking in joy. "Bob's Pizza! Way cool!"

She met his gaze, hers challenging. "You booked it before you even got here? A table for six, was it?"

His mouth twitched; a rueful grin spread over his face. "All right, I lied—but just a little. I *plan* to book dinner at Bob's. For five." He lifted a hand as she started to speak. "It's a celebration and a thank-you, Lissa. To celebrate being with the boys again and to thank you and Jenny for opening your home and family to my kids the past five months."

He kept watching her. As if he knew her reluctance to go to Bob's…or anywhere else. As if he knew the last place on earth she wanted to be was with him.

Three eager, pleading little faces turned to hers. "C'mon, Mum, *please*—we haven't been to Bob's since we first came here," Luke begged.

"And it's the *best* place," Matt added.

Mitch grinned. "I loved the place when I was a kid," he agreed. "I never had a better pizza since."

"It's still the best!" Matt and Luke yelled together.

"*Please,* Mummy?" Jenny's big baby blues were full of wistful wishes. "And I'll tell Daddy we only went with Matt and Lukey's daddy—he isn't gonna go kissin' you or nothin'," she added ingenuously with her sweet lisp. "Then Daddy won't be sad."

After a moment's silence, Lissa felt Mitch's gaze on her. On her eyes. On her mouth. Like he'd planned the exact act Jenny denied. To put his mouth on hers…his lips dancing with sensual care over her throat, her shoulders, and down…

Matt sniggered.

She felt the color rising up her throat and into her face until it scorched her from the inside.

"Jenny, you're a loser," Matt said, laughing, ruffling her golden curls and winking at Mitch, as if he was nineteen instead of nine. "C'mon, get into your togs, kid. I'll play on the water slide with you."

"Cool!" Jenny squealed, and ran to her room for her bathing suit.

"Wanna come, Dad?" Luke asked Mitch, his eyes bright. Bright with hope, and a fear that was too adult, too world-weary. Not wanting to let his dad out of his sight.

Lissa ached for the boy she loved so dearly. Luke still suffered nightmares, with both greater regularity and stronger intensity than the more resilient Matt. Most nights she'd find him sleeping with his twin or with Jenny. *She had a nightmare, Mum,* he'd mumble the next morning. *I was looking after her.*

Sweet, vulnerable, innocent Luke, with a facade of strength to hide his terrified heart. Just like his father.

Lissa watched in hidden hunger as Mitch, his face filled with tender understanding, held his son close. "I'm not going anywhere, mate. Promise. I'm here for good."

"You swear?" Luke whispered.

Mitch crouched down before his son. "Have I ever lied to you, Luke?" Eyes enormous, Luke slowly shook his head. "I promise I'll stay right here. I'll talk to Mum for a little while, and book a table at Bob's. Then I'll jump in the pool with you, all right?"

Even behind closed eyes, the vision remained to haunt her mind. A half-naked Mitch, strong, dark and muscular, playing in the cool, slippery blue depths of her pool...

*Just like we used to.*

Memories flooded her: the sweetest taboo, the forbidden too enticing to deny. Mitch would sneak out the window on hot summer nights, and she'd be waiting for him. And they'd swim and play in scared silence, in the exhilaration of a shared secret. Knowing that if her parents or Old Man Taggart saw them, they'd put a far less innocent connotation on their water frolics.

But it had all been innocent—just as she'd been back then, when she'd believed in love and happy-ever-after with a boy, a man who'd love her and her alone. Forever.

The dream of forever love had stumbled when Mitch left her, then died during her marriage to Tim.

"Yes, Dad," Luke said softly.

Lissa's eyes snapped open to see Mitch mock-slap Luke's bottom. "Then off you go, matey, and have fun. Mum will make sure I don't leave—won't you, Mum?"

Neatly boxed into a corner, she could only nod; but she couldn't hold on to the anger when she saw the soft light filling Luke's dark eyes. The first sign of healing, with the security he so desperately needed. Someone to call his own. A family.

*Like father like son.*

Within a minute all three kids dashed past on their way to the pool. "Take clean towels," she yelled, knowing that, as usual, she'd have to bring them out later.

Mitch stood watching her in silence.

She turned and washed the coffee cups, wishing Mitch's

plan wasn't so damned perfect for everyone except her—
or Jenny, who still dreamed of her daddy coming back to
live with them forever.

Another dream she could never make come true.

*You're so perfect I feel like slime for even thinking about
leaving you, Lissa, but I have to get away...*

Would she always make everyone she cared for so unhappy? No matter how hard she tried, it wasn't enough.
*She* wasn't enough—except for housecleaning or minding
kids, that is.

Melissa the perfect daughter, giving up dreams of university to help her parents run the farm when her sister
Alice took off for Sydney with Brad. Melissa the picture-
perfect wife, allowing Tim to open his gym while she
worked at the local store to pay the bills. Melissa the wonderful mother. Melissa, the woman everyone in town loved
and admired, so loving and giving. Hiding secrets beneath.
Pushing the darkness down deep inside.

Melissa the dream slayer.

"It's all right, Lissa. I'm not going to jump on you."

Startled, she whirled around to find Mitch watching her,
his face shuttered and cold. "Wh-what?"

"You're right. Changes happen, even in Breckerville."
He shrugged as if he didn't care, but the twist to his lips
and flatness in his eyes told her he cared like hell. "You're
not the girl I knew if you get so damn angry about a stupid
pizza or that I wanted a family celebration to let the kids
know I'm thrilled to be back with them. If your eyes turn
to ice because I ask you to reassure my scared and damaged
kid I'll still be around in half an hour. God, Lissa, do you
think I'm so bloody desperate to have you I'd blackmail
you into marrying me through the kids?"

She felt a rising wave of color slap into her face. "Not
me. I don't flatter myself that it's me you want. Just the
family you always dreamed of. Good old reliable Lissa will
take my kids—and me. It's not like she's got anyone else
who wants her!" Then she gasped when she realized what

she'd said. Darn it, did she always have to make an idiot
of herself with men? Her runaway mouth, saying things she
shouldn't think or feel—

Then Mitch riled her with his quiet "Is that what you
think? Is that what you believe, Lissa? That I don't want
you?"

On the defensive, it was her turn to shrug. "Oh, sure.
For cooking. For cleaning. To be there for your kids. Sure
you want me. I get the picture."

She nearly fell over when he burst into huge gusts of
hard-edged laughter. "That's so bloody funny," he gasped.
"Uh-huh. I don't want you. *I don't want you!*"

He almost doubled over he was laughing so hard.

Tears sprang to her eyes. She turned away, determined
not to dash at her face until she was alone. "I said I get
the picture. You don't have to laugh at the idea of wanting
me! Is it so hard to believe any man could look at me?"

But at her dramatic intensity, he only laughed harder.
"Hard to believe—oh sheesh, this is a farce!" Then as she
tried to stalk past him he reached out, grabbing her, halting
her stormy exit. "Oh, no, you don't, Miller. You're not
cheating me of the chance to—"

She struggled against him, terrified of making a complete
twit of herself by breaking down. "To what? Humiliate me
some more? News flash, McCluskey—I don't *do* humilia-
tion. I don't go in for the masochistic side of S&M. Go
find another sucker, you—you *loser!*" she yelled, coining
Matt's favorite expression, trying to pull herself free from
his hand.

"News flash, Miller—I might be a loser, but the only
sadism—no, masochism—I've indulged in in the past
seventeen years has been staying away from you!" But far
from angry, his eyes were bright with fun—the sweet cascade of happiness only Mitch showed so simply and
clearly. She hadn't seen it in so long she ached just watching him. Wishing she could feel what she saw in his eyes.
He was having a great ol' time, teasing her, riling her.

But she wasn't in the mood for games; his light, mocking attitude sparked a fury inside she hadn't known she was capable of. "So why did you do it? Why *did* you stay away from me so long?" she shouted, driven past endurance.

"Damned if I know." He grinned wider and pulled her against him, close, so close she could feel— "So come here and end my misery, will ya?"

She gasped and wiggled, shocked and scared and thrilled by the discovery she'd made: a hard bulge nudging her through his jeans. Was that really—? Could he be—? "Don't order me around, McCluskey," she said, but it was little more than a breathless rush of sound. "I'll be *damned* if I—"

"Lissa, honey, I've waited for this moment for seventeen years. Can we fight later? For now, just shut up and kiss me."

She stared up at him, her lips parted in numb surprise. He sighed again, but it was a soft, sexy sound; the whispering sound lovers make in the night. "Okay, I'll forgive you, but just this once." He bent to her, touching her mouth with his tongue.

Then he groaned with that first touch—with the gentle moan, the shudder of need Lissa could no longer help or hide. She wanted him so badly, oh, how she needed this to be *real*....

And then he shuddered. "Lissa, oh, Lissa, I can't wait anymore."

And finally, at long last, her sweetest girlhood fantasy came to life: Mitch McCluskey, her first and secret love, the man whose shadowy form still came to her bed in the darkness of her dreams, held her in his arms, not as a friend, but a lover. Caressing her skin. Touching her hair. Lifting her face—

And he kissed her.

"I'm in." The tired man hunched over the computer tapped the keys one final time, and, like magic, the database opened to his bleary eyes. After a few more minutes of searching, he spoke to the other man, young and intense, standing in the shadows of deep night behind him. "Yeah, Damon, you were right. It's your boy."

"You're sure?" The young man's eyes blazed, as bright as the other's were weary; but then, he'd woken the former data operator at 2:00 am. Lucky he had a liking for money and a grudge against the Air Force for dishonorable dismissal. "Confirm it's Squadron Leader Mitchell McCluskey of the Royal Australian Air Force?"

The long-haired hacker, as slovenly and unkempt now as he'd once been clean-cut and meticulous, punched more keys. "Here's the list of his career. It's Ex-Squadron Leader McCluskey now. He quit a couple of years ago."

The younger man started. "What? He left the force two years ago?" He frowned and paced the room. "Then why the hell was he in Tumah-ra on recon? Why would the brass let a civilian check out a war zone? Something's not right— something stinks in all this." He chewed the inside of his lip, looking thoughtful. "Or was he there *without* orders— without *official* orders?"

The hacker shrugged. "Final mission or something? A Joan Sutherland command performance for the brass? I dunno. I'm just a computer geek. Anyway, it's the guy you're after. He brought the kid in illegally all right. Here's the printout from DIMA. Careful with them. It's classified." He tossed the sheets over.

The man known to the backstreet hacker as Damon caught the printed sheets from the Department of Immigration, and slowly read them through. "The department wanted to keep the kid in some refugee facility until they sorted out what to do with her, but McCluskey got clearance to take her to a Tumah-ran family living in Darwin. God knows how he managed that—this kind of clearance could only come from the top brass. What the hell's he up to?"

"I don't know, man. I did my job." The hacker held out

his hand expectantly for the envelope Damon held in his fist.

Damon handed the envelope to the other man, with a slow grin, and walked to the door. "This was a transnational crime. No matter how he got the clearance or who got him into Tumah-ra, he broke the law—and someone in high places is covering up for him. It seems Ex-Squadron Leader McCluskey's sins are finally about to catch up with him. One way or another."

The hacker turned back to the computer, placing the envelope beside him, and Damon clicked the silencer on in time to the clacking keyboard. Then, with consummate casualness, he turned and shot the hacker through the head.

The next five shots took out his hard drive.

Within seconds Damon walked out, carrying the hacker's every disk, as well as the envelope containing both his money and the only trace of his fingerprints in this cheap backyard office. He changed his shoes in the yard, and gave the previously unused runners to a grateful drunk in the alley behind the house.

All bases covered—for now.

# Chapter 3

Mitch was finally kissing her....

And oh, how he kissed her.

In dreams her gentle hero, her wandering prince, kissed her in exquisite tenderness and dainty persuasion, showing her how precious she was to him. Then he'd hold her and tell her he loved her and ask her to marry him. Then he'd sweep her up in his arms and carry her to the bedroom...and the loving would be as sweet and tender as the kiss.

*Welcome to the real world, Lissa....*

Either the sun had shifted a million miles closer or Mitch's kiss was hot enough to burn her alive. She was plastered against him from breast to thigh. His kiss ravaged her with a hunger bordering on desperation. He plundered her mouth with lips and teeth and tongue, intense, overwhelming, insatiable. His hands glided, cupped, caressed every inch of exposed flesh, exposing what wasn't open to his search with low impatient growls every time he found a barrier, pushing aside what he could, tearing what he could not. As if he had to know every secret inside her, right here, right now.

This fevered need to devour her—all of her—did not just come from temporary male deprivation. She knew it, could feel it: the fever, the need, was all for *her*. He kissed her as if he couldn't get enough of her...and she moaned, matching kiss for kiss, touch for touch, meeting his need with her own, because she couldn't get enough, either. He was melting her from the inside out. Every flimsy barrier she'd erected against his potent magic puddled like heated rain at her feet. Her body was on fire, her breathing ragged, her breasts swollen, nipples hard. Her belly was a rippling lava pool of heat. She wanted to eat him alive, drink him inside her, suck him in through her very pores....

Drag him to bed and love him all day and night.

"Can you feel me?" he growled too soon, moving his arousal against her without shame or compromise. "I've been this hard all day, knowing I was finally going to see you again. I've been in pain since I saw you in the garden— and right now I'm ready to explode at one more touch— just one. So don't push me, Miller, or I'll show you here and now, where our kids could come in any moment, how much I don't want you!"

She staggered back, groping for support. Her body was flushed with heat, her lips swollen, throbbing with a pleasure bordering on pain—the sweetness of pure feminine sexuality she'd never known. She couldn't speak; she could only watch him, her eyes wide, her pulse pounding. Waiting for the rest of what this new, totally foreign, frighteningly male Mitch had to say.

He followed her like a stalking panther in the jungle grass, moving with sinuous grace and pulsing heat until he stood before her. Breathing. Just breathing. Hot and hard and ready to mate.

Her knees almost collapsed beneath her.

He only touched her chin, yet she felt trapped, helpless, made weak by her own wanting and the once-sure knowledge, untested until now, that Mitch, *her* Mitch, would never hurt her in a physical way. "So let's get this straight," he said softly, his heated breath caressing her face. "No woman would make my boys a better mother than you. I'm not ashamed to admit that—but I want you as my lover, no matter who else benefits from it or how much I need you for the kids. *I* want *you.* I want you in my bed as well as in my life. I want you for *me.* You're like a foreign fever inside me there's no shot for. I always did and I always will want you. Totally. Constantly. Always."

Shooting straight from the hip. No sweet words. No half promises. No winning smile. Just Mitch.

*I can't speak pretty words. I only speak what I know.*

She groped for a chair and sat before she fell down. As soon as she could stop shaking, she whispered, "If…if that's true, why haven't you ever told me?"

He crouched before her; she could see him trying to gauge her reaction. "When you were fourteen, your parents would have stopped our friendship, or Old Man Taggart would have sent me back to the orphanage. Then, when you were sixteen, I was going to tell you, but you started dating Tim first. Then you were engaged—then married."

She felt tears well up. Tears for all the years lost, all the innocence forsaken. The belief in herself she'd never gotten back since she married Tim Carroll, the childhood friend she never should have married at all. "It's too late, Mitch." She choked on the words so badly they came out as a whisper.

"Why?" he asked, just as quiet.

How could she explain? There were only bald words— words she couldn't utter. She swiped at her tears, wishing he'd turn away so she wouldn't humiliate herself by having him watch her crying.

He brushed at her face, more of a caress than a wipe of her tears. "What did he do to you, Lissa-My-Lissa?"

With the nickname he used to give her in private—

coined from one of her beloved Anne of Green Gables books—he melted her. She bit her lip. ''Please, let's not talk about it now,'' she murmured, soft and husky. ''It's not worth it.'' *I just want to forget.*

''It's worth talking about if it's stopping you from taking another chance on life,'' Mitch argued quietly. ''It affects my life, too. And the boys' lives, as well.''

He had a point; but she'd kept silent so long about her marriage, she didn't know how to speak. ''Not yet.'' She twisted her hands in her lap. ''Please. I'm thinking about it. You shocked me, saying it like that so fast, but—I'm not saying a final no. I realize how much is at stake for the boys. And...and for you.''

He pulled her hands into his, kissing each abused finger, slowly and tenderly. She trembled, watching the intimate, sensual act, as if they were already lovers. ''I've waited this long. I can wait a little longer. Take your time. I know it's hard for you to trust me. I've been away too long. I'll go play with the kids.'' He smiled at her in strong, masculine sensuality. ''But you will be mine,'' he said softly, getting to his feet. ''And when you are, there'll be no divorce. It's forever this time.''

Her gaze lifted in teary challenge. ''And will you be mine, or is this marriage-and-forever proposal only a one-way contract? You know, like—you owner, me slave?''

Almost at the door he wheeled back, frowning, searching into her gaze with disturbing depth. But whatever he sought, he obviously didn't find it. ''If you honestly don't know the answer to that question, you never knew me at all.''

She gave a shuddering sigh. ''Maybe I didn't,'' she conceded, hating the sharp dagger thrust of pain the admission cost her. ''And that's no basis for marriage, is it?''

In three strides he was before her, lifting her to her feet, looking into her eyes again. This time she felt as if he read past her words and straight into her soul. ''Where's my brave Lissa gone, who took on all comers that hurt me?

Liss, maybe it's yourself you don't know. It's what's inside you—all the fears, all your anger—you're afraid to let out. You're so scared of life, even healing from whatever Tim did to you terrifies you." He touched his lips gently to her cheek, and she felt her whole face flame—from both the kiss, and his perception. How did he know so much about her most secret self, when he'd been everywhere around the world but near her in twelve long years?

Mitch sighed at the implicit rejection, but in sadness, not impatience. "Oh, baby, whatever it was he did to destroy your self-confidence, I can fix it if you'll only let me."

Again she wanted to cry. After six years she thought she'd become an expert at shutting off all feeling except with the kids. Yet she'd been with Mitch less than two hours and she'd fallen apart, not once, but twice. He'd done it again, he'd woven the Merlin wand over her soul, making her think, feel, *want....*

She couldn't afford to want—not Mitch. He'd only walk out again. Sooner or later everyone walked out on her.

She lowered her gaze before he could see the hunger growing, screaming inside her like a living thing, *I want, I want, I want.* "It wasn't Tim's fault." She balled her hands into fists to stop the nervous twisting. "He didn't want to hurt me."

"Yeah, right. That's what they all say. I thought you were too intelligent to fall for such a pitiful line." His tender understanding vanished like a shimmering water hole in the desert. "'Sorry, I couldn't help myself—I fell in love,'" he mimicked, a painful if unconsciously perfect parody of Tim's words to her the night he walked out. He gripped her arms, his gaze burning into hers with frightening intensity. "Grow up, Lissa. Wake up! Men have been saying that crap since the dawn of time, making the same lame excuses for their behavior, and women swallow it, forgive them and let them home when they're tired of that little piece of variety. All his life Tim's done whatever the hell he liked, and let others pay the price for his selfishness.

And if I knew where he lived I'd go and shove his damn line down his lying throat!'' She was stunned, unable to speak, as he stared hard at her. ''I thought you were smart.'' His voice lashed at her like a low predatory snarl of a panther on the hunt. ''The guy left you. He's been gone six years. He slimed on you and screwed around on you and left when you were pregnant with his own kid. Why the hell are you still loyal to him?''

Trembling inside as they stood face-to-face, their bodies almost touching, she still managed to face him down. ''He might have left me—but you see, *he* comes back. He calls to see if I'm all right, that I'm still alive, if I need anything. He might be in love with someone else, but he still looks after us, fixing stuff, painting, maintaining the house for me. He helps me with the kids, he's been like a father to the boys, as well as Jenny. He loves them all.'' And she held his heated, angry gaze with her own fury, burning inside her with an intensity hotter and stronger than ever after twelve years. *''He still comes back to me*—and that alone would earn my loyalty, if nothing else.''

''He comes back to see Jenny. He calls to ease his guilt over leaving you—he knows you won't take anything from him, with that damn-fool stubborn pride of yours. So he comes back once a fortnight like a conquering hero, plays with the kids, pats you on the head with a few household jobs and gets free sex in gratitude for his sterling efforts.'' He was openly furious now. ''Which part of that particular form of care turns you on, Lissa? Is that what you call a relationship? Or don't you care, so long as you're not alone for those few hours before he goes back to his other lover? You certainly have changed, if you've sunk low enough to swallow such a pitiful amount from him.''

She shivered, sick to her stomach with his calculating assessment, as if he'd dissected her soul to find the disease within. But she couldn't answer him. Even letting him think she was a fool of this caliber was better than his knowing the truth.

He shoved his fists in his pockets, his dark gaze tight and brooding. "I wish I knew why the hell you still love him," he said quietly. "Why, Lissa? Do you even know?"

Unable to stand any more, she turned away.

Moments later he stalked out the door to the kids.

The sight of him playing with the children, his strong dark face alight with love and laughter, was more than she could take. She stalked out to the market garden, cursing herself for her stupidity. She might have won this round in keeping her secret—but was maintaining her pride intact worth the ultimate cost? Deep inside she knew that, through her damn-fool pride and stubbornness, she'd won one fight, but she might well have lost something far more precious than a battle with the truth: the implicit trust and faith she'd always had with Mitch.

"That's enough, Burstall. You hear me?"

The young man in uniform stiffened; his strong, square jaw tightened. "It's the truth, sir. He smuggled the kid in, and it's not the first time, is it? What happens to the kids after? Are the adoptions legal or bought? What level clearance does McCluskey have, to keep breaking transnational laws and getting away with it? What brass is in on this? This case involves people smuggling at its worst, sir. And you know that yourself, sir!"

A short silence, his commanding officer clearly shifting, on edge. "It's commendable that you have such eagerness to fulfil your work, Burstall, but this time I'm giving you a direct order—to leave it. Leave Squadron Leader McCluskey alone."

"But he's not a Squadron Leader now, is he, sir. He left the Air Force two years ago."

"How do you—damn it, that's highly classified information!" his commander barked, half starting up from his chair, his face purpling. "If you've been using our computers to break access codes for more dope on McCluskey, I'll personally see you get a dishonorable discharge from all duties—anywhere! No more investigation into this. You're not to gain access to check on those adoptions. Are we clear on this, Burstall?''

"High connections giving you pressure, sir?" Damon taunted softly. "Has McCluskey got a politician in his payroll? Seems so—and he'd need one pretty high up to keep this under a tight lid. The immigration minister? The prime minister?" He let his gaze, flat with accusation, speak for him. "It's harder to fight this filthy trade when those at the top are involved. It makes it hard to keep your own job, doesn't it, sir?"

The commander's heavy-jowled face reddened. "That's enough, Burstall. There's more going on here than you know or need to know. Leave Squadron Leader McCluskey alone. That's an order!"

With open reluctance, Damon took the hint, saluted his commanding officer, turned on his heel and left the office.

So he couldn't use his computer anymore. It was probably safer not to. Anyway, it'd be a snap to find another ex-military hacker with a mercenary soul. It was amazing how easy it was to find people with a grudge against the forces these days.

# Chapter 4

**D**amn it all.

His facial muscles ached with the forced grin for the kids' sake. He wanted to yell, throw something, punch his fist through the wall at the back of the house—the fresh-painted wall that bore testimony to Tim's ongoing care of his family.

"Hey, Dad, catch!"

Automatically Mitch dived for Luke's tossed ball and threw it back, lifted Jenny in the air for her catch and throw, all the while his thoughts stuck on Lissa like lava to rock.

Oh, yeah, he wanted to hit something all right—but most of all he wanted to put a fist through his thick skull for letting himself get caught up in dreams again.

The price he paid for dreaming was way too high.

He knew all right. He'd been paying the price ever since Tim beat him to asking Lissa to the school formal. And then he'd asked her to every social function in Breckerville after that, until everyone in town assumed Tim and Lissa would marry. And he'd taken off to the Air Force as if the hounds of hell chased him, going after the only dream he had left.

"Piggy in the middle!"

Mitch took the part of piggy, wondering if his smile had gone into atrophy yet, it had been plastered there so long.

Damn Tim, too. Man, he'd love to ram his fist down Tim's throat! If he'd stayed around, Mitch wouldn't be going through this turmoil of anguish and fear and hope and sexual hunger.

*Liar.*

His hunger for Lissa was unending: a gnawing in his gut that hadn't even dwindled in seventeen years, let alone died. Whether she was married or single only made a difference in his hopes for the future; the need remained unchanged.

Which was why he'd stayed away from the only real home he'd known for so long. He'd gone through hell on earth for years, watching Tim and Lissa holding hands or sharing the occasional gentle kiss. But the thought of Tim touching her body, moving inside her, gave him the most primitive of urges—to wrap his hands round his best friend's throat, throw him bodily away from her and take up where Tim left off.

No! He still couldn't handle that Tim ever touched her at all. Oh, how he'd *ached* to be Lissa's first love and lover...her last love and lover. As she would be his. First, last and only.

He'd requested a base in another state when he heard of their engagement. He couldn't tolerate constantly being near the woman for whom he felt such addictive love and powerful, forbidden lust—never touching her, never knowing her kiss. The craving he couldn't conquer or kill off.

Lissa. Always Lissa. Forever Lissa.

He'd only come back to Breckerville for the wedding because Lissa had begged him to. He hadn't been able to make himself let her down. Then he'd made the mistake of his life, having one or six beers too many and he'd let the whole town know, in his damn-fool speech, that he was hopelessly in love with the bride.

But Tim knew. Tim had always known how he felt about Lissa. So why had Tim thrown him out of their lives? It wasn't as though Mitch had had the gall—or the guts—to make a move on her.

But today he couldn't rein in his hunger for her anymore. How could he control the bounding of his heart when Lissa said she was free? How could he tell his crazy heart *not* to hope…or keep his stupid mouth from blurting the proposal? How could he hold back from taking her in his arms, kissing her and touching her sweet honey-toned skin when she'd made it so clear, even unconsciously, that she wanted him?

*She wants me.*

The words thrummed through his body like a fevered pulse in the night. *She wants me.* That was such a bloody miracle to his starved body, and the need and hopes he'd kept under control too many years, that he'd all but jumped on her. He'd forgotten all his good intentions and eaten her alive like a starving man at a banquet, tearing at her clothes to touch her when he should have been giving her the tenderness and the gentle wooing she deserved.

But Lissa didn't want restraint. She wanted heat and fire and passion. He'd only been here two hours, and with one kiss—one mad, glorious kiss—her eyes and body told him she was ready, no, *burning* to make love.

She could deny it forever, and he'd know it for the panic-stricken lie she told. When he'd shown her the physical evidence of how much he supposedly *didn't* want her, her body spoke to him with an exquisite, fiery eloquence that negated any terrified utterance coming from her mouth, before or after.

*She wants me.*

Something walloped into his head. "Oooof!" He fell backward into the water, glad of the full dousing, cooling his brain and libido. He had to put this on hold or he'd tear back inside to Lissa—and the kids might end up seeing him act in a way the kids should never have to see.

The boys had had too much of seeing how badly adults can behave from their mother, and Jenny was just starting to warm to him, seeing him as a friend of the family. If he blew it now, family harmony could be ruined for the next decade—that was, if Lissa ever let her barriers down enough to show him what the hell was going on to make her back off from his proposal as if he was the devil incarnate.

"I booked the table at Bob's for you."

The cool, gentle voice turned the refreshing water around him to a seething cauldron, scalding him from the inside out. He turned to her, hoping the instant fire in his body from just hearing her voice didn't show in his eyes. He had enough to do, fighting her current demons without adding more to it.

But she'd brushed her hair, falling over her shoulders in a cascade of sun-kissed honey; and the simple sundress she wore, with spaghetti-thin straps and gently molded bodice, fanned flame to bushfire as wild and unstoppable as the statewide burn he'd helped fight in '94. Dumping fifty choppers full of water had barely touched 'em—and the coldest of showers wouldn't douse the heat blazing through him now.

Keep it cool and friendly. You can do it. You always did before. "Thanks." He barely managed not to croak. "What time?"

He watched Lissa's tension fade with his prosaic remark. "Six. Jenny's usually in bed by seven-thirty."

"Sounds good." He hauled himself out of the pool and reached for a towel. "C'mon, kids. Better start getting ready. I need to iron my clothes, if that's okay."

"Uh, yeah. Um, fine. I…"

Her voice had a strangled tone to it—the suffocated sound of a woman in sexual thrall. He looked up from toweling himself to find Lissa's gaze fixed on his bare chest. Then it traveled over every part of his bare skin, slow and dazed, her lips parted, her eyes a dark, stormy gray. She seemed mesmerized by him, head to foot. The delicate flush from the line of her bodice to her cheek told him exactly where her thoughts were.

Same place his were, every time he looked at her, or even thought about her.

The pool. The bed. Hell, the floor or the paddock where they'd talked so often as kids. Cool, slippery loving, heated sex in tangled sheets…the untamed mating of mustangs in the wild. Any or all of the above, so long as it was just them: Mitch and Lissa and nothing between.

"Yeah." He moved the towel, opening it a little wider to reveal more of his body, reveling in her fascinated stare, the rushes of air he could hear moving in and out of her sweet lips. As her eyes caressed his swim trunks—and the obvious arousal beneath—her tongue delicately moistened her mouth, slow and sensual, and he struggled to hold in the groan of painful glory. She was so aroused, so lost in wonder just looking at him, she was all but unconscious of it—and reminding her now would only send her running again. "Where should I do it?" he asked softly.

"In my room," she whispered, then blinked, as if thinking, *What am I saying?* But she didn't retract it—and hope soared inside him. He wanted her so much he was in pain.

Would she come silently to him in the night, bring him to her bed? Or take his hand and lead him out to make love in a warm summer night, in a paddock lit with a million stars?

"Silly Mummy," Jenny giggled. "Why would he put the iron in your room? It wouldn't fit in with the bed there!"

He watched Lissa shake herself. "Oh. Of course. Silly me." Dull color replaced the sweet, sensual flush of moments before. She clapped her hands, reverting to the in-control mother. "Go in and get ready kids, or we'll be late for our pizza."

"Yeah! Pizza!" All three bolted to their rooms.

She turned to him, with the first genuine smile she'd

given him all day. "We have a spare room. It's next to mine. I'm in Mum and Dad's old room. Yours is my old room. You remember. Take your bags and change in there. You'll stay with us until you fix up the Taggart place, of course. It's unlivable as it is now."

Better and better…this couldn't have been more perfect if he'd scripted it himself. Lissa had just said far more than her simple words. By letting him stay—by giving him her old room—she'd given him a message. She was willing to offer him a second chance to be trusted. She'd give his idea a twice-over before she threw him out.

And maybe, just maybe, she wanted him to stay near her.

"Thanks, Lissa." He started to move past her, but paused to gently brush his mouth on her cheek.

She almost stumbled back, as she had after he kissed her—no, *mauled* her—in the kitchen. "Good old reliable me." She flashed him a wobbly grin.

He knew that look, that gorgeous, wonderful, green-light look of feminine desire and uncertainty; uncertain of what, he could also read in her eyes. Gently he lifted her chin. "You know, magazines and books say men find unpredictable women a real turn-on. Maybe I'm a freak of nature, but the woman who's always turned me on is beautiful in her serenity. I like knowing she's there when I need her. I love that she doesn't put on an act to be interesting. She's herself, and happy to be. She's so naturally sexy I can hardly breathe when I'm around her." He placed her hand over his thundering heart. "This is what reliable does to me, when you're the one who's reliable. Is that a good enough definition for you, Lissa?"

She couldn't look up, but her fiery cheeks and trembling lashes told him all he needed to know. "Mitch, I…I need time. I can't believe what you're saying—that you want me," she whispered in an almost despairing tone.

His heart soared, for the despair came from Lissa's waging an inner battle against her demons. Within a day he was winning the fight for her body and heart against her

old friends of pride and fear. "I'm not going anywhere." *Ever.*

"Thank you." Suddenly she wrapped an arm around his
neck, her gaze lifted, showing him the aching depths in her
sweet gray eyes, her mouth parted, wet and glistening,
matching his hunger with her own. "Mitch, I need time,
not gentleness. I need to know this is *real.*" She muttered,
almost to herself, "I need to feel alive again...."

He pulled her up hard against him and put them both out
of their misery with another deep, hot kiss, all but exploding in the fire bursting to life between them. Hands and
lips and tongues, meeting, mating, eagerly seeking more.
Finding his sun-kissed wet skin, fresh and bare, she roamed
with hands and mouth, making the softest of low purring
growls in her throat with every touch, every taste of him.
She kept pushing closer and closer, rubbing, touching, tasting, clearly reveling in his aroused state. He was too—in
the tautness of her nipples, the way she caressed her most
intimate self on him.

Beautiful, so beautiful. Loving Lissa was hotter, sweeter,
richer than any fantasy he'd ever had—it was like discov-
ering rum-laced mocha chocolate after a lifetime of making
do with cheap instant coffee. The warm silkiness of her
skin...the fire in her touch, in her eyes, in her kiss. The
luscious sexuality wrapping itself all around and between
them like a living entity only added to the sweet splendor
of being with her, touching her. *Let this be the start of
forever....*

"Mitch," she mumbled through kisses on his shoulder.
"Don't sleep in the spare room. Make love to me tonight."

"Are you sure?" he murmured urgently, caressing one
small, perfect breast—fulfilling a seventeen-year fantasy
and more than halfway to exploding with the potency of
one touch.

Looking up at him, her lips swollen, her delicate body
all flushed, she answered, "More than sure." She glanced
down to where his hand cradled her breast, and drew a
ragged breath. "I need to know you don't have hidden

agendas. I don't want to play Carol in any Brady Bunch fantasy. I have to know you want me—*me*—not someone for your kids or the family you never had.''

If she'd dumped a bucket of ice water over him he couldn't have killed his desire more effectively. He gawked at her. ''Where the hell did you get that crazy idea from?''

She shrugged. ''It'd be a normal thing for a guy to want who grew up the way you did, Mitch. You've never had a family, so you want one now, and I'm convenient. You know me, and you know the kids love me. And it's normal and healthy for you to want a mother for your kids after all they went through with Kerin.'' Her sudden tension, the shuttered look in her eyes, told him her inner self screamed against the lies she uttered. She didn't want anything to do with his so-called *normal* desires.

Whatever it was she was hiding from him, he had a hell of a lot to prove to her yet; his words, his kisses hadn't penetrated beyond the outer shell of her shattered self-esteem.

What the hell had Tim done to her?

''Can you doubt right now how much I want you?'' He moved over her, letting his hardness speak for itself. ''Does it feel like I'm playing Mike to your Carol?''

''Prove it,'' she muttered fiercely.

The fiery sexuality in her challenge hit him hard and fast, smashing all his good intentions. He growled in her ear, ''Baby, if you don't control this, I'll prove it all right. Because I'm about to lose control. Big-time. So either we hold this off until tonight, or I hitch up this pretty dress of yours and give you all the proof you need. And I swear to God I won't last longer than three seconds, I'm so damn close. And not for any woman—for you. Only you, with your sweet body and mouth made for sin.''

She leaned on his chest, breathing in high, tattered gasps. Apparently, she believed that much—at least for now. ''I wish we could,'' she whispered so low he could barely hear her. Then she whirled away, walking with an unsteady gait to the house.

"Lissa?"

She looked over her shoulder; her eyes smoldered with need so raw, heat so intense it made him ache all over again, burning alive in the fire erupting beneath the calm surface of her. "Prove it—and not just with pretty words or a few kisses." She drew a deep, shaking breath. "I want us to be lovers—constant lovers—for six months, maybe a year, before I'll tell you whether or not I'll marry you. I can't—I *won't* give you any more than that. Not now. Maybe not ever."

He dropped the towel at the same time his jaw hit the ground. "What the *hell* is this—"

But she'd already run into the house.

Slowly, he picked up his towel, rubbing his body by reflex, though it had already been dried by the sun and Lissa's eager hands. Hands he wanted to bear his rings. A life he wanted to share, a body he did not just want to have fun with.

What was going on here? Why on earth did his traditional Lissa want to shack up with him? Was she trying to tell him she wanted him but didn't need him in her life beyond sex?

Anguish tore and clawed at his gut, hurt his very soul…all he'd ever known or thought, every certainty he had, blown away with the blasting force of a few words. An offer that probably figured as most men's fantasies come to life left only a bitter taste in his mouth.

There was no way he could leave it like this, or accept it.

What Lissa demanded went against everything he'd ever wanted or dreamed of—and ran counter to her own intrinsic nature. Something had hurt her so badly—damn, he wanted to *kill* Tim for whatever it was he'd done to her—that she was fighting *herself,* all she'd once believed in, to have him prove his need for her.

But he had a card to play—one fabulous ace. He could turn the sweet unexpectedness of Lissa's hot sexuality back on her.…

If she wants me she's gonna have to come get me—on my terms.

He only hoped like crazy he could hold off his own desperate need to make love to her until he knew the secrets hiding behind the barriers in her pretty, suffering eyes.

''Reliable,'' huh?

She'd done it! Even now, she could hardly believe she'd said it. She'd given her demands without negotiation. She'd thrown down her gauntlet, shown Mitch in unmistakable terms that she was *not* the old Lissa Miller—the innocent, vulnerable, gullible, *available* girl he'd known. She was a woman now, with a woman's emotions and needs, and she wasn't ashamed to tell him.

Okay, maybe *embarrassed,* but not ashamed. She had no need to be. She'd put up with far less than second best once, and she'd never do that again—*especially* not with Mitch. Second best with Mitch would only pave the highway to hell. She wanted to be so much more to him than a convenient wife and mother.

After Tim left, a few men had showed interest in her, but none of them had remotely appealed to her or begun to patch the deep, dark abyss in her self-confidence from Tim's desertion…from the life she'd shared with Tim, long before he left. Starting with their honeymoon…she shuddered with the force of memory of those two horrible weeks.

No! She didn't *want* to remember. All she wanted was to forget—as Tim obviously had. Apart from the money he scrupulously paid every month for Jenny's welfare, he'd put away all thoughts of their disastrous marriage and reverted without any trouble to being her best mate and helper. As if nothing had ever happened to interrupt their twenty-year friendship.

It wasn't going to happen with Mitch. She'd be damned if it would! If he ever walked, it would be because *she* wanted out. And *he* wouldn't forget her—she'd make sure of it. He'd wake up nights with sweat pouring down his face and body, dreaming of what it had been like for them, craving more—

She felt a slow smile curve her mouth…hmmm. Made for sin. Oh, if only she could do it, make him want her so badly she could—

The doorbell rang. She moved to answer it, knowing the kids wouldn't bother and Mitch was probably still reeling in shock from her ultimatum. She grinned wider. She liked that idea.

She opened the door to a man with plain brown hair, a quiet manner, a common gray suit and strangely anonymous dark glasses. "Melissa Carroll? We need to talk. Privately."

A quarter of an hour later she shut the door on her unexpected visitor, blinked and checked her watch. Five o'clock. She'd opened the door at nineteen minutes to five, thinking she had some measure of control over her world.…

Now she knew it for the lie it was. Everything she once thought she knew was upside-down; everything had changed. Sick, shivering, scared to her marrow, she had no choice but to go on with this miserable charade with Mitch. Even if the man in gray who'd come to the door hadn't demanded her total cooperation, and that she keep Mitch in the dark, she would have gone through with it for Matt and Luke's sake. They'd been through enough tragedy in their short lives without knowing that their beloved father, far from being an honorable squadron leader in the Air Force, a hero from East Timor and Bosnia, was nothing more than a—dear God, she couldn't even *think* the words. Oh, that poor little girl.…

*Damn you, Mitch! Damn you!*

*Fool!* Why did she ever think she could trust him? Why did she ever kid herself into believing he'd ever really want her?

"Da-ad! C'mon, Dad, we'll be late!"

Despite feeling as if he'd been hit by a truck by Lissa's ultimatum, Mitch grinned. Matt had bounced back from his momentary bout of insecurity, already taking him for granted again—just as a kid should. ''Coming!'' He emerged from the room to find his sons bouncing with eagerness outside his door.

Luke immediately grabbed his hand, his eyes still dancing with shadows. Mitch swung him onto his hip. ''Still here, kiddo. I promised, didn't I?''

Luke's whole body relaxed; he smiled and nodded. Matt, with an empathetic look on his face, also hugged his brother, in the total understanding that comes with being an identical twin. They might be as different as a kangaroo and a koala, but their bond was unbreakable, their empathy beyond what even the most loving father could relate to; he was just glad they had it. And it was proven again. Luke flushed, knowing he'd acted like a little kid—and Matt immediately said, ''Cut out the girl stuff, Dad. I'm *hungry!*''

''Me, too!'' Luke wriggled off his hip and bolted toward Mitch's car, parked out the front. ''C'mon, Jen, stop puttin' girly ribbons in your hair. We wanna eat!''

''Yeah!'' With one of the despised ribbons floating from her hair, Jenny tore out the door without so much as a glance at him. He chuckled as the kids fought over who had to sit in the middle. Oh, Matt and Luke were part of a secure family all right.

At that moment Lissa emerged from her room next to his. He felt her presence, though she didn't speak. He slowly turned to her, wondering what she'd say next to stun him—

He almost reeled back in shock at the sight of her.

She was trembling, wraithlike in sudden ethereal paleness. Her eyes, dark and blank with horror, looked at him as if she'd thought he'd sprouted horns in the last half hour. He didn't need Matt and Luke's silent form of communication to tell him something was wrong—very wrong. Something connected to him.

''Lissa?'' He started toward her. ''What is it?''

She cringed. Oh, dear God, Lissa literally cringed from

him. "We'll be late for the dinner reservation. We'd better go," she whispered, as if she couldn't speak any louder.

If he weren't so damn scared he'd laugh in her face at the pitiful excuse. They'd be almost the only people at Bob's on a Wednesday night, and she knew it.

"The kids are hungry." She spoke as if the fact was something profound. Her eyes couldn't meet his. Her hands twisted around each other, and she bit the inside of her cheek—classic signs with Lissa that she wanted to bolt.

*From him?* Simple fear upgraded to sheer terror. "Lissa, you look like a ghost. Are you sick? Let me help you." In a lightning move, he grabbed her hands before she backed off again.

She worried her cheek even more but left her hands passively in his. "I'm fine. It…it's the heat, and the garden's worrying me. If I don't harvest enough to sell at the country market at Bathurst, I'll fall behind in my mortgage on the farm—"

"I'll help you. I can harvest fruit and vegetables as easily as you, Lissa. And if we're late, we can use my courier plane to fly them to Bathurst to make the market."

"All right. Thank you." She looked down and away.

If anything, the acceptance of his offer made her tense even more. Her sweet spunk of this afternoon was gone, vanished like the Phantom down his tunnels. Her hands were so cold he wanted to shiver…and he wondered when she'd tell him the truth. Or if she would at all.

He chaffed her hands, trying to inject his warmth into them. "Lissa, can't you trust me enough to tell me what's upset you?" he asked softly, wishing, hoping to reach her shielded heart. Her eyes lifted to his for a brief moment, flashing with hot resentment, a fury he'd never seen in her, even after he'd proposed today. Then, as swift as flight, it was gone and so was she, retreating inside herself. The vivid, passionate woman who entranced him half an hour ago was encased again in delicate ice, frozen in time— lovely and pure, cold and lifeless as the ship's figurehead he'd likened her to before. Lost in the mists of time, with no one to sail or steer her back to port. A dead woman still breathing. "Maybe I'm hungry, too. We should go."

He couldn't leave it like this, even though he knew he was digging a deeper hole for himself. He loved her too much to leave her suffering. "If it's money you're worried about, baby, don't. If you marry me you'll never have to worry about anything again." He clicked his tongue savagely. "Oh, damn. I know I put that badly, but I want to take care of you for the rest of our lives." He lifted one hand after the other to his mouth, warming her with his inner heat. Loving her like crazy. Wanting her to belong to him, with him, forever. Yes, damn it, wanting the family he'd never had...but only with her. "Marry me, Lissa."

There was a long, dreadful silence before she spoke. "Is that what you want, Mitch?" Her voice was trembling so badly he had to strain to hear her. "You really want that?"

"Yes," he answered without a second's hesitation. "I'd marry you today if I could."

Lissa shuddered. Oh, God, she shuddered—and it wasn't in passion or joy. "All right," she murmured. "Whenever you want."

He had his answer—she'd marry him—but her dull, lifeless tone ripped him apart from the inside. She didn't want it; she didn't want *him*. It half killed him to put the words together, but he managed it, for her sake. "Lissa, if you don't want this—if you don't want to marry me—"

Absolute, unbelievable terror flashed in her eyes for a second, long enough to drain her face to pasty white. Her eyes skittered around the room, as if seeking something out. "No, no—of course I want it. I said so, didn't I?" Her eyes returned to his face, filled with pleading anguish. "Please, Mitch..."

Oh, help. If he were any sort of honorable man, he'd retract his proposal now, give her more time—or give her freedom. But he suddenly discovered he wasn't honorable enough for that.

Or was it that? Some gut instinct he had to work with told him that she needed him—now more than ever. He didn't know what happened in the past half hour, but he knew Lissa was in trouble. Trouble bad. Trouble deep.

Whatever she was hiding from him was bad news. Someone or something had put her under compulsion to agree to his proposal, and he realized that, like Lissa, he had little choice but to go on with it until he got the truth from her…one way or another.

Was this a Nighthawk-related thing? Did someone know?

By marrying her, he could find out.

Stupid jerk—you're lying to yourself! After seventeen years aching for her, I'd take Lissa any way I can have her.

Not much of an officer and a gentleman after all.

So he quietly said, "Thank you," and released her hands, walking beside her out to the car.

Opening the door for her, he saw a tear fall onto the step as she passed him. She was shaking so badly, she held on to the post to walk down the stairs and again to walk through the gate. It amazed him that she even made it to the car.

More than anything he wanted to take her in his arms, hold her and reassure her, melt her fear into trust, kiss her ice into fire. But his gut screamed at him to back off, give Lissa space and time until he knew what was going on. Because he had a bad feeling about this whole situation. A feeling that a hell of a lot more was going on than just Mitch McCluskey and Lissa Miller alone. He had a premonition, a gut-gnawing feeling that the Nighthawks were mixed up in this somehow…and the lid of four decades of highest-level secrecy was about to come off.…

In an explosion of nuclear proportions.

## Chapter 5

He was beginning to wonder if they'd get past the wedding vows before he found out who was holding what threat over Lissa.

Some spy he was. He couldn't even worm information from the woman he was going to marry or listen in on those whispered phone calls that came night and day. All he knew about her was that she was a fabulous cook, was utterly devoted to the kids, had a home security system to rival the best stores—he'd yet to discover why—and that she was rather a good kickboxer. As were the boys. They took lessons together every Monday and Thursday. He'd watched her last week. She'd dropped her opponent in moments without breaking a sweat. The master said she was the best and most determined student he'd ever had. She'd already reached intermediate stage—and she'd make advanced by the next meet. Six plus continuous kickboxing matches would clinch it.

Lissa—*kickboxing?*

This latest mystery felt like the tip of the dinosaur's tail.

The final piece of the puzzle to whatever the hell was going on.

He couldn't involve the Nighthawks in this yet; it was too personal. If he told Anson, he'd have to bug Lissa's phone, put hidden security cameras everywhere and, worst of all, give daily reports to his boss on Lissa's behavior.

Mitch couldn't do it to her, even though he damn well knew she was doing it to him.

She made the most piss-poor Mata Hari he'd ever known, but it made her maddeningly adorable. Asking fumbling questions about East Timor. About where he went on his courier flights. Sneaking glances at his log books to make sure.

He walked in the door from dropping the kids to school, knowing the wearying battle, the guarded questions, would begin again as soon as she heard his news.

About to push open the kitchen door, he heard her strained voice, arguing with a defensive weariness that hurt him. She must be talking to her contact again; and, just as obviously, she'd waited for him to go before calling him.

Hating the necessity, he pushed the door ajar and listened in, hoping to hear something, anything to give him a clue.

Her voice was almost desperate as she spoke.

"No, you can't—not this weekend. I'm sorry. Yes, I know, but—I know that. Have I denied you? Just listen, all right? I...I have something to tell you." Mitch heard her drag in a deep breath. "I'm getting married, Tim." A short silence. "What do you mean, how? The same way anyone else does. A man asked me and I said yes!" Another silence. "Yes," she said, sounding defiant. "It's Mitch. Just like you always said it would be."

Mitch had had enough. He pushed the door wide and strode in. Lissa gasped as he grabbed the phone from her slack hand. "G'day, Tim. Mitch here," he snapped into the silence. "I'm back and I'm marrying Lissa in ten days. You got a problem with that?"

After a moment Tim's deep chuckle came over the line.

"No, mate, why should I have a problem? I've only waited for it since the day I walked out. What took you so bloody long?"

"A small matter of not knowing you'd gone," he replied dryly.

"Another thing that's my fault, eh?" The laughter was gone now. "I knew where you were. I could have told you—I *should* have told you. And I should never have married her either. I know that. I was selfish and I stuffed up your life for years—yours and Lissa's both. I knew I was screwing up big-time, and I did it, anyway. I punished you both for my mistake. I'm sorry, Mitch."

"Bloody hell. You haven't changed, have you?" he growled in exasperation. "Do whatever you want and give the grand apology after. And the worst of it is, you always mean it. Well, it's twelve years too late as far as I'm concerned. I might have to put up with you coming here—you're Jenny's father and I wouldn't stop you seeing her if I could—but you so much as touch Lissa's hand from now on and you're dead meat. Got that?"

Another short, pregnant silence. Then Tim chuckled again, his good humor as unbreakable as ever. "I guess I deserved that—all of it. About time you got your own back on me. Have you told Lissa you love her yet, or are you still too shit-scared?"

"Go to hell," he replied without heat, starting to enjoy the conversation. Tim's charm, his rueful honesty about his failings and the ability to apologize with sincerity, had always been his saving grace—and the thing that stopped Mitch from belting him to hell and back, more than once. "Just remember what I said."

"Yeah, yeah," Tim laughed. "The obsession lives on. Mitch, my old mate, you know what I reckon? It's way past time you told her the truth. And I think it's time Lissa told you some things you obviously don't know. Put her back on, will you?"

"Yeah, bye." And he hung up.

Lissa rounded on him. "What did you hang up for? I was talking to him about arrangements for Jenny! And as for that warning, you can just—"

"Mind my own business?" he suggested, the very essence of blandness in his tone. "Um, that's what I thought I *was* doing, Lissa. Warning him off my woman. My wife-to-be."

Her jaw set. "Fine," she muttered through gritted teeth, and swung away, cleaning the breakfast dishes with such force she cracked a plate. "Damn!" She threw the plate in the trash and kept thumping crockery in the sink.

He grinned as he grabbed a towel to wipe up. Her evident frustration was so cute...and he hoped its origin was as sexual as his own. "Um, you might want to turn the taps off there, unless you usually like to mop the floor with used dishwater."

She didn't even look at him. She snapped the taps off and continued abusing the cups and plates.

*Stop jerking her chain and get to the point.* Mitch gritted his teeth and plunged in to give her the news he'd been putting off all morning, since Anson's 5:00 a.m. call. "I have to go away for a few days. I'll be back by Sunday, maybe Monday."

The crashing stopped. "Oh?" There was a wealth of casual inquiry in her voice, but he wasn't fooled. Her every nerve was on the alert. "Setting up the business?"

"A job I need to do before I can set up. That's all."

"Where are you off to?"

Even with her back still turned, he saw her thumbnail move to her mouth, chewing, chewing. "First to Canberra, then a little place up north. You wouldn't know it."

"Oh." Her other hand was making a fist, releasing. Tugging at her simple sundress. A teardrop of perspiration trickled down her neck. "I've never been farther away from here than Sydney," she remarked, as if it were no big deal. "Maybe I could come on the trip with you?"

"Not this time," he replied, just as casually, his gut seizing. "But I'll take you wherever you want on our honeymoon. You still haven't told me where you'd like to go."

She pulled her hair out of its ponytail, shook it out and turned to smile at him over her shoulder. "It might be a good chance for us to be alone," she said softly, using her mouth to wickedly stunning effect.

Oh, hell. The bad hats must've been piling the pressure on her to mammoth proportions for her to start trying to seduce him; she'd barely touched him since his first day back home. He gulped, fighting temptation with the last threads of his self-control. "Next time. I promise."

The quick flicker of emotion, gone in an instant, socked him in the jaw like a TKO. Terror. Devastation. Anguish. Then she plastered a smile on her face, sultry and feminine, and fake as the sensual look in her eyes. "Please, Mitch. Please take me with you. I want to be alone with you. I...I could help you. We could do anything. Anything you want."

Oh, man—if she'd given him that look, that promise, without the knowledge that someone was out to destroy him through her, he'd have been in fool's heaven. As it was, her words only hurt. "Lissa, can we stop playing these games and talk?"

The flare of panic flashed again and was gone. "About what?"

He could feel terror simmering beneath the projected calm in her voice. "About why you're looking through my things. About why you're asking me about my work in the islands. About why you stopped touching me after the first day, and made excuse after excuse for us not to make love for the past three weeks."

Silence. A quiet as dark and stricken as the guilt and driven need in her eyes.

He drew in a harsh breath and said the hardest words he'd ever had to say in his life—risking his dreams, his hopes, his future in one sentence. "And I want to know

why you're marrying me when it's obvious you don't
want to."

A slow, shaking hand covered her mouth. "Mitch…"

He had to physically force himself to stand still, to not
reach out and give her comfort—the reassurance of touch
he needed as desperately as she did right now. He balled
his fists at his sides and breathed between the slamming
beats of his heart. "Baby, talk to me. I know something's
going on—that someone's got you scared. But whatever
they think they've got over you, I can fix it. Just trust me,
Lissa. I've never lied to you, and I won't start now." He
closed his eyes as she gave a silent, gulping sob. "I'll let
you go if I have to. I'll leave here, if that's what you want.
Just don't shut me out."

"Shut you out. Shut *you* out?" With startling suddenness
she laughed, loud and strong and totally fake. "Boy, have
you got a vivid imagination! Who do you think you are,
James Bond? Looking through your things! How would
you know, with the mess you keep in that room? And I
shut you out? About what? And as to questions about your
work, isn't that what all couples do?"

"Lissa—"

She shook her head and put a finger to her lips. *Shut-up,*
she mouthed, using their one-time favorite method of quiet
communication. *It's about time you finally caught on.*
"Where did you get all this rubbish about someone scaring
me?" she laughed. "Have you *seen* anyone? I've been too
busy with the kids and the wedding to see anyone. I've
barely had time to call Mum and Dad in Europe to give
them our news." Then her mouth moved, silently speaking
words echoing the terror flashing in her sweet eyes.

*The house is bugged.*

Oh, my God. So it was true.

She giggled, sweet and false, keeping up the charade.
"And as for sex—honestly, Mitch, can't you think of anything else? For goodness sake, there are times of the month
a woman can't make love, not to mention when the kids

walk in with nightmares! Of course I want to marry you. We have the rest of our lives to make love, after the wedding, when it won't damage the kids and Jenny's accepted that I won't be getting back with Tim.''

*It's there.* She pointed to the picture of the Pears soap baby in the bath. With one step he could see it hiding between the frame and the wall. The cheap kind of bug made and sold at electronics stores.

Okay. They could work with this. Their invisible friend wouldn't be able to hear them with that crappy piece of work if they whispered softly enough…but no doubt within seconds they'd come to check on the sudden silence.

Welcome to the Twilight Zone…he had the weirdest sense of unreality, the sublime and the ridiculous. Breckerville and Lissa. Home. Love. Peace. Where life was always serene and nothing bad would ever happen.

Where spies listened in and threatened the one person he'd always been sure would have a carefree life.

For God's sake, *Why?*

His scalp crawled. ''C'mere, baby. Sorry I've been stupid. I was just scared of losing you.'' He held out his arms, sweating on the hope that she'd get it. Then they could talk, just like they had from their windows in the old days, when they'd turned lip reading into an art form.

She walked into his arms, moving against his body with the sensuality of an iceberg, her skin cold and clammy with fear. ''They won't hear us at this pitch,'' he whispered into her neck.

She nodded. ''Kiss me, Mitch,'' she said aloud, her voice pulsing with sensuality. She breathed in his ear, ''There might be cameras, too, but I don't think so. I've looked.''

He kissed her, long and deep, touching and caressing her for the silent listener's benefit. ''Keep it up,'' he mouthed into hers. Relieved beyond words she'd decided to trust him, furious enough to kill whoever the hell it was doing this to her. ''What the hell's going on?''

"Talk," she whispered back. "We've kissed long enough."

She was right. He rushed on, "Sorry I've been so stupid. I just love you so much, and the thought of losing you…"

She shuddered so delicately only he felt it. "I love you, too, Mitch." The words, warm and soft, came out frigid on her lips, as insincere as the words of love he'd just given.

Damn! After waiting half a lifetime, it shouldn't be like this. None of it should be like this. But there was more at stake than his relationship with Lissa. He had to find out what was going down here, or the vital work of the Nighthawks would be destroyed. He kissed her jaw, her ear and murmured, "Who is he?"

She tugged at his ear with her teeth. "I don't know. He said you left the Air Force two years ago." She moved against him, moaning. "Darling, that's so good…"

My *God*. That was highly classified information! His cover was blown even before he set up a courier business. Anson would roar like a wounded tiger when he knew. "Let's go to bed." He cupped her bottom in his hands, his body taut with fury and unwanted arousal. "Is there anything on you? Any bugs?" he whispered.

"No. Just in every room. I think he did it when we were at Bob's the first night."

Damn and double damn.

She let her hands roam under his shirt. "I don't want our first time to be in the bed I slept in with Tim," she said in a strangled sexual mutter. "That's why I've held off, darling—not because I didn't want to. Let's make love outside, out by the water hole, where we were always together as kids."

"I'll buy us a new bed this afternoon." He chuckled aloud for the bug, but in truth stunned by her quick thinking and clever manipulation. She'd woven truth and lie, using her real life and his to find a way of getting privacy their silent watcher would find hard to doubt. And heaven help him, he was horny as hell, turned on beyond belief by the lightning change in her, by her intelligence in a terrifying situation—by the sexual game they had to play. "I'll grab a blanket."

"Mmmm…" She kissed him again. "Two blankets, darling, just in case anyone comes and sees us." Another soft, melting kiss, her eyes flashing. "He's not far away. He'll probably watch us. We'll have to make it look real—but it damn well better not be until I have answers," she whispered fiercely into his mouth. "Don't take long," she moaned aloud. "I can't wait…"

And he'd thought her predictable? Sheesh. She could win an Academy Award for this performance. But while the Nighthawk in him cheered her on, the man wanted more.

The next kiss he gave her was deep and hot and *real*. Grinding against her, getting even hotter when she pressed back, kissed him back with a passion she couldn't possibly be faking. "Is this exciting you as much as me?" he growled in her ear.

She grinned up at him. "Probably more," she whispered, "since I reckon you're probably used to it. I haven't had this much fun since I always beat you and Tim and Sally Jones at Spy versus Spy. Oh, Mitch! Now!" she cried aloud.

The memory hit him. How had he forgotten? Lissa always found the treasures buried on school orienteering games, always knew who murdered who, and where, whenever they played Cluedo, and always topped them at Spy versus Spy. Her nickname at school had been Nancy Drew. She'd been so known for her love of intrigue-type stuff she'd been voted "girl most likely to join the FBI."

So make use of it now, if only this once—then get her right out of it.

"I'll get the blankets." In her ear, "You'd better control this if you want it to stay fake, because I'm way past that."

She lifted a brow. "I like that idea," she purred, loud enough for the bug to pick up, low enough to sound saturated with sex. "Being on top. Hmm." *Try it and you're dead,* she mouthed.

He laughed and nuzzled her neck. "You're driving me nuts, Miller, you know that?"

Both brows lifted this time. The look in her eyes was pure, undiluted satisfaction. "Get the blankets." *Bug is in the hallway beside the linen cupboard.*

So she'd conducted her own search, but was smart enough to know not to destroy any of them. Good Lord, she was treating this dangerous situation like their old games...and it was working. Did he know her at all? He'd underestimated her in more ways than one. Even her clumsy attempts to look through his things now held a chilling new meaning. Dear God, she'd been all but dropping written signs for him to pick up, and he'd missed every sign.

"Go get the blankets," she purred again, her eyes telling him something else...but what?

He nodded and ran for the blankets, and had an inspiration.

After a lightning check of the house, he returned to find her with two pieces of underwear in her hand, hers and his. *Props,* she mouthed.

He shook his head with an amused grin. He'd never have thought of that. He wouldn't have wanted to. But she was right. Their first time—and it would happen soon—wasn't going to be where someone could listen in on them or see them.

She took his hand and led him out into the warm, dreaming sunshine. "Where?" she whispered.

Aloud he said, "Not the water hole, baby. Too many creepy-crawlies.... Behind the pool," he murmured for her alone. "The steel fence and the filter will hopefully interfere with any portable listening device he aims out here."

She nodded, kissed his palm and wrist, and walked toward the pool. Taking one of the blankets, she frowned. "Thermal blanket?"

"Privacy, baby. Can't have neighbors watching us." He pulled the foil-covered blanket over the pool fence as far as it would stretch. Then he crouched down behind it, lying on the blankets with her face-to-face. "Interference. It won't last long before he gets around it, so talk fast. And we'll have to undress while we're at it and make the right noises."

"Of course. I'm not stupid." She covered them both with the thin cotton sheet he'd brought out and pulled her shirt off. "Did you leave the Air Force two years ago?"

"Yes." He threw his T-shirt over his head and sent it sailing across the yard.

"Oh, Mitch, darling…" She wriggled against him, driving him crazy. Then her shorts flew across the grass. "What were you doing in East Timor, then? Were you ever there at all?"

"I was there briefly. Training some of the younger guys on stealth work. After that, I was sent to Tumah-ra, an island northwest of Darwin. Oh, baby," he moaned aloud, losing his shorts, and most of his self-control with it.

She wriggled away from him, her eyes warning him not to try it. "I know where Tumah-ra is. I saw a piece last week about the hidden war there, the world's reluctance to get involved until—" She gasped. "You took the footage. The baby at the mass grave."

He nodded, struggling to hold back. "That's part of my job."

Between soft sighs and moans she whispered, "Who do you work for? And is that where you've been when you disappeared on your 'courier' runs? To see her? Or was it to do more spy stuff?"

"I can't tell you without clearance." He groaned again and mouthed, *I heard a car door shut.*

"Yes, oh, darling—that's so good! But not good enough, McCluskey," she whispered. "You want my trust? Well, I want more answers, and I want them now!" Her bra came off. "Make it look real. Put your hands on me."

"We'd better stop whispering. He might have portable sound surveillance on us." Oh, man, he was touching her naked breasts, her nipples flush against his chest, tight and hard, exciting him almost beyond thought. He caressed her until he thought he'd go insane, landed a gentle kiss on one taut peak, then reared back before she slugged him. *Who is this guy? What did he say to you?* he mouthed.

"Baby, oh, baby, I want you now!" She flipped her spare undies onto the grass. *Don't even think about doing that again!* But her eyes, silver and burning hot, belied her threat. *He was from ASIO. He showed me ID. He said you stole that little girl—that you've been smuggling children into Australia and selling them to rich adoptive parents. He also said you're a spotter pilot for people smugglers from the Middle East, watching for the Coast Patrol and warning them.*

Holy-moly. Someone was out to get him, and get him good. If this story leaked, it would not only destroy his career and put him in a cell, it would blow the Nighthawks apart. But—

*This is all wrong, Lissa. People smuggling isn't within ASIO jurisdiction. It belongs to DIMA—the Department of Immigration—Customs and the Federal Police.*

His spare undies went the way of Lissa's. "I can't wait any more, Lissa. I need you!"

If only she knew how true that was. He needed her on this. He needed her to believe him. He needed to make love to her so bad the pain was exquisite...and he had to know she wanted it as much.

Her startled eyes told him he'd scored a hell of a point with her, telling her about DIMA. *Can you prove that?*

He pulled the foil blanket on top of them, hoping like hell it would give interference for thirty seconds. "Let me get a clean computer and Net access and I'll prove it in seconds," he whispered, barely making a sound. "This guy doesn't work for ASIO any more than I do. His bugs are cheap electronic-store stuff. If he was ASIO—or had official clearance to watch me—he wouldn't need bugs or cameras. Satellites do most of the surveillance work these days, and good bugs are the size of pinheads. This guy's a rogue, working alone—and until I know what he's after we have to keep up the act. Only for a day or two.''

She wriggled against him and moaned, ''Oh, oh, oh! But—''

''Seduction and bugging and threatening innocent people went out with the Berlin Wall. If ASIO or the Feds suspected me of people smuggling they wouldn't have involved you, an innocent bystander. They'd track my plane and check my mileage and radio contacts against my logbooks for discrepancies. A real ASIO officer or Fed can do that with a computer and satellite in hours, and I'd already be hauled in somewhere for questioning.''

She threw off the blanket and rolled beneath him, taking him with her; then she cried out as though he'd just entered her. ''Mitch!'' *Who do you work for?*

''Lissa, oh, Lissa.'' He was dying by delicious, agonizing degrees, so close he could feel her sweet wetness through her underwear, and knew she wanted him as much as he was aching for her. So far away, because if he blew it now and lost her trust, he'd never have it again. *Come with me to Canberra this afternoon. If I get clearance I'll tell you everything.*

She nodded and pulled him down for a sweet, unexpected kiss. *Thank you, Mitch. Let's finish this farce.* She softly kissed him again, then cried out his name, shuddering.

He groaned and jerked on her as though he'd just finished—and she'd never know how damn close he was to the real thing. ''He'll probably bug your things,'' he whispered in her ear. ''Let him do it. Let him think you're with him still. I can't bear to leave you,'' he groaned aloud. ''Come with me to Canberra. We'll have a few days to ourselves.'' *Don't leave my sight until we go. We'll play devoted lovers if he follows us. We'll have to share a room.*

"I'll call Tim to get the kids," she said softly, searching his eyes. *He threatened to take Matt and Luke away, give Kerin's family custody, unless I cooperate with him.*

Damn it—no wonder she'd turned so frigid on him. The one way guaranteed to make Lissa obey any order, believe any lie, get information from him and betray him. She adored his kids, and their bastard voyeur had used that. Any last lingering traces of anger against her melted. She'd been trying to save Matt and Luke from the years of misery he'd endured as an unwanted kid, until he came here. He felt humbled she'd given him a chance at all, let alone trying to tell him almost from the start. She must still care about him to do that—she had to have forgiven him, too, just a little, to risk it all and tell him.

Maybe, when all this was over, he had a chance to make this whole farce a reality.

But now wasn't the time to talk; it would blow everything. "I need to go by tonight. Call Tim and tell him we'll drop the kids at Bankstown Airport by six," he said aloud, then whispered, "When we get there, take Tim somewhere safe without any bags or purses. Tell him what's going down and get the kids away from Sydney, Breckerville or anywhere else this guy knows you've taken them. Mmm…I wish we had more time now," he groaned aloud.

"I can hardly wait until tonight. I want to make love again." Then she suddenly wrapped her arms around his neck, holding him tight. "I'm scared, Mitch," she breathed in his ear.

"Me, too, baby. Me, too." He wanted to reassure her, to tell her he could fix all this, but he'd had it with lies and half-truths. He was sick of the whole crappy sham life he led for his job. Now he'd come full circle: it wasn't just him, but Lissa, even Matt and Luke, who would also pay the price for the cheap adrenaline rushes he'd had every time he was sent on a mission. Lissa's life had fallen apart because he'd had the appalling arrogance to think he could save the world, that he could make other people's lives better because his own was a nightmare.

He knew better now, because he had more to fight for. He couldn't save the world. All he could try for was to save his own small corner of it—the woman he loved, the kids he adored. This was his real fight. To keep his family safe.

To make Lissa trust him again. To make her want him again. To have her want him to come home for good. To be his woman forever.

Lissa wrapped the thin white sheet around her near-naked body and got to her feet. "I'll call Tim."

"Will he come?" He tried to hide it, but the strangled note came through in his voice, seeing the silhouette of bare honey skin he'd just touched and kissed and lain on, without the fulfillment he craved like a pulse-pounding addiction.

She smiled, that gorgeous mouth curving in haunting knowledge and feminine arrogance: a woman coming alive from self-imposed sexual exile. She might be scared—he didn't doubt it—but she was also reveling in every second of this, especially knowing she'd made him suffer with their blanket charade. "He owes me. He'll come."

A shaft of pain lanced through him as he wondered just why Tim owed her and what for, but he knew better than to ask. "Good."

Her eyes flared for a moment. He'd managed to surprise her with his restraint, and he grinned. Oh, he was gonna love every second of this. After waiting half his life, finally the battle was on. Mitch and Lissa, locked in the unspoken glory of sexual war between man and woman. Take no prisoners. All or nothing.

She walked toward the house, leaving her clothes behind on the grass. Her hips swayed beneath the near-transparent sheet. As fresh and natural as a frolicking breeze in sunshine, as mysterious as deep night. A woman in every sense—and his body throbbed with promises unfulfilled.

Then he turned to pick up their clothes and saw the man watching from the other side of Old Man Taggart's land. The sun glinted off the binoculars gently swinging around his neck, as if they'd just fallen there—and on the cold dark barrel of the gun following Lissa's progress into the house.

Point made.

The man in gray chuckled as he drove off, leaving a half-naked, furious McCluskey panting behind him.

No license plates for the gallant squadron leader to trace. The car make, model and color one of the usual choices of impoverished farmers' teenagers, common around here in the grassy fields, dumped and torched by night.

He'd created a role his replacement could slip into with no difficulty at all. A generic white shirt, gray suit and dark glasses, frightening in their quiet anonymity. A standard-issue gun common among law enforcement officers across Australia.

Pointed at McCluskey's woman.

He liked the idea of scaring McCluskey…and his woman. Fear tended to make little country-mice women like Lissa Carroll do *anything* to end the terror. Begging. Panting. On her knees.

Oh, yeah. Nice image. McCluskey's woman, that sweet bundle of sin with the deliciously wicked mouth, on her knees for him…

So much for the last of the red-hot lovers. McCluskey had done her over in less than thirty minutes flat, and no repeat performance for him to watch, either.

He liked watching—but better still, he liked *doing*. He could do a much better job of her than McCluskey. What a loser. First time on a blanket in the backyard, for Pete's sake, like a horny teenager in a backseat. Oh, yeah, he knew how to please a woman far more thoroughly than that. And one day soon, pretty Lissa Carroll would know all about it.

He liked delicate, haunting women like Lissa; so much

to discover beneath the quiet shell. And when the mystery was over, they were so easy to break. Meanwhile he could enjoy what that luscious mouth could do to him. He'd make better use of that sweet mouth than McCluskey had dreamed of. Yeah, there was something…something about Lissa Carroll he wanted—all for himself.

But it was far more important that using her mouth and body would turn that jerk McCluskey inside out. Ruin him for life. Yeah, he'd break McCluskey all right…and he liked that idea best of all.

# Chapter 6

*Damn!*

Mitch watched in helpless fury as the car disappeared. So what happened now? Were all bets off, now the man had shown himself? Did their watcher know that he and Lissa faked it just then? Did he realize Lissa now had an ally? Or did he and Lissa and their gun-toting voyeur have to keep playing this perverted little game right down to the finish?

*Who the hell was he?*

Another car passed. The woman driving gave a slow wolf whistle. "Hey, darlin', you advertising?"

Oh, sheesh—he had nothing on but his briefs! He swore and stalked back across the long-fallow fields to Lissa's place to hop into his jeans. Then he ran inside to Lissa. Had she seen that jerk's gun on her? Was she as scared as he was?

She was dressed again and on the phone, but she turned to him as soon as the door opened. *Did you know him?*

He shook his head. "Play the game," he whispered

softly in her ear. "He knows I saw him. If I don't tell you about it I look bad, and if you don't tell me, he thinks you're with him—and he's secure." He wanted to draw her close, to caress her sun-kissed honey skin beneath her loose lemon top—wishing he had the right to stroke her and give her the physical comfort they both needed.

Her head fell to his shoulder, crowding in close, needing the contact as much as he did, but she kept talking. "We'll see you at the airport at six, Tim. Don't be late. We want a few days alone together before the wedding and for once you're going to put your life on hold for me. Got that?"

He could hear the chuckle as Tim evidently agreed.

When she hung up, he held her by the arms, caressing up and down her silky skin, soothing, reassuring her, even as he spoke with heavy sexual intent for the listening device. "Let's pack our things, baby. Don't pack too much, and nothing heavy—all summer gear. You won't need much of anything where we're gonna be." With a lightning decision that he knew he'd get in really hot water for later, he mouthed, *Insect repellent. Covering hat. Dark-green or long-sleeved clothes if you can. Netting if you have it.*

With a startled glance of comprehension—for though high-altitude Canberra could get really hot on occasion, it was rare to need big hats or insect netting—she nodded, gave him a slow, scared smile and laced her fingers through his. "Come and help me, then I'll help you. And maybe we can play in between. Tonight seems a million miles off."

Clever, clever girl. Her words were shy, just a touch sultry, and the little quiver in her voice could be discounted as post-sexual nerves. Let their listener make of that what he would.

He followed her into her room and sat on the bed, watching her shaking hands haul out an overnight bag. "C'mere, baby. Let's play first." He pulled her on top of him, laying her cold hands on his warm, naked chest. "Did you really share this bed with Tim?" he breathed in her ear, because he was curious—because he wanted to distract her from her fear. Because he wanted her hands on him again.

After a startled moment she shook her head with a little smile. "I burned the damn thing in the back paddock and bought a new one with the divorce payout," she whispered. She looked down, saw her palms flat against the curling hair on his bare chest. With slow, lingering touch, almost as if she moved against her will, she caressed him, filling her hands with his skin. The look in her eyes was one of total wonder. Sweet joy. Surprised innocence. An arousal so new, so life-changing, he had the answer before he asked the question.

"So you haven't slept with him since the divorce?"

Her hair, warm and smelling of jasmine, grass and sunshine, tumbled over her face as she leaned down and pressed a slow, hot kiss on his chest. "Jerk," she mumbled. "Do you think I'd make the same stupid mistake twice?"

He chuckled, low and rich, wanting so bad to make this real, but mindful of the bug behind the headboard he'd found earlier on, and the silent gray-suited menace not too far away, he kept his hands to himself. But unable to entirely resist temptation, he lifted her face and kissed her open mouth.

Then Lissa sagged on him, whimpering, her hands going to his hair to hold him there. The kiss went on and on, lips and tongues dancing, breath mingling with the moans they both couldn't help. Their hands exploring, drinking in the warm textures of the other in wondrous discovery.

How could a kiss be so sweet, and so impossibly saturated with sexuality at the same time?

Because I'm kissing Lissa, my sweet, sexy surprise package of woman—and she's kissing me.

And *man,* how she was kissing him, touching him—giving him the unmistakable green light to go, with two glorious, bewitching words. "Touch me…" Her hand guided his beneath her summer top to find her silky bare breasts beneath.

With a little groan of exultation, he touched, caressed—and slowly he drew a chocolate-tinted nipple into his mouth.

Lissa gasped and writhed against him. ''Mitch,'' she moaned—this time soaked in real passion. ''Yes, Mitch, oh, yes...'' Her voice had a high-pitched lilt to it, telling him she was filled with the frantic, hot, mindless urge to mate...just like him. And suddenly the fresh, clean-smelling room held the heady scent of sex. The one response a woman couldn't possibly fake.

Still suckling her, he touched her beneath her skirt, feeling the delicious wet heat through her panties. She bucked against his hand again and again, creating her own friction until his hand slipped inside the cotton barrier, and his finger gently stroked and circled her where she had to have him, where she ached and pulsed and pounded for release; and within moments, she shuddered all over, cried out his name and collapsed on him, in the most beautiful surrender he'd ever known. A surrender that held no losers—they both claimed victory.

He kissed her hair and held her, feeling content. ''We have to go,'' he whispered eventually.

She lifted her face. It was flushed, flooded with dazed wonder, satiation and renewed need. ''But Mitch, you didn't...''

He smiled, and touched her warm cheek. ''But you did, Lissa. You did, and that's enough for me.''

Total confusion filled her eyes: a stunned, glazed look. ''But how can it be—''

Hoo-wee. She truly didn't know. Tim must've been a hell of a loser in bed. ''I can wait,'' he murmured, with a quick glance at the back of her bed.

Instant comprehension: all her rosy color faded. ''Oh, God, he heard me,'' she breathed in his ear. ''He heard me... That filthy creep listened in on my most private moment...'' She glared at him in bewildered betrayal. ''How could you? How could you remember, and still go on?''

He muttered a curse, holding her close as she tried to pull away. "I'm sorry, Liss. I forgot, too, until just then." Still she struggled against him. "We have to keep up the whole lovers' thing until we find out who the hell this guy is, why he wants to destroy me and why he just pulled a gun on you!"

She stilled so completely he wondered if she'd fainted. He cursed himself. Maybe she hadn't seen the jerk, after all.

Then she sighed. "Tonight's your turn, then. I'll make sure of that."

Her voice was filled once again with the sultry saccharine sweetness of the fake siren. Lissa the consummate actress was back, with a vengeance.

He was still unforgiven.

Tim's fair, handsome face showed up stark and pale against the fading glare of a hazy city dusk when he and Lissa returned from their little walk around the fuel-and-tar-scented airport. Through the passing lights of early-evening traffic, his eyes met those of his one-time best friend in a silent question.

Mitch handed Lissa her bag, lifted his brows and slowly nodded.

Tim invoked the name of his savior beneath his breath, then said levelly to the kids, "Hey, guys, I've got a great surprise for you. Just wait till we get into the car!"

"Yeah!" Matt bolted without a backward glance; and Jenny, after unsuccessfully trying to get Tim to tell her what his special surprise was, followed Matt to find clues.

But Luke glanced from Mitch to Lissa, his eyes filled with the same old question, the same fear. The need for love and reassurance that would take years to fade, if it ever did.

Lissa hugged him. "Luke, darling, I'd never, never leave you. Neither will your dad. We're just going away for a few days, okay? We'll call you every day on Uncle Tim's cell phone.''

"Your mum's right." Mitch bent to his son. "Matey, hear this now. I'm your dad and I love you kids more than anything in the world. I never left you and I never will. If Kerin hadn't taken you away from me, we would always have been together. But we always will be from now on. What Mum says is the truth. Trust us. We're just going away for three or four days. Okay?''

"Yes, Dad," Luke whispered, shadows in his hurting eyes.

Tim joined in. "Matey, I swear the fun'll only last three or four days with me before Mum and Dad are back to drive you nuts, so you'd better make the most of it!''

With another of those heartbreakingly uncertain, haunting smiles of his, Luke nodded. "Okay, Uncle Tim.''

Tim clapped the boy on the shoulder. "Good man. Liss, my little love, why don't you take Luke to the car? I wouldn't mind catching up with my old buddy Mitch for a few minutes. You know, male bonding, swap war stories, etcetera.''

"We don't have time, Tim," Lissa replied, her voice sharp. The warning carried itself clearly to both men.

"Lissa, sweetie, trust me. You have time. Say goodbye to the kids," Tim retorted, in curious gentleness.

With flared nostrils and gritted teeth, Lissa herded a reluctant Luke to the car waiting fifty meters away. "Poor Liss always had too much pride for her own good," Tim said softly, watching his ex-wife walk across the car park. "She'd really rather you walked through life not knowing the truth—even if it means losing you.''

Mitch faced his old school friend squarely. "Spit it out, Tim. I'm sick of working in the dark with her. We're in the middle of a bloody serious situation here and we don't have much time.''

"I'll protect those kids with my life," Tim said quietly. "I'll take 'em where he couldn't possibly find them, and he'll have to walk over my dead body to get to them. And you'd better do the same for Liss or I'll kill you myself.''

Mitch rounded on him. ''If you still love her that much, why the bloody hell did you ever leave her?''

Tim met his accusing gaze without flinching. ''Because, though I love her to death and always will, I'm not the man for her. I can't give her what she needs.'' He shrugged and said simply, ''I'm gay, Mitch.''

''Oh, crap!'' he gasped without thinking. ''You had twenty girls before Lissa. You were married to her more than five years, and all over *her* like a bloody rash for three years before that!''

Tim's mouth quirked. ''Ever heard of denial, mate? That's what those girls were for me—and what my marriage to Lissa was. I loved her like crazy. I still do. I wanted to believe it was the right love—that if I married her, my attraction to men would die out. I hoped, almost believed it was teenage stupidity, a passing thing I'd get over with the right woman. But I only made Lissa unhappy, in and out of bed.''

''Let's skip that part, shall we?'' Mitch growled, wanting to deck him for ever having Lissa in bed, feeling totally flabbergasted by Tim's unexpected revelation. Tim Carroll, who could barely keep count of the girls he'd bedded, was gay?

Tim said seriously, ''Do you think I *want* to talk about this? I can't leave it out. If it weren't at the heart of all the problems you have with Lissa now or will have in the future, I wouldn't bring it up at all.''

His gut wrenched. ''So she's told you we have problems.''

''No, mate. She didn't have to. The tension's so thick I could make a gourmet sauce with it.''

Mitch shrugged. ''So you know what's causing it. Get to the point, Tim. We're in a bit of a hurry escaping some jerk after Lissa with a gun, if you haven't noticed.''

''Yeah, okay—but this is hard to talk about, so give me

a minute.'' Tim shook his head. ''She's scared of sex. She thinks she's no good in bed—that she's incapable of turning a man on.''

Mitch stared at his old friend and swore. Hard.

Tim sighed. ''You know how she wanted to be a virgin till her wedding night? Well, she was—and for two weeks after that.''

*''What?''*

''It took me all the honeymoon to make love to her—and it was a nightmare.''

Mitch blew out a sigh. *Sheesh.* No wonder Lissa was so tetchy about sex. No wonder she wanted them to be lovers so long before she'd marry him. ''Go on.''

''We wrote it off at first that were both upset about what I did to you, me being drunk, and grieving over the way you left. But deep down I knew we had a real problem. My love for her is what I'd feel for a little sister, if I had one. Touching her felt so damn wrong I couldn't get past it. What she didn't realize—and probably still doesn't—is that she never wanted me, either. We should never have been anything but friends.''

Mitch said slowly, ''But if you knew that, why would she—''

''Because we grew up together! C'mon, mate, *think!* You were there. She heard the rumors, talked to girls in the locker rooms. I might be gay, but she knows I was more than bloody capable with *some* girls. A lot of girls. Just not Lissa.''

He felt the blood drain from his face. Good God. What must that have done to Lissa's self-esteem?

''In five years, it was only good once. *Once.* After I'd met Ron, my partner of the past six years—but I didn't act on the attraction. I still wanted to deny what I was. I came home from the gym where I met him, tortured about my life, and saw my beautiful Liss waiting for me, so lonely, so glad to see me. It was the only time I didn't have to pretend she was someone else—I just wanted to give her all the love I had, all the care she deserved. We conceived Jenny that night." He sighed. "I left two weeks later."

Mitch growled an expletive.

Tim shrugged. "Yeah, I'm a bastard. But whether or not I meant it, whether or not I could have changed things, doesn't help Lissa now." Tim's eyes met his. "Think about it, Mitch. You know Liss as well as I do. How many other lovers do you think she's had to show her she's a desirable woman?"

A home question. Oh, yeah, he knew Lissa, knew her romantic idealism, her dreaming soul, her hidden hopes and fears. So she'd been alone since Tim left. She'd gone through twelve years of thinking of herself as undesirable, unwanted by any man...and he'd never come home to her because he hadn't wanted to see her happiness or loving sexuality with Tim.

Happiness. Sexuality? Dear God.

Tim went on with his demolition job on everything Mitch believed about the past fifteen years. "Do you get it now? I had to tell you, because the damage has never been undone. She's never let another man within ten miles of her since I left. I sure as hell can't fix it. So that leaves you."

"Yeah," he sighed. "Me." Me who's blundered from the minute I got home. Me, who thought of "perfect solutions"—more reasons to destroy her self-esteem—because I was too bloody scared to tell her the truth. And now she doesn't trust me enough to hear it.

Tim's hand gripped his shoulder. "I know why you're hanging back, mate, but you have to stop it. Tell her you love her. *Show* her you want her—seduce her. Believe me, she wants you. She always wanted you, and far more than she lets on. Have you touched her? Let her know how much you want her?"

"Mind your own business," he growled.

Tim laughed. "Good. No worries, mate. I'm outta here.

I'll head up the north coast. I'll call you with our location—''

"No," he said sharply. "Don't. Don't tell the kids the name of the place where you are, either." He found he didn't give a damn about Tim's sexuality, what happened to make him realize it or what he'd done after. All he knew was that he could trust Tim with their kids. He handed Tim a card, plain and unadorned, but for eight numbers. "Call that number if you even *think* you're in danger. Someone will be there fast. I'll have people ready on hand between Coffs Harbour and Byron Bay to protect you."

Tim stared at him, frowning. "Who are you, Mitch?"

He returned without a second's hesitation, "A man who's giving up his current life and job for his wife and kids. So keep them safe, Tim."

"With my life. You just take care of Lissa." Tim turned back to him after walking a few steps, his face relaxed, like a huge weight had been lifted from him. "When this is over, we'll have to go somewhere for dinner, or do something with the kids. Sort of nice, the three of us together again. But now it's the way it should have been from the start—you and Liss together, me the friend. I don't regret making the mistake—we wouldn't have Jenny without it— but I do regret like hell what I've done to Lissa." He added slowly, "Jealousy's a bloody rotten thing, isn't it?"

He grinned in the near darkness. "I didn't think you'd know all that much about it."

Tim's smile faded. "I probably know more about it than you ever will—and Liss is the one who's paying the price for it. Call me. See ya." Tim waved and faded into the gathering dark.

Within moments Lissa returned. Even in the soft purplish darkness that comes between dusk and night, he could see her face, pale and proud and aloof. Every line of her carefully held body read *back off*. "Let's go."

He climbed into Bertha's cockpit without a word, and radioed the little-known, barely used airstrip outside Canberra, to notify them of their ETA. Then he sent out a message to the other Nighthawks on their exclusive channel, hoping someone was out there to tell Anson what was going down.

Within moments, he got an answer. "Flipper here, Skydancer. All clear for return?"

"Extra package arriving. A real live wire. Will need supernatural briefing before recent package heads north, Flipper," he informed Flipper, an ex-Navy diver and pilot who, with Irish, a crazy bush pilot, had been his backup in Tumah-ra. Flipper was now on recon looking for some black-market arms dealer's lady on the run, under the guise of an investigative reporter.

"Will do, Skydancer," Flipper answered, and signed off.

The drill would be in place in half an hour. Whatever happened to them now, the Nighthawks would be protected—and he'd protect Lissa with his life.

Lissa gazed at him, her brows lifted. "Well, I suppose 'livewire' is an upgrade from 'reliable.'"

He grinned. Let her think she was the "package." If their silent watcher was listening in, all the better. "I think so. You've managed to surprise me from the first day I got back," he said, and waited for the defensiveness to begin.

She settled back in her seat and buckled up. "Good," she sighed. "I'm glad I've managed to surprise someone in my life. So did Tim tell you about how he wished it was you in bed with him on our wedding night instead of me?"

He gasped, coughed, choked on air. *"What?"* he finally spluttered.

"Oh, I see. So he took the coward's way out, told you he was gay and stuck to my more embarrassing moments in life, huh?" She peered at his face. "I can see by the stunned look in your eyes that Tim left out some of the interesting bits, like the fact that he was in love—but with you, not me. Yes, indeed, it was a strange wedding night. Both the bride and groom wanted the best man in bed with them instead of their spouse. Wouldn't that story go down well in one of those true confession magazines?''

"Rio Delta Bravo. All clear for takeoff. Rio Delta Bravo, do you read?''

He couldn't respond. His mind was totally blanked out and his hands nerveless, useless. Lissa picked up the receiver and said blithely into it, ''Yes, we do read. Thank you very much.'' She replaced it and smiled at him, sunny and unruffled. ''Um…Mitch? You can take off now.''

Slow, disbelieving, turned to her. ''Is that *true?*''

''Uh-huh.'' She singsonged the word. ''That's why he remained in denial for so long, darling—besides feeling so obligated to stay with poor unwanted little me. He was fussier than the average guy. He wanted you, and until he met his partner, Ron, he never met another man who—to put it delicately—lit his flame enough to leave me. So at least I didn't have to worry about diseases. He swears he was faithful to me until the day he left. Um, I think you'd better start the plane, or the control tower people will start worrying.''

He couldn't tear his gaze from her, so bloody flabbergasted he couldn't think. He'd always thought himself a modern, open-minded kind of guy—he hadn't put a foot wrong when Tim told him he was gay—but he couldn't be open about this. The thought of Tim—oh, holy Hannah, his best mate back then—Tim, who'd seen him in the buff so many times…and oh, man, he'd probably been horny, staring at his naked body like a lovesick girl. Listening to him rave on about how much he adored Lissa. And though he'd never discussed it, Tim knew he'd rejected every sexual advance from every bloody girl in Breckerville who approached him, so that his and Lissa's first time could be together.

Oh, yeah, Tim knew him well enough to let Lissa be the one to give this juicy tidbit to him—and no wonder Tim hadn't told him or tried anything on him years ago. He'd have thrown up, beaten the crap out of him, never spoken to him again—in essence, shown in every way an insecure and lonely teenage boy can that the answer was and would always be *no*. And if Tim had *dared* touch Lissa after that—

Was that why Tim snatched Lissa from under his nose in the first place?

*Jealousy's a bloody rotten thing, isn't it? I probably know more about it than you ever will.*

"Rio Delta Bravo, we have two crafts in line behind you. Please notify if you're experiencing difficulty."

Startled, he grabbed the receiver. "Rio Delta Bravo, all clear for takeoff."

He glanced at Lissa as he started the plane in motion. She looked like a doll carved from alabaster—beautiful but untouchable, cool, not quite human. A tiny smile curved her mouth. Oh, yeah, she was enjoying this, wanting to put him on the back foot—and her use of the word *darling* was a dead giveaway. She wanted their unwanted listener to have something to think about besides how she came apart for him in bed this morning.

But she was also telling the truth—a truth that tore her world and sexual self-esteem to shreds, and left her doubting his motives for wanting her. If he told her he loved her now, she'd probably spit it back in his face—and that was leaving out the fact that she thought he was a bloody people smuggler.

Then when they were in the air, the rest of her blithe recital finally hit him. "You wanted me, too, Lissa?" he asked slowly. "You married Tim, wishing he was me? You wanted me to make love to you?"

"Oh, yeah. I was even sillier over you than Tim was." She turned to look at him, her eyes bright with self-mockery, the hatred of unresolved grief turned inward to anger. "You were my white knight, the man who'd save me from the biggest mistake of my life. My gallant flyboy hero, whom I adored so blindly it felt like sacrilege when my fiancé touched me." She laughed, and he knew this conversation had become personal—way too personal. She'd forgotten about their silent listener, and she'd probably hate him again for that later. "You wanna know how dumb I was? Even after you left for the Air Force, I had the stupidity to hope you'd fly back for me, and we'd fly away together. Then I was romantic enough to hope you'd come home to stop the wedding. Then when you came home and did nothing, I prayed you'd stop it at the last minute. Oh, God, how I prayed you'd object, tell me you loved me, and marry me yourself. What a dumb jerk, huh? I begged God for years that one day you'd love me as much as I loved you. You have no idea how much I worshipped you back then."

Hoo, boy, was this a day of stunning revelations. *Both* his best friends in love with him? Unable to take it in, to realize or truly believe what she was saying, he said, "You *loved* me back then? Not like a friend? Like a woman loves a man?"

A light, bitter laugh. "Oh, yeah. Dog-like devotion on tap. From the moment I saw you, you could have snapped your fingers at me and I'd have followed you to the ends of the earth. If you'd held out your hand to me at the wedding I'd have left with you without a second thought."

"Then why the hell did you marry Tim? Why did you go out with him in the first place?" he demanded, scraped raw with betrayal. More than fifteen years of their lives wasted! All the love he'd needed from Lissa—the true sexual romantic love he'd spent his life hungering and craving for—had always been there, and he'd never seen it. He'd missed every sign, blind to her need, and he'd thrown it all away. And why? Because—

Because you never had the guts to tell her, either.

He flicked a glance at her and saw anything but love in those soft, dove's eyes. They glittered with her own sense of betrayal—the unhealed fury of a rejected woman, an unseen love turned sour. "Because he *asked* me to his school formal, his special night, and you didn't. Because, like any normal girl, I wanted a boyfriend. I was sick of waiting for you to make a move on me. I kinda figured after two years or so that it was never going to happen for us. So when Tim asked me, I thought I may as well get on with life.''

She shrugged. ''I married him for the same reason. Because he seemed stable and secure, and he wouldn't take off on me. But in the end he did. Just like you—except you left me for a plane, and *he* left me for another man.'' She laughed, but the sound grated harshly. ''Funny how a few years thinking about that rubs the glamour off silly childhood dreams. There is no knight on a white horse, no hero to love me and no happily ever after.

''This is a beautiful view,'' she suddenly said, watching the Sydney skyline beneath them. ''You know, I never flew anywhere before today.'' She smiled and patted his cheek. ''Don't look so stunned. Like I said, I got over my stupid dreams of you years ago. We can be friends, lovers, get married—whatever. It doesn't really matter.''

''Like hell it doesn't matter,'' he snarled. ''I never rejected you in my life!''

''True.'' She laughed, that pseudo-cute, bloody irritating tinkle of sound—irritating because it meant she didn't believe a word he said. ''You just never wanted me—until now, it seems. Who cares? We're grown-ups. Let's just enjoy what we have now.''

He opened his mouth and slowly shut it. The last half hour had been too filled with shocks; his brain felt scrambled. If he said anything now, it would only come out wrong, words that would alienate her more.

But there was no way he'd leave it like this for long.

The rest of the trip to Canberra passed in silence. But if Lissa thought she'd escaped his questions by turning it all around on him, then maybe she didn't know him as well as she thought, either.

The moment he cleared security with Anson—and made sure their listener couldn't hear a thing—reckoning time would come...for both of them.

# *Chapter 7*

$A$ sleek sedan waited for them when they landed at the hidden airstrip in the quiet, dark countryside just outside Australia's capital city. Lissa watched in silence as Mitch felt under the license plate and came up with a set of keys. Then he glanced to the right. A set of headlights flicked on, then off.

What did that mean? That Mitch's mysterious boss wanted to see him immediately? Or that the car was clean, safe from bugs or bombs? Or no one was nearby to follow them? Well, well. Whatever organization Mitch was involved in, she couldn't accuse them of being sloppy.

He opened the passenger side for her, still in grim silence, and she wondered, with a grin, if he was still in shock. Hmm. She'd better leave any further revelations until tomorrow, or he might run them off the road....

Never underestimate a woman. Especially not this woman.

He appeared to drive with total certainty, turning without pause from the airstrip into one street, into another then

another, onto the Federal Highway, taking back roads from
there through Queanbeyan and into Canberra city, all in
darkness.

"I think you forgot to put your headlights on, Mitch,"
she said softly.

He swiveled around to look at her. She nodded. *We're
alone. No one's following us.*

He nodded to her handbag. *There's a directional device
as well as the two bugs in your bag.* But he said, "Oops,
so I did," and switched the lights on.

Oops indeed. The bag was bugged; she'd known it and
still botched their cover. And she thought she was so clever
taking the initiative, checking for signs of a car tailing
them, making the decision they'd be better off looking like
normal motorists. She'd only made it easier for the gray
man to find them now.

She blew out a breath. It seemed she had more to learn
before she started doing Mitch's job for him, but she
wouldn't leave him to it, either. For the first time she was
right in the middle of Mitch's world. After a quiet, dutiful,
merry-go-round life, she was finally riding the roller
coaster, right in the front seat…and she intended to enjoy
every moment of the ride.

At the next light he turned her face to his. *Swap seats
as fast and quiet as you can.* "One kiss," he groaned, and
rolled beneath her while she slid over to the driver's seat,
making a moaning sound. By the time the lights changed,
they were ready.

Were they fooling the gray man? Was he nearby? Adrenaline hit her in a rush. If he could see them, he'd know
they'd changed seats. But could he get here so fast?

At the next lights he breathed in her ear, "Next right,
and keep going around the block slow, but don't stop. Pretend we're lost." He handed her a small tape recorder.
"Press Play when I'm gone, and follow my prompts. Don't
stop driving."

She nodded and watched Mitch wind down his window.

''Where are we?'' He sounded frustrated. ''I thought we were on—there's a kid on the crossing!'' Lissa slowed the car with a squeal of brakes, and Mitch vaulted out the window without a sound.

Heart hammering, she drove on and pressed Play on the tape. ''Can you see the turnoff for Braddon?'' His voice came from the little speaker. ''I booked into a hotel there, and we'll lose the booking if we're not there by eight-thirty.''

''Um—I think we just passed it. These roads in Canberra are so weird, aren't they? Everything goes round in circles. Maybe we should double back to the last turnoff.''

''Okay. Good idea,'' the disembodied voice said a few moments later. ''Let's do it.''

He'd known she'd think of something to say. Her heart soaked in warmth. He trusted her, at least that far.

If only she could trust him at all.

When she came back around, she slowed at the crossing, and he emerged from a shrubby bush carrying a case. He vaulted straight in, as quick and quiet if he jumped into moving cars every day.

Maybe he did. What would she know? He'd disappeared from her life for years and then reappeared like magic. Seeming so much like the Mitch she'd loved with all the depth of her romantic girl's heart—yet a stranger. A man with edges. Secrets. Edges of danger that excited her... secrets that scared the living daylights out of her. And an untamed sexuality she suspected she'd only glimpsed so far.

How could a man like Mitch, always on the fringes of risk, leaping from the brink of a cliff, want *her?* At first, yeah, for the family he'd never had; she'd understood that even as she hated it. But now? Dared she believe him when he said he wanted her, only her? He seemed to be burning alive for her, but as she'd found out over the past few weeks, nothing with Mitch was what it seemed.

Like it had been with Tim.

Yet with Mitch, finding out the lies beneath the secrets wouldn't just break her heart—they would change her world forever.

So find out if he's really one of the good guys. Oh, Lord help her if he turned out to be in organized crime, an adoption ring or people smuggling. The men who ran those gangs were absolutely ruthless. People who got in the way of their schemes tended to disappear without a trace.

It was only then she realized the enormity of her own risk, the depth of the abyss she stood near. If he was using her for a respectable cover and the gray man had blown it, Mitch could be taking her somewhere now to kill her. He could have seduced her, filled her head with lies and doubts, turned her around with her own body's betrayal and was just waiting for the opportunity to—

"You were right. Here's the turnoff."

She started, put on her indicator and braked for the road Mitch indicated, her heart pounding and her scalp crawling where sweat trickled. Her hands shook so badly she could barely turn the wheel. The road wasn't the turnoff for Braddon, a well-lit, safe and respectable suburb of Canberra.

Where were they going?

Did she dare ask? Or should she now be grateful the gray man had slipped those devices in her bag? If Mitch tried to hurt her, she only had to scream and—

Was the gray man even in the Canberra region yet? Or was he listening from a safe distance—safe for him, but too far to save her if her risk blew up in her face?

*Trust me, Lissa.*

Her chest ached so bad it was hard to breathe. If there was one thing she'd always been sure of, it was that Mitch would never hurt her. Now, in a darkened city street with a man she no longer knew, she had nothing, no certainties, not even seeing the sunrise tomorrow, or be with her beloved kids again.

What was it with her, that she always went for the wrong man? First she married Tim, who never wanted her at all, and left for another *man*. Then Mitch, the man she'd always hungered for, had in his absence become either a spy or an international criminal—and to find out which, she'd put her own life in deadly danger. She had to keep faking the intimate act she'd only ever wanted to do with Mitch. If only she'd had the guts to throw herself at him all those years ago, he'd still be *her* Mitch, a respectable Air Force Squadron Leader, not—

She shuddered as the cold sweat ran down her back.

She jumped as he touched her arm, gentle and nonthreatening. "Oops. I just went past the place," he said very softly.

She bit back an apology, did a screeching U-turn and blinked at the long, beautifully lit driveway before her, leading to a lovely house on a large, fenced acreage. A very pretty Tudor-style house, which proclaimed itself to be a B&B.

Illogically she felt reassured. Would he kill her in such a nice, respectable place as this?

No, but he can seduce me into believing his story, then— Then what?

Nothing. Not if he couldn't seduce her. And it'd be a cold day in North Queensland before he'd get her to fall into his arms so easily again. Not until she knew beyond all doubt that Mitch was one of the good guys. Not until he'd proven his claims about the gray man to be true.

And told her what his real job was, what it was for, and why the gray man had dragged her into it.

Mitch booked them in as Mr. and Mrs. Kendall, holding on to the case and their overnight bag like grim death. The woman who signed them in and showed them to their room was chatty, yet somehow it seemed a false brightness. Her glance kept flicking to her, as if she couldn't understand why *she* was there with him.

Did the woman know Mitch? Had he stayed here before—and with whom? Another woman or just other spies or other criminals? Maybe this place was near a casino.

She'd heard crooks laundered their money through casinos and expensive hotels.

Their room was quiet, quaint, dainty, with an enormous bathroom and spa bath. It had upper class and big nightly rates written all over it.

Whatever Mitch did, he must get paid well, at least.

The woman closed the door behind them, and they were alone. And for some weird reason, when it should have escalated, her fear evaporated. She felt only nervous excitement, the adrenaline of anger and the unknown bubbling through her bloodstream like dry ice. "Well, this is very nice," she remarked, her tone mild, slightly nervous—making her expression cold and sarcastic.

He was already watching her, had seen the challenge. He nodded, apparently accepting her mistrust. "Beautiful. The spa's fantastic. Come and try it with me—there's nothing like making love in hot bubbles."

She lifted her brows. "I can hardly wait," she breathed, as she walked over and swiftly, silently frisked him.

*Good girl.* He did the same to her, his eyes gleaming with cool approval. Still holding the case, he took her handbag, put it on the bed and held out his hand to her.

Confused, she let him lead her into the bathroom, watched him put the case down and run the water. "If you think I'm going to make love in there with you—"

He twisted his face to her and grinned. "Well, a guy can always hope," he said softly with erotic meaning. "But if not, our being in here together has a couple of good purposes."

"Which are?"

"One, since we're both clean, any listening device he has aimed at us or hidden in our stuff won't transmit clearly over the water; two, it gives him time to search our room if he's here, and we've given him a good reason why he can't find a way to be alone with you tonight."

Chills raced down her spine. The gray man, going through her personal things—getting her alone…

She was alone with Mitch but felt no fear. Did that count for anything? Could she trust her instincts, or would he only make a fool of her, then betray her?

"Get in the water, Lissa."

She started. He already had his shoes and socks off. "What?"

"We don't know what he might have on us from outside," he answered, his voice soft yet heavy with strange sorrow. "If he's really ASIO, or with some criminal organization, he could have access to more sophisticated hardware than he's used so far. He could be watching us through night goggles outside the window. He could have heat detectors on us I haven't found yet. We said we were going to make love in here, so let's give him another show."

She felt the blood leave her face. She swayed. "I can't do this. Mitch—"

"Trust me, Lissa. I won't hurt you." He unzipped his jeans, stepping out of them to reveal his long, strong legs. "This has been a bloody hard day for you. It's been a hard few weeks for both of us. Neither of us wants our first time to be some stupid jerk's private peepshow. I know, baby. I understand. This is work only." He shucked his T-shirt, still watching her, the act sterile and erotic at the same time.

She searched his eyes, uncertain. Terrified. Yearning.

Slowly he lifted her hand to his mouth, kissing the palm. "Lissa, one day you're going to realize just what you mean to me—what you've always meant to me. But now's not the time or place. When this is over and I have you safe, we're going to make this real. So real you'll never doubt how much I want you ever again. But for now, trust me—at least in this. I respect you too much to make you subject to a lousy Peeping Tom."

After a long, hanging moment filled with tense waiting, she nodded. "All right."

"Thank you." He slipped each button of her sundress from its sheath, one after the other, until the dress pooled at her feet on the floor and she stood before him clad only in simple cotton bra and panties. A sight she saw every day. Nothing special.

But Mitch dragged in a harsh breath, his gaze glued to her body. "Dear God, you're lovely," he whispered, and unhooked her bra, letting it fall on top of the dress, revealing her naked breasts. One hand lifted to her, then fell. "Beautiful. So beautiful." His voice came out strangled with need.

He'd already forgotten they were supposed to be putting on an act. His hands were shaking and he was hard, so hard and big through his briefs there was no way she could doubt the reality of his words.

He wanted her so bad he was shaking....

She bit her lip, fighting her own need galloping away with her, a stallion let free on a wild mountain, no fences or boundaries. "Mitch, you said we won't—we can't—"

"I know," he groaned quietly, reaching out to lay his hand gently over her breast, caressing with exquisite care. "Just one kiss. Just touch me once, Lissa, one real touch, and we'll start our stupid game. Please, baby. I want you so bad."

He stood before her, all but naked, this big, magnificent male animal, in anguished arousal for her. For *her,* Lissa Carroll, who'd never known how to arouse a man in her life.

Caught in the dark, throbbing wonder of returned hunger, her fears flown on the night wind, she found the courage to do what she'd wanted to for more than half her life.

She removed his last barrier and hers. She stepped into the spa with him and then pulled him to her. She slowly caressed him, taking his hardness in her hands, exploring, feeling his heat, his need for her. Drinking in the hoarse cry he gave, his bucking motion into her hands, the agonized pleasure in his voice, in his face.

She'd never known desire this intense, or felt the urgency to touch a man so fiercely. Giving Mitch sexual pleasure was the headiest magic she'd ever experienced. Hungry for more, she cupped him, leaning forward to kiss his chest, nip his ribs, his stomach, with the surging of the hot, wet, soapy bubbles caressing their skin—

"Baby, stop. I've wanted you too long. I can't hold off," he groaned through gritted teeth, his face beaded with sweat. "I want this so bad, but I'll lose it right now if you don't—"

Tenderness and power flooded her. She felt like a sorceress, a queen of enchantment, a sexual witch who could bring this man to his knees with her hands and mouth. "Good," she whispered, and caressed him again and again, and, lifting him out of the water, pleasured him with her tongue, just once.

With a harsh shout, he pulled her up and kissed her, hot and wet; then she felt the pulsing of his climax against her skin before the warm water washed it away. He collapsed on her, his face in her neck, tangling his legs with hers; and she ran a hand through his wet curls, feeling utterly content. A woman at last.

"I'm sorry," he murmured, when he finally had his breathing back under control. "I never meant it to go so far. I promised you I wouldn't—"

Funny, but right now she didn't care if that creep watched them or not, or if Mitch was a good guy or bad. She just felt—how could she describe such a feeling of total peace and happiness? "You didn't do it, I did. And I enjoyed every second of it."

He gave a low, sexy chuckle. "Witch. I think you wanted revenge for this morning—and you got it, all right. That was amazing. Having you touch me like that, after spending half my life fantasizing about it—"

Oh, heady stuff. He'd fantasized about her hands on him, just as she'd dreamed of his hands and mouth on her. And now she understood what he'd meant this morning: bringing him to fulfillment was enough. More than enough.

She pressed the button for the jets to start again, and

spoke over the noise, needing to know just what sort of man she'd just seduced. "So who are you, Mitch Mc-Cluskey, and what is it you really do for a living?"

He shook his head, still lying on her shoulder. "Tomorrow, I promise. For now, let's forget it all. I feel too damn wonderful to start up the tension again."

Their position, the act they'd just shared and his acceptance of her power, made him curiously vulnerable to her. She discovered she didn't want to know what he was, who he was. Not now, not yet. She just wanted tonight. One more night before her illusions either came to fruition or shattered in her face.

"Okay." She lifted his face and kissed him. "Tonight."

He smiled and pushed a lock of hair clinging to her cheek. "I used to dream of this, Liss. It was my constant fantasy, when we swam in your pool. You'd play with me, so innocent and wet and sweet and sexy, and I'd be envisioning you naked like this, looking at me like you wanted me."

"I did." She gave him a self-deprecating smile. "Well, I wasn't naked, but I looked at you like this all the time—whenever you weren't looking."

He shook his head against her skin. "How was I so blind that I never saw it?"

"I was blind, too. I never once saw you looking at me like that, either." She shrugged. "I couldn't tell you or show you. I never for a minute thought you'd ever truly want me. So many girls at school had a thing for you—the pretty, sexy girls—and I was just the girl next door. I wasn't like them. I couldn't risk losing our friendship by telling you or coming on to you."

He kissed her throat, making her shiver. "Oh, baby, I wish you had, because I was an even bigger coward than you. It was always there for me, too, Lissa—always. It always will be, till the day I die. I never so much as looked at any girl but you, until after you married Tim. Even then, even with Kerin, I felt like I was betraying you."

With those words, *you married Tim,* the shadows came creeping back in. Specters of the past, rattling chains on their wrists and ankles, crowned and garlanded with doubts of the here and now. Taking her prisoner without a word. "Don't. Don't say it. No promises, Mitch. No more pretty words until you tell me what's going on. I have to know the truth first. I can't play the game."

His smile faded. "Then what was this?"

A click, and the ghosts chained her. "This," she said carefully, "was sweet revenge, McCluskey. This was me, enjoying sexual power over a man for the first time in my life. I needed to know—"

"What? What do you need to know, Lissa?" he asked, harsh and just a touch bitter. A predator after truth, and all man—a strong, naked, virile man.

And aroused again. The proof lay big and hard on her thigh.

Her nipples peaked against his skin and slid over his chest, hot and wet. With a smoldering look in his eyes he slid the other way, making her moan at the delicious friction.

She pushed him off and looked away, splashing her face, but the heated water only made her more breathless, the heat outside match the pulsing fever within. "So, do you think our good friend has finished his job in there?"

With a leisurely motion he catapulted out of the spa. "I'll check." Without bothering to towel himself off, he picked up the case he'd brought in and pulled an odd-looking contraption out of it, aiming it at the door, waving back and forth. "There's no one there now, if there ever was. Maybe he hasn't caught up with us yet." He opened the door and padded out, carrying the case with him. He turned to her, not bothering to hide his aroused state. "Come to bed." It wasn't a request. It was a gauntlet thrown down, a challenge issued. Mitch, hard and hot, naked and wet, shooting from the hip. *Trust me, Lissa.*

Her gaze fixed on his gorgeous body, she uttered in a

strangled tone, "I'll just stay in here a few minutes. I, um, I need to…"

Mitch smiled sadly, with just a touch of coldness, and she shivered again. He said, "Sure," and closed the door for her.

And for some reason she felt it again. She'd won a battle, kept her pride, but she'd lost something—just a tiny piece of something infinitely precious in the process.

But this time she could identify the loss. Mitch's heart, Mitch's trust…and Mitch himself. He was withdrawing from her.

She was losing Mitch. *Her* Mitch. The boy she'd so blindly adored—the man she'd never been able to put behind her. The one her heart refused to forget.

Oh, how she wished to God she could believe all he'd told her! Oh, how she wanted to know she could trust him. But this could so easily shatter in her face—just like her marriage to Tim. Tim acted like he couldn't wait to make love to her—until he married her. And she'd been trapped in a nightmare world of half-formed fears and doubts, walking in the shadows of wondering, Why? Even when she found out the truth about Tim, she still knew one thing— he'd been with almost every girl in town before her. What did more than five years of being unable to want her say about her ability to arouse a man?

If the same thing happened with Mitch, she'd want to die.…

With a strangled sob she turned on the spa jets and cried her heart out.

When she came out, wearing the fresh clothes he'd put just inside the door for her, she found a different man in the room. A man wearing dark jeans and a black polo shirt—cool, elegant, almost lethally sexy. He sat leisurely on a swivel chair before the cherrywood desk. He didn't bother to turn as she opened the door. "You like solitaire?"

Oh, this man looked like Mitch, sounded like Mitch. But

this was the man with secrets; this man wore danger carelessly tossed over his shoulder like a jacket on a hot summer night. The tenderness in his voice was gone, replaced by cool unconcern, the blazing need in his face now casual concentration.

This was the man he'd been hiding from her since he came back into her life. Mitch the spy.

The mysterious case was open, a hollow showing where the small laptop computer he now used had been.

But there wasn't a card game on the screen. The title read:

DIMA—Illegal Migration Issues

Border Control

The Division has the key responsibility to ensure Australia's border is an effective barrier to persons who have no legal entitlement to enter. It also has responsibility to prevent the travel to Australia and entry of those whose presence in Australia is not in the national or public interest.

Policy and procedures for border control activities are formulated and monitored by the Division and delivered in the States and Territories by Australian Customs Staff.

Unauthorized Arrivals

The Division is responsible for the coordination of entry and removal of unauthorized arrivals, regardless of mode of transport to Australia. DIMA airport inspectors undertake entry processing of unauthorized arrivals at airports, with referral to a senior officer located in Central Office, on a case by case basis.

Compliance and Investigations

The Division undertakes enforcement, deterrence and compliance awareness strategies. These activities include the investigation and prosecution of offences under the Migration Act, the location and removal of unlawful noncitizens, and data matching with other Commonwealth agencies.

She finished reading the screen, saw the official Australian government stamp on it and nodded, squelching the small spurt of guilt struggling to make itself felt. "Can anyone see us?"

He jerked his head at the window. "Lead-lined curtains. Lead in the walls. This is our safe house; all the workers here are trained operatives. I called Tim. He and the kids are fine. We'll call again tomorrow when we have another phone. We need a clean source this guy can't trace, just in case."

"Then what was the point of all the pretence with the woman at the desk earlier? Why say our spy could listen in on us or break in?"

He didn't even look at her. "You're not the only person with trust issues. I had orders from my boss and the others here. They wanted to see if you'd follow my lead. If you could be trusted to see the bigger picture."

She felt a slow smile curve her mouth at that. Hmmm. And Mitch was unhappy? Maybe they were checking her out for more than he was telling her right now.... "You could have called me out to talk to the kids."

He didn't even turn around. "I tried. You were crying too hard to hear me. I figured the kids were best off not hearing the tears in your voice, in case it scared them."

She made no excuses. After talking to Tim, he must know as well as she did why she'd needed the release of tears. "All right. But I want to talk to them tomorrow."

"Of course." After a short, awkward silence he went on. "I checked the room with the heat detector. No one has been in the room but us since we got here. No one's close enough outside to use the bugs—at least not for the next five minutes. I can't guarantee it after that, so we have to watch what we say."

She aimed a glimmering smile his way. "Heat detectors, huh? No carefully placed hairs on our luggage or invisible powder for fingerprint identification?"

"I don't do Hollywood stunts. The heat detector tells me if someone's been here in the past few minutes, where they went when they were here...and to do that, to break in here at all, he'd have to be a trained professional. So my guess is, this guy isn't."

His voice was terse. Withdrawn. "How disappointing," she said with a mock sigh. "Your marvelous whiz-bang heat detector thingamajig doesn't give you a magical computer reading telling you who it was, and who he works for?"

Her gambit worked: he gave her a slow, reluctant grin. "I'm not Tom Cruise, Lissa. I only get as high as Mission Difficult." He waved at the screen. "Is that enough for you for now, or would you like more proof our boy's not what he says he is?"

It was more than enough: it told her all she needed to know. The Department of Immigration controlled illegal immigrants. The gray man had lied to her. Mitch had not. The gray man had pulled a gun on her. Mitch had bolted after the man to protect her. "It's enough. Who do you say *you* are?" she asked, soft with meaning.

The phone buzzed once and was abruptly, eerily silent.

"There's two bugs in your bag, one directional tracker, and we don't have time to talk. That was Mabel. She's been watching the road for us. A car just turned into the outer road. It could be our boy. He's had time to get a commercial flight down here by now and track us." Once more he gave her that look—and something inside her told her he was giving her one last chance. "He'd be within range now."

The phone buzzed again once, then stopped. "The car's slowing down outside the driveway." He said no more, still watching her, the integrity in his deep, dark eyes damning all her doubts.

The next move was hers.

Don't be a fool. Give him what he needs, at least until he gives you reason not to. She drew a deep breath, and nodded. "What do we do?"

Though he didn't smile, she felt his body tension relaxing. He closed down the computer, locked it away in a safe in the wall behind the desk and got to his feet. "We go to bed." He looked at her, hiding all expression.

She pleaded silently; he shook his head, and she sighed in relief. Neither of them could stand another performance of pseudo-sex like this morning. Not here, not now. Not tonight. This had gone way beyond games for both of them.

Thank you. She took his hand and followed him to bed, where they lay fully dressed, still, tense, unmoving. And she felt lonely—lonelier than all her years alone. Mitch was right beside her, yet he'd never seemed farther away.

Then after a few minutes he sighed and drew her into his arms. "I don't care about tomorrow. I need you now, Lissa. Just let me hold you tonight."

The whispered words in the dark planted a tiny bud of hope in her soul. "Me, too." She wrapped an arm around him, laid her head over his thudding heart, and a sense of deceptive, unquiet peace touched her spirit: two children alone, huddling together in the eye of a storm, waiting for the worst to come. "Tonight," she whispered back. "Hold me. Just hold me."

And for the first time in years she just fell asleep. She slept wrapped in his arms, feeling safe, feeling *cherished*— for the first time in so long, not alone anymore.

Six hours later they lay in almost the same position, holding each other close—and the storm broke.

The door burst open without warning; two men in flak jackets rushed in, brandishing guns. "Stay where you are! Federal Police! Put your arms above your heads and don't make any sudden moves!"

Lissa screamed at her abrupt awakening and shrank

against him. But Mitch, who'd been waiting for it to happen, wished only for ten minutes more, another hour, another day. For the time and the courage to make things right with Lissa. To gain her trust before he did what he had to do and risked both their lives to fight for what was right—and to fight for her love.

But time was up. He could only lift his arms above his head, advise Lissa to do the same, and allow the two men with guns to cuff him and take them both in the unmarked dark car to the nation's capital for questioning.

# Chapter 8

"What the hell is this, Skydancer? The most bloody juvenile way known to man to impress a reluctant girl-friend?" Nick Anson demanded in open fury. "You want to take her to Tumah-ra with you? What alternate universe are you living in? Our work is more important than your love life. And if you don't know that, it's time to get out of the game!"

Mitch didn't flinch; he'd expected it from the moment Irish and Braveheart burst into their hotel room this morning and "arrested" them both. "Of course I know, sir," he replied, with all the military formality Anson insisted on whenever he was in the Australian headquarters. *Complete and total professionalism can save lives. Always keep your distance with operatives.* "I didn't have any choice but to bring her into it."

"There's always a choice," Anson barked. "Don't be so bloody melodramatic!"

"Someone bugged Lissa's house, sir. He claimed to be ASIO. He threatened her with losing custody of my sons if she didn't find proof that I'm a child smuggler and spotter pilot for people smugglers. Then he pulled a gun on her.''

Anson stared at him. "You *know* that?''

"I saw him, sir. I saw the gun. I have one of the bugs here.'' He pulled out the plastic bag holding one of the de-activated listening devices from his jacket. "I left the other one working, so he'll believe Lissa still doubts me. Dust it if you like, but I doubt we'll get anything.''

"Don't leave me in the dark, Skydancer,'' Anson demanded irritably. "Fill me in.''

With that acerbic demand, Mitch told his superior the whole story, as far as he knew it.

Anson reacted exactly as he had—in utter disbelief. "This has got to be someone's idea of a joke! Look at this stupid bug—it's made in Taiwan! And ASIO don't do smuggling stings. That's the Feds' jurisdiction!'' His commander looked likely to tear his hair. "This is a script straight out of some rerun of *Dragnet!*''

"I know, sir.'' Mitch nodded. "I knew that at the beginning, but Lissa's a civilian, a mother whose kids have been threatened. She didn't know who was telling the truth until I told her and downloaded the proof from the DIMA file on the net last night.''

"Did you use a clean source?''

"I picked up the laptop from here as soon as we landed in Canberra, sir, plugged into my cell phone line.''

"Good. At least that's one thing we don't need to worry about.'' Anson paced the room, and asked him, "You think this is personal, or a hit at us all?''

"I don't know, sir. Not yet.''

Anson gave Lissa, standing still and silent beside Mitch, a glance of pure male frustration, and Mitch knew he'd be chewed out later for insisting on her being a part of this conference instead of leaving her outside the room. Too bad. "And you had to bring her here. You couldn't have made up something plausible?''

"No, sir. Not until I know what's going down with this

rogue. He made it clear to me that he wants to hurt her. If I want her to stay alive I have to keep her with me. Lissa and I are getting married next week,'' he said simply. ''Requesting formal permission to hand in my notice when this case ends, sir.''

''Permission denied,'' Anson snapped. ''You signed a three-year contract and you'll fulfil your final year.''

Mitch felt his jaw set, hard. ''We have three children, sir. My kids need me at home.''

''I don't need reminding of your children, Skydancer. You wouldn't have your sons at home—and neither would your fiancée—if I hadn't found them for you and made all the arrangements for them to be with her.''

He felt Lissa start beside him, but still she remained quiet. She'd been silent from the moment Irish apologized to her for the cuffs as soon as they were inside the safe building.

He was grateful for her instinctive wisdom. Nick Anson, ex-CIA operative, had a perpetual mistrust of ''outsiders''—those outside the military—that ran too deep to be mere prejudice alone, but whatever had happened to him, his boss kept it to himself. ''I know, sir, and I've thanked you over and over for that,'' Mitch replied now, ''but I still had to stay away from them another five months during the problems in the Java and Arafura Seas. I don't want to be away from them that long ever again. I've risked my neck for national security and regional stability enough times. I won't do it again, not for any other reason. My sons are emotionally fragile. They've been hurt enough by their mother. They need to know I won't take off without notice, and they need to feel secure that I'll come home in one piece.''

''Risk is the nature of our beast.''

''For single guys like you, sir, and Flipper and Braveheart and Irish and the other Nighthawks—even Songbird and Heidi love the game. But it's not for me anymore. I have a wife and family who need me and I won't leave them alone or at risk.''

Anson's fair hair glinted in the artificial light of the office. ''The contract's nonnegotiable, McCluskey. Our work's too important to throw away. I feel confident that when your lady knows the score about what you do, she'll agree with me.''

Lissa, her gray eyes wide in awe—by what she'd heard, or, like many women, by Anson's rugged, Nordic god looks, Mitch didn't know—ventured a smile. ''Maybe I will, sir. 'Skydancer' has this annoying tendency to want to overprotect me. He doesn't know what I'm capable of doing on my own.''

He grinned at her and rolled his eyes. ''I've been learning lately, Lissa. Constantly learning.''

She smiled up at him, with a sweet relief in her eyes, and belatedly he realized he hadn't smiled at her since last night. ''Good,'' she teased, looking so dainty, as ethereal in her faerie-like loveliness as ever—yet he knew she could kick his arse into tomorrow without breaking a sweat. ''Welcome to the twenty-first century, my gallant squadron leader—um, ex-squadron leader.''

''Ah, I see your lady has spunk and sass.'' Anson gave Lissa his slow, reluctant grin—the smile guaranteed to make Songbird and Heidi, their two female operatives, plus most other women, weak in the knees. ''I like her, McCluskey.''

Mitch flicked a glance at Lissa, who was watching his boss in turn. While he could see she wasn't immune to Anson's lethal, unconscious charm and lazy, deep New Orleans accent, he could tell it didn't go beyond a natural inclination to look. There was no flicker of feminine awareness in her eyes. He grinned back at Anson. ''So do I, sir.''

Anson waved them out, too absorbed to even notice, let alone worry about Lissa's reaction to him, too obsessed with saving the world to notice any woman at all—even the gloriously beautiful, sophisticated Songbird, and the equally dedicated-to-the-cause mountaineer operative, Heidi. "Take her to Tumah-ra if you have to. But tell her only what she needs to know, in a soundproof room in this building. Don't give any names of our operatives."

"I don't know their names," he retorted dryly. "And, sir, I think it's better if we talk out in plain sight. Our boy will be timing us if he followed us here, checking who owns this place and drawing his own conclusions. Which could rebound on the Nighthawks. If he's after me, it's best if the Nighthawks don't appear in this at all." He hesitated. "Livewire in bag, sir."

Anson nodded. "Okay, Skydancer, we'll do it your way. A thirty-four. Who do you want?"

"Angelo. Just the bag. We're clean."

"I know that," Anson retorted in withering sarcasm.

Of course he knew. The electronic detectors and portable sweeps inside the building here put Australia's international airports to shame.

The door opened behind them. The interview was over.

"Thirty-four?" Lissa asked softly, in the outer office.

Mitch led her to the front offices, lifted her bag from the security cupboard and lifted his finger to his lips.

She nodded.

They walked out onto the sunshine-soaked grass verge outside the building, leading to a park. "What the hell's going on, Lissa?" he snapped, his eyes darting side to side, looking for a tail. "Why did those goons drag us out of bed and down here at six in the morning? What did they say to you?"

"They strip searched me, of course—single mother farmers are obviously *so* dangerous to the Australian public! How would I know? What did they say to *you?*" she retorted, continuing the argument they'd started this morning after Irish and Braveheart cuffed them. "After all, it's not like *I* disappeared anywhere the past twelve years. I don't fly planes into dangerous places. *I* don't consort with drug-addicted prostitutes!"

Oh, she was *good.* He felt a crazy urge to laugh. Lissa had missed her calling in life. She could've made a fortune as a soapie actress or radio talk-show host. He led her down the street into the tree-lined park that bordered the Nighthawks' headquarters near Lake Burley-Griffin, holding her arm as they walked along the winding path beside the man-made lake. "She was not a drug addict when I met her. And you're on dangerous ground, talking about Matt and Luke's mother like that," he growled.

A quick flash of worry came and went in her eyes, seeing his reassuring twinkle. "And what a mother she was! I'm their real mother and you know it. The only good thing she ever did was give birth to them—after that she dumped them on you, kidnapped them and damaged them just to get back at you for not paying for her drugs, or for standing by her in the first place, marrying her when she was having your kids!"

Mitch stopped in his tracks. "Where the hell do you get off talking like that? My relationship with Kerin is none of your damn business!"

"And why don't the same high-minded principles stop you passing judgment on my relationship with Tim?"

Passers-by were staring, looking away. Hurrying on. Wild ducks quacked, flapped their wings and took off into the bright, clear sky—and a thin dark boy came out of nowhere, snatched Lissa's handbag from her shoulder and tore off.

"Mitch!" she screamed. "That kid stole my bag. Stop him!" And she bolted after the kid.

Mitch overtook her in seconds, sprinting in the same direction the boy had run. But the kid jumped into an open dark car without plates, looked at him with a big, smirking grin and slammed the door shut. Within seconds it was gone.

Lissa joined him moments later, panting. "I hope I'm getting that bag back. I was fond of it."

Man, he'd never have thought Lissa would think so damn

quickly on her feet or get the deal so fast. "I'll get you a new one this afternoon, I promise." Under the pretence of comforting her, he held her close. "Angelo signaled to me that someone's following us, so I'll make this quick. We'll get a bus to the nearest police station and notify them about the bag. We can talk while we're on the bus—the engine and talk around us should interfere with any signal he sends out. You all right, baby?" he asked aloud, caressing her, kissing her face.

"I want to go to the police," she hiccupped against his chest. "He'll sell my bag for drugs!"

"That's what kids do these days. Welcome to city life, Lissa. This is why I want to bring the kids up in Breckerville."

"Huh!" she said, recovering in an instant. "What planet are you living on? Armed robbery and assault's three times higher in country New South Wales towns than in Sydney, and double that statistic again for single mothers like me. I've been robbed four times since Tim left. The last time they put me in the hospital. Matt and Luke are probably safer in Bondi Beach than Breckerville."

*"What?"*

She shrugged. "Why do you think Tim checks on me so often? Why he's done repairs around the house so much? You know now it sure wasn't for sex."

He felt sick, like he'd been kicked in the guts. His stupidity and selfishness in never coming home, never checking to see if Tim had left her alone, so small and vulnerable, made him sick. And all because he thought he loved her too much!

But who did he love more—her, or himself? Love took risks, and all he'd done was protect himself. Damn his cowardice! Maybe Lissa was right in what she'd said last night in the plane. Maybe he'd never cared enough, never loved her enough. He should have come home, stopped worrying about *his* feelings and taken care of her. Then she'd never have had to live alone for the past six years. She'd never have been burgled or injured. And maybe, just maybe, she'd have some faith in him right now. "When? Who did it? How badly were you hurt?"

"I had a broken nose, a few strained ribs. Nothing life changing. But I don't own a VCR or computer anymore—it's too much of an open invitation. He was a local brat on ecstasy—he's long gone, disappeared to Sydney, probably dead or on the Wall," she said tersely, referring to Sydney's notorious area for boy prostitutes. "Tim got us a security system. Tim's partner, Ron, built me a pull-out cupboard for the microwave and coffeemaker, to hide them." She shrugged again, like it was no big deal. "I got out of hospital about two months before you called me about the boys." She grinned. "Now you know why the family takes those kickboxing lessons you hate. I wanted the local punks to know we're not such an easy target anymore."

He lifted her face, the awed glow in his eyes serious. "Baby, I'm so proud of you. For your strength. For your optimism. For your courage, after all you've been through. I just wish I'd been there for you. But from now on you're not alone—and if you give me a second chance with you, you never will be again."

The shutters came down. "Mitch, I don't—" Her eyes darted sideways, then back to him. "Kiss me, Mitch. I'm not as brave as you think I am...." When her lips met his, she murmured into his mouth, "He's there. At the other end of the park. See him?"

He maneuvered her around under the guise of tender kisses. "Uh-huh. He can't have any long-distance equipment or he wouldn't bother to show himself. My guess is he's trying to intimidate us. Let's find that bus."

They stalked to the main road, holding hands, and he didn't have to tell her not to look back. They climbed on the first bus they saw, Lissa wailing that she didn't *like* this park anymore.

He'd never have thought of that, either. "You're an awesome actress, you know that? Just who is the agent operative in this couple?'' he murmured, as soon as the bus lumbered off and he was sure no one had followed them onto it.

Lissa faced him, her eyes glittering, and he knew the games were over for now. ''I don't know. Why don't you tell me about it, *Skydancer?* Tell me who you are, who that man is and what this organization does and why?''

Crowding close, he murmured all she needed to know for now into her ear. About his reputation as a rebel in the Air Force—taking stupid chances with his life and his squadron to help people in need. How it resulted in a phone call two years ago from Anson, ex-CIA and head of an international group of operatives known as the Nighthawks, with head offices in Virginia, London and Canberra. What the Nighthawks did. How Anson offered him a place with the Nighthawks, doing what he did best—search and rescue in war zones, saving women and kids and political refugees. Offering Mitch an irresistible cover by having him appear to remain with the RAAF, and bona fide work with the Vincent Foundation—feeding kids and women in desperate need. The promise to find Matt and Luke, to get them back from Kerin. A guarantee he need only do backup, part-time work if he got the boys. The RAAF's total cooperation with his cover, proving to him that the Nighthawks were definitely on the up and up. With the good guys.

Slowly she nodded. ''Did you bring that little girl illegally into the country?'' She pretended to nibble his earlobe, then she giggled as an old woman huffed about declining morality in Australia. ''Now I'm a wanton woman! Oh, this is fun. I haven't had this much fun since we played spy games as kids!''

Fun? He was going insane. ''I don't know about you, but I want the real thing,'' he growled in her ear. ''I love being this close to you, touching you, but I hate knowing it's all fake. I want to get you naked again—totally naked— and not have to worry about listening devices or anything else but pleasing you. I want to make love to you so badly, and I want *you* to want me, to make love with me, too.'' He looked in her eyes and found a compelling mix of heated desire and haunting uncertainty. ''I want to see you—all of you—and touch you without games or doubts. I want to touch you all over—kiss your breasts, your face, your gorgeous bottom. I want my hands and mouth on every part of you until you scream my name again, scream for me to be inside you. I want to lie on you, to be inside your body, then have you take control of me. I want you to ride me until we both collapse. And then I want to start again, and then again. I—''

''Stop,'' she whispered, sounding anguished.

*Tell her. Let her know how much you want her.* It was time to take Tim's advice; they'd already lost so many years through his own stupid dread of losing her. ''You don't want me anymore? You don't want me as much as I want you? Because my fantasies and needs are at the point of no return. Yesterday and last night was incredible, fantastic—but I need to be inside you, Lissa. I want to feel it, to be with you all the way.''

A tiny gasp told him she wasn't just listening but living and reliving his words in glorious Technicolor. ''Tell me you want me like you used to, even if it's just a little bit— please. Don't punish me for the gutless wonder I used to be, for letting you down by not coming home. I always wanted you. I wanted to tell you so bad, baby. But you were everything to me. *Everything.* I'd have gone berserk if you didn't want me. I couldn't face thinking about you going to bed with him, wanting, aching for it to be me. I knew if I stayed around, you'd end up knowing how hard I get just from being in the same room as you. But I'm willing to risk it all this time, if you are. I'll tell you how much I want you—I have to have you.'' He tried to gauge her reaction but failed. ''I need to know how you feel, too.''

Silence; she hid in his shoulder. He closed his eyes, waiting, hoping for the smallest sign from her—a sign of passion, of need...of trust. And that, he found, he wanted most of all. Her trust. But he was getting nothing, nothing at all....

Then a shuddery breath filled his ear. "Yes. If it really matters—if this is the honest truth—I want you. I want you like crazy. I've never wanted any other man this way. Only you." A sigh. "The man in the gray suit just got on the bus. Did you bring that child into the country illegally?" she asked again.

"Yes." He didn't turn around. "No more now." He held her close, in a mixture of play-acting and dead-serious desire. "Let's look out for a cop shop."

"I want to look at mug shots," she said venomously.

He nuzzled her neck, feeling, oh, so happy. He hadn't blown it. She still wanted him; she trusted him enough to stay on the plan, even after what he just told her about the little girl, Hana. "Oooh, baby, you turn me on when you're vicious."

She giggled before she could catch it. "Behave yourself, will you, McCluskey? That poor lady behind us looks like she's about to have a coronary as it is."

"Give our listener a sign," he murmured. "Shake your head or whatever he's waiting for."

"I already did," she said simply. No big deal. "I think he wants to talk to me."

"I don't care what he wants. The kids are safe, Lissa. His hold over you is gone. And you're not going to be more than ten feet away from me until I've put him out of action."

She put a hand on his thigh, caressing him. "Threat or promise, McCluskey? Because I think you'll find I can look after myself. Stop underestimating me, Mitch. If I was an operative, wouldn't you use me?"

He wouldn't hesitate. "But they're trained operatives."

"Then train me."

He shuddered, but the agent in him knew she'd be an operative to equal Songbird or Heidi too damn fast. Her capacity for acting, for enjoying danger, already equaled anything he'd ever done or felt. "But they know the game, they realize the risks."

She laughed softly in his ear. "I think I'm getting the idea. I've been playing the game the past few weeks—and playing it well, so you tell me."

*Damn, I wish she'd stop making sense!* "They don't have kids."

"You have kids. You've had them the whole time, even if you didn't know where they were. You took the risks, knowing Matt and Luke had no one to rely on but you."

He opened his mouth and closed it. He had no answer for that one, and she knew it.

She lifted a brow. "Well? Got any more buts?"

The only ones he could think of he couldn't say. Not now, not yet, not in a crowded bus—not until he found more courage than he had at this moment. *But I wouldn't be frightened as hell to use the other female operatives. Though I'd risk my life to save them, they'd be calculated risks. I wouldn't take damn stupid risks because my heart was involved.*

*I wouldn't want to give up and die if I lost them.*

He thrust a hand through his hair, feeling beads of sweat trickling all over his scalp. "Not right now. Give me a minute."

She chuckled, low and soft. "Oooh, baby, you turn me on when you're frantically trying to protect me from myself."

For the first time since joining the Nighthawks, agent and man were tangled beyond unraveling. He turned her face to his, and kissed her, long and hard. "You're driving me crazy, Miller."

That low, rippling laugh came again—the one that sent hot shivers down his spine, hard and wanting. "Good." And she nuzzled his neck, then ran a slow tongue along his skin to his ear. "Now let's get back to work. I'll let him know I'll meet him somehow. Any ideas? I can slip out when you're making your statement to the cops. And don't worry about me, I'm far from helpless. I didn't come third in the last State Intermediate Championship in kick-boxing for nothing.''

Uh-huh…and no doubt she can shoot a can off a fence at five hundred meters, throw knives at the heart and break a man's neck in seconds.

He shook his head; he felt like someone had opened his brain and poured mud in it. And to think he'd been so surprised when she lost her temper the first day.

His every illusion of her seemed destined to shatter. His gentle, home-and-hearth Lissa, who'd barely left Brecker-ville for years, had wild and dangerous depths he'd never even dreamed existed—and he suspected he'd get more than a few shocks before this case was complete.

He just hoped he could keep her away from Anson from now on, because after a few minutes he'd see the incredible potential in her. The potential Mitch would give anything not to see right now, or to remember she'd always had, the potential he'd chosen to forget.

She had the guts, the fire and the intuition—not to mention the exceptional thirst for danger, and the level of self-defense skills she needed and twice the enthusiasm. Sheesh, give her six months and she'd outclass him on any op Anson sent them on. If she went with him, that was. And if any other Nighthawk met her, they'd love her—literally.

And then he'd lose everything he'd ever wanted.

# Chapter 9

"It's time to talk with our friend," Lissa murmured in his ear outside the police station. She'd given her statement and checked out mug shots without success, but they'd expected that, since Angelo was an operative in training. "He's looking twitchy."

"I still don't like this," Mitch muttered. He had a real bad feeling about this. About letting her out of his sight at all.

She smiled up at him, confident, sure, sexy as hell in those snug jeans, her burnished hair loose, the golden tips glowing in the sunlight. "I'll be fine, Mitch. Stop worrying. Wait here. I'll be back in ten minutes."

"Lissa—"

She touched his face. "Turn two of your favorite words round on yourself, McCluskey. *Trust me.*"

He watched with a slow-growing sense of dread as she slipped away across the small park to a quiet alley in the shadows of an old building where the man in gray waited for her. And while he couldn't see clearly, Mitch would later swear the filthy jerk had a smug grin on his face.

His cell phone beeped as he sat at the park bench watching the shadowed alleyway, timing the minutes before he went in there to get Lissa to safety. ''Yeah.''

''Where's your lady, Skydancer?'' Anson asked tersely. Oh, help. He didn't like that tone. ''With our boy.''

''Get her out of there—now. Angelo took shots of our boy while he was following you, and while we don't know who the hell he is yet, he sure ain't ASIO, CIA, MI5 or any other respectable organization. I'll send more news when I have it.''

The line went dead…and Mitch bolted at a dead run for the dark shadows where the stranger had Lissa.

''We have to hurry,'' Lissa said, panting, as she reached the shadows where the man in gray waited for her. ''McCluskey thinks I'm looking for a washroom. I've only got a couple of minutes.''

''What have you got for me?''

''Nothing but suspicions. If he has anything incriminating he's hiding it too well for me to find it.''

''It's been three weeks. The Feds pulled you out of bed this morning—a bed you've been sharing with him. You must know more than this by now.'' A small, chilling silence. ''You aren't protecting him by any chance, are you?''

''The Feds just wasted two hours, asking me a pile of useless questions about conditions in Bosnia and Indonesia—places about which I know nothing. They also asked me about McCluskey's living habits—again, I'm ignorant. So don't waste my time on more stupid questions. I know nothing about McCluskey. Whatever he is, he's good at hiding it.''

''Didn't he give you any pillow talk? Come on, you've

been sleeping with him,'' the man said in cold impatience. ''He must have told you something. On the plane last night—anything?''

Lissa stared into his expensive dark glasses, seeing only a mirror of her own face. She found no clue as to his emotions. ''If he's a spy, what would he tell me? You heard him yesterday. He knows I've been going through his things. He got suspicious when I wouldn't sleep with him. So I did—just like you asked me to. Makes a nice change from celibacy, and he's not bad in bed, but no, I'm not protecting him. He thinks I am, though. He thinks I *trust* him.'' She used the word like an epithet. ''I don't trust any man.''

''What about me?'' The gray man touched her hair in a lingering caress. ''Do you trust me, Lissa?''

She jerked her hair out of his hold. ''Don't flatter yourself. I'm doing this for my kids.''

He laughed. ''Smart girl. I wouldn't trust me, either.'' A finger trailed down her face, making her wonder if he wanted her or just wanted to intimidate her.

She allowed the touch, willing her face to remain still and cold. To give nothing away. ''So what now?''

If he was taken aback by her coolness, he didn't show it. ''Same. Stick with him. Do whatever it takes. Just get evidence of what he's doing. These smuggling rackets are ruining Australia. Illegal migrants are taking jobs from decent Australians, draining taxpayers' money with legal arguments to stay here, and using our hospitals. They form gangs in our cities and criminal rings. Conditions at our refugee facilities are unsanitary for the real, honest refugees of war or political turmoil. And people like McCluskey continue to bring them in for money. They don't care what they're doing to our country.''

It sounded so plausible, so passionately delivered. What was his real agenda? And how did he expect her to answer? ''I don't care. I just want my kids safe.''

''Spoken like a true mother.'' The words were light,

amused even, but she felt some gut-level attraction simmering beneath. He wanted her, and didn't care if he showed it. He touched her face again, running lightly over her skin. "Pretty Lissa with the beautiful eyes and sensual mouth. When this is over—"

"You'll go back to your world, and I'll go back to mine. And we'll never meet again. Goodbye." She turned away.

He swung her round to face him. "Don't turn your back on me." His snarl was soft with menace; yet it struck her with a sense of wrongness. Like he was hiding laughter beneath the words. "Don't ever turn your back on me."

"I don't know what sort of women inhabit your world, but I don't put up with being mauled. I might have to get information for you to keep my sons, but that's *all* you'll get from me!" She pulled her arm free, her breast heaving. "I said goodbye."

With a small, taunting grin, he covered her heaving breast with his hand, groping her. "But *I* didn't. I didn't dismiss you yet, sweet thing." He ran his hand with deliberate insolence down her ribs toward her panties. "I can do better than him, Lissa. Twenty-nine minutes, seven and a half minutes. I can last much longer than that—and it wasn't that good for you, I could tell. I can make you scream for me."

He'd *timed* them? And he wanted the same thing from her. He'd been turned on by listening to them! Bile rose in hot burning chunks up her throat, and her temper flashed. She ducked, spun and lashed out, catching him in the inner hip with the full weight of her leg—and he staggered backward into the wall, a look of comical surprise on his face.

"Sorry," she said, with just the same touch of insolence he'd used on her. "You see, I don't do intimidation, and shows of power don't turn me on. Don't touch me again without permission."

Like a flash he was standing again, white-faced and furious, holding a gun right against her forehead. "Don't you dare walk away." The gun touched her breast like a lover. "Get down on your knees and apologize for hurting me."

"You don't scare me." Her heart was pumping hard, but still she forced her chin up, facing those frighteningly face-less glasses with all the defiance she could summon. "You won't hurt me. You need me. McCluskey's obsessed with me—you heard him. He's wanted me for years. No one but me can get what you need from him. You know it and I know it."

"I'll find another way if I need to. I don't need you—except maybe in bed." The gun caressed her mouth now. "Pretty-mouthed Lissa. I want you to do things to me with that mouth—"

"Lissa, duck."

Mitch stood at the end of the alley, holding a gun aimed right at the gray man's head.

The man just smiled and pushed the gun inside Lissa's mouth.

Mitch didn't budge; his eyes and hands holding his gun remained rock steady, but Lissa could see the sweat beading his brow. "I don't know who the hell you are or what you want, but so help me God, if you don't get that gun off my woman I'll kill you where you stand."

He wasn't joking.

The gray man appeared to consider Mitch's ultimatum for a few moments. "No...you don't know who I am, do you?" He smiled at Lissa then, and ran the cold barrel of the gun over her mouth once more, with a little smile. "Good girl, Lissa. I'll see you soon." He turned and walked around the corner, whistling softly.

Mitch grabbed her in his arms, pulling her away from the alley and into the safety of the sunshine at the front of the buildings. "Are you all right?"

She turned on him. "You almost blew our cover, you idiot! I was fine! I can look after myself! I had him convinced you know nothing and I don't trust you, and you had to come charging over like some cheap Bruce Willis impersonator, ready to save me! Damn it, Mitch, I'm not helpless. Trust me for once. Let me help you bring this jerk down without treating me like some fragile porcelain doll!''

She stopped, panting, at the look in his eyes, suddenly cold with warning. It was only then she realized Mitch wasn't holding her, he was frisking her; and when he withdrew his hand from her breast pocket, Mitch held another listening device.

So that was why the gray man groped her.

She closed her eyes. ''I'm sorry,'' she whispered.

He threw the bug down and stamped on it. ''Too late now for regrets. Let's get out of here. Fast.''

He grabbed her hand and they bolted in a stumbling dead run across the park, waiting with every step for the hit; but they made it to the main road, unmolested. They melted into the rush of lunchtime workers, heading west to the main city street.

''What now?'' she panted, rubbing her ribs to relieve the stitch in her side.

''Back to the plane,'' he murmured. ''We're getting out of Canberra.'' He used his cell phone, asking Anson to send Mabel with their clothes to meet them at the airstrip.

She checked herself over again. ''Is there any more on me?''

''Did he touch you anywhere else?''

''He ran his hand down my shirt to my pants. He kept touching my mouth.'' She shuddered.

He leaned over, checked her pants pockets and cuffs. ''You're clean now.'' Then he smiled and brushed her mouth with his, in a kiss that had little to do with passion and everything to do with tenderness. ''Totally clean, baby. Forget the filthy creep. He'll never have his hands on you again.''

She nodded, upset by her own naiveté. She was so protected, the gray man made her feel soiled with a touch, a dirty smile and lewd suggestions. ''How are we getting to the airstrip?''

He pointed to the row of taxicabs lining the front of the shopping mall ahead of them. "First stage."

But he held her back when she headed for the front cab. "The third one. He hasn't had time to pay more than one of them."

He handed her into the cab. She hid a smile, wondering if she'd ever change his perceptions that she was delicate, fragile and feminine—if she'd ever conquer his need to protect her.

It wasn't so bad, feeling cherished. Sometimes.

"The nearest Suzuki dealership." Mitch added quietly to her, "I'll buy a motorbike and we'll ride from there to the airstrip."

She blinked. Okay. This month appeared to be the time for crowding a whole world of new experiences into her narrow life. "Do we have to leave now? Maybe he doesn't know about us. Maybe he hadn't switched the bug on yet when I said all that—"

He took her hand, caressing the palm. "If he didn't then, he does now, Lissa. I broke it. He'll draw his own conclusions from the silence, for sure. Which puts you in danger." He turned her face to his. "We're not just leaving Canberra. We're leaving Australia for a few days."

She gasped. "Oh. I mean, you said something to Anson about Tumah-ra, but I never thought—"

"Don't say his name in public, Lissa." He smiled to soften the words. "I thought since you were worried about what happened to Hana—the girl I got out of Tumah-ra— you might like to see her reunited with her grandparents, aunt and uncle and cousins."

"We're flying to Tumah-ra?"

"After we pick up Hana in Darwin. The Australian government wasn't too impressed with my methods of saving Hana. They don't want any international wrangling over her or diplomatic incidents over my supposed kidnapping of a child. They don't even want to get involved in the war until the UN says to go. It's election year and they're trying to look like white knights for the electorate. Anson found some extended family who are very happy to know she's alive. I'm taking her back home.''

''That's, um, good.'' Awed, she murmured, ''Mitch? I don't have a passport. I've never needed one.''

He grinned. ''It's all arranged already. Mabel's bringing it to the plane now. I brought your birth certificate and a recent photo of you from home, and Anson pushed the paperwork through.''

So while she'd been going through his stuff, he'd been going through hers? Admiring, indignant and confused, she wanted to laugh, cry and tear his hair out. ''The advantages of being a spy?'' she murmured in his ear.

He tipped her face around to meet his. ''I'll do whatever I can, use whoever I have to, to keep you with me. I don't care what consequences come after. I'm keeping you safe. He'll never get to you again, Lissa, never touch you again. Ever.'' He drew her against him, and she could feel the heavy thudding of his heart. ''It scared the hell out of me when I saw that gun on you the first time. Then today, when I saw that jerk using it like a sexual toy on you, I knew there was no turning back. Anson agreed with me when he told me to tell you everything and take you with me. Welcome to the world of the Nighthawks, Lissa. Welcome to my world and the advantages it can bring.''

Her heart almost burst in the fierceness of her joy. Finally she was inside Mitch's world, a full part of his life. He trusted her enough to bring her in from the outer fringes.

*But would it ever have happened if I hadn't been in danger?*

Fifteen minutes later Melissa Carroll, single mother and up-till-now overlooked country mouse, was wearing a top-class helmet and thick leather jacket, sitting on the back of 1250cc's of off-road power. Ready to do a runner out of Australia like a common—no, like a high-powered criminal, a drug dealer or child smuggler. A hit man's woman.

A failed media baron's wife, she thought with a half-hysterical giggle.

Or a Nighthawk's woman.

"Hold on tight," Mitch said.

She wrapped her arms around him, snuggled in to his big, strong body and closed her eyes as he took off.

He rode like he drove: with total and superb confidence.

"Does Matt know you can ride like this?" she yelled over the rushing wind in her ears, trying her best to keep up with his balancing moves as they turned corners.

"No way," Mitch yelled back. "He'd drive me crazy wanting to learn." Then they hit the open road, and the rush turned into a roar as Mitch turned speeding into poetry in motion.

Within minutes they were at the airstrip. He flew over the bumps on the runway until he reached the hangar, standing open and ready.

The placid, middle-aged woman from the B&B waited beside the plane, wearing a seventies style print dress, reading glasses perched in her iron-gray curls—and a vicious-looking assault rifle in competent hands.

More and more Lissa felt like Alice falling down the rabbit-hole....

Mitch hopped off the bike, took his helmet off and held out his hand for hers. "We're taking the bike with us. We'll need transport in Tumah-ra in case snipers hit us and we need to land before we reach the hangar. The militia hijack planes, if they can get to them first."

"Nets and greenery already in there with the usual kits." Mabel swung the rifle around to her back. "Plane's clean and ready to fly, Skydancer. Here's your new passports. You're Mr. and Mrs. Alan Sinclair of Turramurra, newlyweds and all over each other like a rash. You're on your honeymoon, and your wife wanted an adventurous holiday. If the militia catches you, you found the little girl wandering and you're taking her home. If they probe, you're really philanthropists with secret militia sympathies. You own shares in the oil company of their choice. You want to donate fifty thousand to their cause in return for shares later. Your stuff's packed, including jungle greens. They'll protect you in the trees, but you'll look like stupid gung-ho amateurs if you're caught." She held out some papers and a wad of money to a startled Lissa. "Anson said to give these to Countrygirl. She's good at keeping secrets, or so he said, and with that Madonna-like face and a few tears, they'll be less likely to strip search her. And if they try, she can do a Charlie's Angels on them. I hear she can really kick arse."

Mitch's face darkened. "You can tell Anson for me that my fiancée won't be back on after this."

"Don't answer for me, *Skydancer,*" said Lissa. "I can handle my own life." She frowned and asked Mabel, "You've been checking on me?" She knew Mitch hadn't had time to tell anyone anything about her—and obviously hadn't wanted to, by the scowl he wore.

"Anson did. Of course he did, as soon as he knew you were going to marry Skydancer." Mabel gave Mitch a swift grin. "As I'm sure you were aware, Skydancer, he found a lot more than he bargained for. Welcome to the Night-hawks, Countrygirl."

Curiouser and curiouser: a month ago she was a ne-glected dirt-poor farmer and single mum, now she was an international spy. She blinked again, took the papers and money and smiled back. "Countrygirl? Who thought of that?"

"Anson, of course. He gives us all our names." The woman lifted her brows at Lissa's surprise. "You didn't think Mabel was my real name? Don't give me yours, ei-ther. I don't want to know. It's safer if none of us knows anything."

Mitch, his face dark and brooding, hauled the bike onto the plane. "Tell Anson I'll be taking Bertha from Darwin on. She's been spray painted since I got back. The kanga-roo's gone."

Mabel patted his shoulder. "It's only paint, Skydancer."

"It's obvious you're not a pilot," he retorted.

Mabel laughed. "I'll pass on your obvious displeasure at Anson's offer to Countrygirl."

"Like that's gonna make a difference, if 'Countrygirl' wants the job," he snapped. "Tell Anson I really appreciate his courtesy in discussing the matter with her, or with me, before he enrolled my fiancée in the job I want the hell out of!"

"No, you don't." Mabel kissed his cheek, then pinched it, chuckling. "You're as addicted as the rest of us, Skydancer. Puff off all the steam you like, but you're an adrenaline junkie and hero wannabe, and you always will be."

Lissa smothered her grin and climbed into the cockpit. "Bye, Mabel. See you again sometime."

"Not if I can help it," Mitch muttered, and slammed the door shut on the Cessna.

Mabel winked at her, hauled the rifle back over her shoulder and returned to sentry duty as Mitch, still muttering beneath his breath, prepared for takeoff.

She pressed her nose to the window as they lifted up into the sky, still marveling at the wonder of being in the air. Only her third flight, and she was hooked.

"Try to get some sleep," Mitch said, his tone sour. "It's a seven-hour flight to Darwin, and it's gonna be a long night."

Her stomach rumbled. "I can't sleep now—I'm hungry," she replied apologetically. "I don't suppose Mabel packed food? We didn't get to have lunch."

Without a word he handed her a Snickers from a pouch in the backpack between them.

"Mmmm." She sank her teeth into the chocolate bar, mumbling in ecstasy at the rich, sticky sweetness. "I don't know what it is about having a gun put to your head and running for your life, but it makes me really hungry."

He shook his head as he set course northwest for the Northern Territory. "And I thought I knew you so damn well. Is *anything* about you the same as when we were kids?''

''Yeah, I still like Spy versus Spy.'' She lifted her chin. ''Baby, if you want a sweet little mousy wife who'd stay home, mind the kids and knit cardigans, you shouldn't bring spies and secrets home with you to tempt me with a life I always wanted. But I must say in your defense,'' she added thoughtfully, ''I didn't remember all of this about me, either, until the gray man bugged the house. So I guess you can say I'm as surprised as you are by my sudden penchant for action and excitement.''

''My old mate, the adrenaline rush,'' he said quietly.

''Hmmm. I suppose so. I guess I have something to thank our voyeur for, after all,'' she finished with a grin.

''Well, if we're going to share excitement, do you think we can share food? That was my last Snickers, and I don't want to stop before Birdsville. The pub there has steaks to die for.''

''Birdsville,'' she murmured dreamily. ''The Outback. I always wanted to see the Outback.'' She broke off half the chocolate and handed it to him.

''You won't see much of it today. It'll be sunset by the time we get there. Darkness comes quick in that part of the world.''

''And you've seen so much of the world, haven't you? Not like me. I've barely ever left Breckerville.''

There was a small silence. Then he said, ''You never had to leave it to know it's home, Lissa. You don't have to see the horror and violence in the world to appreciate the peace you've already got.'' He spoke in a jerking tone. Then he plunged into his half of the chocolate, as if he knew he'd said too much.

There was a small white line around his nostrils. His eyes were shadowed with anger and something else—disillusionment?

She sensed he was making an enormous effort to talk so

casually to her, and she could read his thoughts as clearly as her well-loved *Anne of Green Gables* books.

"Don't do this to me, Mitch," she said quietly. "I didn't ask for this to happen. But now that I've been dragged into your world, I won't scream and faint so you can play the big he-man protecting his woman. If you want a gentle, innocent homebody for a wife, you'd better start looking elsewhere. Because I won't pretend to be what I never wanted to be. I've had to live this boring, stay-at-home life for the past twelve years, and I won't do it again so you can fulfil your dreams. You've had enough of yours come true. Now it's my turn to live!"

He glanced at her, his eyes filled with ghosts of the past. "You were that girl once. You would have done that for me—once."

"Yes," she replied bluntly. "And I'd have been fool enough to think I was happy. But that girl's gone. The girl who adored you with all that puppy-dog devotion is gone forever."

His jaw clenched. "So it seems."

She bit her lip. "I see. It's not really me you want, is it? It's the past. I represent the security you always wanted."

"I told you before that's not true," he growled.

"You told me that the first day, before you knew what I'm like now. Before you saw that I could take care of myself. I've grown up, become a woman—and I'm not the woman you imagined I'd be."

"That much you got right." His laugh held no amusement. "In all my dreams of you, I never saw you checking the house for bugs, kicking a spy's butt or joining the Nighthawks."

"And it bothers you—that's what gets to you the most. You don't want me to be part of your world. You want me in the past. You want a haven from all the war and horror you've seen, to help Matt and Luke forget the pain they went through with Kerin. You want a mother, a lover, a friend and counselor—but essentially a woman without needs of her own. I'm not a real person to you. I'm an ideal.'' She almost choked on the words. ''Did you know, Mitch, or did you fool yourself into thinking that you really wanted me? Maybe you even thought you were in love with me. Maybe you even called it love. But it's really a foster kid's infatuation with what you think I am—what a family woman should be.''

When he spoke this time, it was in grim desperation. ''Lissa, I'm taking you to Tumah-ra—a war zone, for crying out loud! Would I do that if I thought you were just some stupid ideal?''

''Oh, yeah,'' she said gently. ''To protect me—to save me from the big bad wolf. To keep me in character, your gentle goddess who knows nothing about the seamy side of your life. But the first time I stepped off the pedestal, you were outta there. You can't handle me being less than your perfect ideal. You didn't see me protect myself, did you? But then, you don't want to know about that, because it makes me real!''

''Lissa, don't do this to us! Don't say it.''

''I have to.'' She was shaking now; she had to force down a huge, hard, hurting ball of anguish in her throat. ''Sorry if I've shattered your illusions and dreams, but I don't want to be your haven. I don't want to be some warped representation of home and hearth, the little woman waiting for her wandering hero to come back to her. I've been that all my life. I've been daughter and friend, wife and mother. I gave up my dreams of university to help Dad on the farm, then I did it again for Tim's gym. Then I had Jenny, then Matt and Luke. But it's finally my turn now. I want to *live*—and since it seems you can't accept that, you'd better start thinking up how to tell the boys they aren't getting the family you promised them.'' She looked down at her lap. ''The wedding's off.''

''No. I can't accept that. I won't accept that!'' Mitch was shaking himself. He hit the auto-pilot button then held her by the shoulders to turn her to him. His eyes blazed.

''Baby, it's not like you think at all. Don't judge me until you've seen what I'm talking about. Give us a chance before you blow it all off.''

''There is no us. I only agreed to marry you in the first place because that man insisted I do what it took to get evidence against you, to keep you with me. Then I wanted it to be real.'' She pressed her lips together, gritted her teeth, but the tears came anyway. ''There never was a real chance for us, except in our imagination. I think we made ideals of each other based on how crazy we were about each other as kids, and neither of us were lucky enough to meet anyone else who fulfilled our ideal. Maybe one doesn't exist. We're dreamers, Mitch,'' she whispered, trying to smile through the tears raining down. ''Both of us. But we're not kids anymore. We can't force each other into moulds that don't fit, whether we want each other or not.''

''I don't want to force you into anything. I don't want an ideal. I just want you!''

She shook her head. ''You didn't trust me today. You came in with guns blazing. You didn't give me a chance to deal with him.''

''Why don't you ask me why, Lissa?''

She looked at him, but the words wouldn't form.

He sighed. ''Anson told me to go in and get you out. And you'll learn soon enough that you just don't disobey Anson.''

She nodded reluctantly. ''Will I learn, Mitch? You don't want me in the Nighthawks.''

His eyes went dark, like a light snapped off. ''No. I don't,'' he agreed, his voice quiet—too quiet. ''Why don't you ask me about that, too?''

She wiped tears from her face. ''Why don't you ask *me* what I want for my life, instead of assuming you know? Why don't you ask me why I *want* to join the Nighthawks?''

''You don't know what it is you're joining!''

''And you knew all about it when you signed up with

them?'' she challenged. ''You left the Air Force before the
peacekeeping force was needed in East Timor. So besides
flying, how much Air Force training in peacetime Australia
helped you with what you needed to do with the Nighthawks?''

''Okay, not much!'' he muttered. ''But I know now, and
I know it's not for you.''

''Based on what you knew of me as a kid, or what
you've seen me do the past few weeks?'' Silence. She
sighed and turned away, tired of crying but unable to stop.
''Just answer this, Mitch, based on what you've seen of me
the past few days. If it weren't me in question—if I were
any other woman than sweet little Lissa Miller from your
Breckerville memories—would you still *know* I couldn't
handle what's entailed in being an operative for the Nighthawks?''

That silenced him, too. But oh, how she'd hoped it
wouldn't.

She watched in helpless anguish as he resumed control
of the Cessna. ''Please, don't say any more. Let's just get
this over, let's bring this guy down, get the kids safe
and—''

''And?'' he asked quietly. ''What then, Lissa? What do
we tell Matt and Luke—Luke, whom we both promised
we'd never leave? That we'd always be together?''

''I don't know!'' she cried, finally beyond tears. ''I don't
know, all right? All I know right now is I'm thankful we
didn't get in too deep, that I didn't fall head-over-heels in
love with you all over again. We'll think up something to
tell the kids.''

''You'll have to, Lissa, because I won't lie to them. I
still want to marry you. I won't cancel the wedding.'' He
sighed again, and spoke with quiet despair. ''Give me two
days, Lissa. Two days to convince you you're wrong about
us—that if I'm wrong, I can change how I think of you.
That we do have a chance together. That what we have
could be as real as our dreams.''

She shoved half a fist in her mouth to stop the hysterical laughter emerging. "Mitch, we're gong into a war zone!"

But he only nodded. "What better place to prove I trust you, by putting my life in your hands, and yours in mine?"

Startled, she turned to face him.

He smiled grimly. "This is as real as it gets, Lissa. I've always worked alone. I've never trusted anyone. But in the next two days I'll have to. Because any decisions I make will affect the rest of your life—and yours will affect mine. Matt, Luke and Jenny's as well…and Hana's, too. We have to do this together, for all our sakes. No arbitrary decisions or orders. Joint decisions. If we can do this, we can do anything. If I prove I can do that, will you think again about our life together?"

She wanted time to think it through—but he was right. There was no decision. This had to be. If they survived the next two days, maybe—just maybe—they could make a life together, too.

Slowly she nodded.

The stiffness of his spine visibly relaxed. "Thank you." Then he turned the plane toward far-west Queensland, to the tiny Outback town famous for its yearly insane horse race, its one pub and nothing else. As he guided the Cessna groundward the sun dipped and fell, and they flew right into a harsh, unforgiving land, all ochres and copper and rust and the flaming dark red of blood, in a violent and glorious sunset.

# *Chapter 10*

The adorable little dark-haired child's face lit on seeing Mitch the next morning. "Nicker! Nicker!"

With a grin Mitch dropped to his haunches and held out a Snickers—one of an amazing supply, almost into the hundreds, he'd bought that morning near Darwin airport. "Go for it, kid."

With a look of ecstasy Hana devoured the chocolate, smearing a good portion of it over her face in her hurry to get it all in. Then she gave Mitch a timid smile. "Tanks you."

He touched her grubby cheek. "*Wala pong anuman,* Hana."

Hana's face lit up at his use of Tagalog; she nodded, with a beaming smile. Then she dragged him to a small table, where she got out a pack of cards, and they were soon embroiled in a falteringly bilingual, very intense game of Snap.

Lissa watched him playing with Hana, touched anew by his rapport with kids—any kids. For a man never brought up in a family—whose own last name came from the priest who ran the church orphanage where he'd been dumped— he had such innate tenderness and empathy. He never wasted time with self-pity but got on with living, making the best of what he had.

"Would you like a drink of tea, Lis-sa?"

Lissa turned to the smiling Tumah-ran woman. "Thank you, Lily. I would."

The little woman bustled around her simple kitchen beneath the ceiling fan, cheerful amid heat so humid she could wring out her clothes. If she hung them on an outdoor line they'd still be wet tomorrow. The whole house—the whole city of Darwin—had a heavy odor of steamy heat and the doubtful swirling freshness of an afternoon storm coming.

Lissa used her handkerchief for the fiftieth time to wipe her perspiring face, but it was so damp it was of little use. She felt limp and languid, puddling from the inside. "Is Tumah-ra as humid as Darwin?" she asked Lily, wondering if, like a character in a book she'd read in childhood, she would literally melt away in her own sweat. How could people live here?

Lily frowned and tilted her head. "What is—"

Lissa bit her lip, then she fanned herself and wiped her forehead, using the same sort of verbal sign shorthand she'd seen Mitch use with Hana during the Snap game. "Tumah-ra same?"

Lily smiled and nodded. "Hot. Very hot. Rain."

Lissa sighed.

Lily patted her arm. "Very nice, Tumah-ra. Pretty. Much tree, pretty water...coral. Nice. Before soldiers come and...and—" She frowned, then said triumphantly, "Shoot 'em up!"

Lissa gasped at the terminology. "Are you sad, Lily?"

Lily turned to her, with a heart-wrenching smile of sadness and bravado and acceptance all in one. "Tumah-ra very pretty. Very nice. Find oil, it go bad for money. My brother, he die fighting rebels. My sister, she disappear. We lucky here, my husband, me, my son, be refugees for one year, maybe two. But one day go home. Make house again. Make village back. Find my father. He we not find to go on boat.'' She shook her head as Lissa's eyes filled with sympathetic tears. ''No, Lis-sa. My brother, my sister in God's hands. We have good life. This bad thing for now— only now. One day soldiers go home, and we go home. Make Tumah-ra pretty again.''

She couldn't answer Lily. A queer pain streaked through her, an aching wistfulness. Lily and her family—not to mention Mitch—had known so much less of love and joy and family security in their lives, yet it was she who held back, who refused to rebuild her world when it fell apart. She who kept others at arm's length for fear of being hurt.

When had she lost that optimism, that willingness to see the brighter side of life? When had she become so much less than the woman she'd once wanted to be?

*Give me two days, Lissa. Two days to show you that our lives can be as real as our dreams.*

Maybe it was time to start dreaming again. If anyone deserved to have their dreams come true, it was Mitch. Why he wanted to marry her, why he wanted her at all, she had no idea. But if he wanted this to work, she could at least give him these two days, for his sake. And for her own. For something told her this was her final chance at life. If she threw this away—whatever it was she and Mitch had—then cynical loneliness would set in her heart for good. She'd become another deserted wife and single mother, complaining about the price of education, interfering with her kids' choices in life because she had no life of her own, and then, finally, she'd grow old alone, bitter and angry, wondering why her kids no longer came to visit her.

She couldn't live that way. She didn't *want* to live that way, nor did she want to live for the past anymore. Something had to change. It was time to let go of the fears she'd held almost as friends for too long—the false friends who'd robbed her of her chance with Mitch. Who'd helped her settle for Tim. Who'd allowed local kids to rob her four times before she fought back. Who whispered in her heart that Mitch would desert her again if she let him into her world. That if she trusted him again, he'd only let her down.

*Give me two days, Lissa.*

"Lis-sa?"

She smiled into the anxious soft eyes of her hostess. "Thank you, Lily." She took her cup of tea and gave Lily a swift, impulsive kiss. "Thank you."

With the empathy born of her turbulent life, Lily didn't need to speak. The understanding hovered in the air between the women. A defining moment passing in gentle silence...and Lissa knew she'd never be the same.

She was making him nervous.

It was late afternoon by the time they made it to the island. Mitch requested permission to land at the only civilian airstrip left in Tumah-ra not taken over by the rebels yet. He wondered what was going on with her. She must have a hundred questions about what would happen next, where they'd be going, what to do if they got caught. But beyond halting attempts to talk to Hana she'd said nothing beyond, "Look at the ocean. Isn't it a perfect shade of turquoise?" or "The forest looks so cool and lush."

Perfect. Cool. Boy, was she about to learn. It was hotter than Hades down in that jungle, and perfection was an illusion, a conjurer's trick of smoke and mirrors, gone with one pull of a trigger. Or a thousand. Death in steaming heat, fighting for a deceptive treasure beneath corals that would destroy the island.

For the thousandth time he wished he'd sent her with Tim and the kids to safety, even if it meant losing her trust. At least she'd be alive and safe.

What had he been thinking to bring her here? Trouble was, he hadn't been thinking straight. He'd gone with his damn fool heart and bloody gonads, the need eating him alive—the need to have her near him, obsessed with the need to make love to her.

Damn his insecurity and unfounded jealousy of Tim, his need to prove God knew what to her. And damn her need to prove she could live in his world, a world she'd never needed to know about.

The unreality of the whole situation hit him. Sweet, gentle Lissa Miller was going into a war zone. She had no idea what she was in for, and he'd promised not to protect her.

Heaven help them both.

He landed, steered Bertha into the high-security hangar built especially for the Air Force but used by the Nighthawks, and pulled out the motorbike before he locked the massive doors.

Lissa, with Hana perched on her hip, frowned. "Mitch, there's three of us. How do we fit on one bike?"

He shrugged. "We make do. This is Tumah-ra, Lissa. There's no road rules, the taxis have all been confiscated by the rebels or blown up, and buying a car—if there's any to buy—will only yell to all the organized gangs and looters that we have money." He pulled the license plates off the bike, tore a jagged line across the seat with a long-bladed knife from his backpack, and smeared dirt and tire black all over it. "That'll do."

He looked up to find Lissa shoving the money Anson had given her into her running shoes in two flat piles. Then she pulled out a mirror and made herself up, putting a dark foundation all over her exposed skin, and liner on her eyes and brows to give herself an Asian look. She pulled her hair under a ratty baseball cap and rubbed dirt over her face, hands, neck and upper chest not covered by the long-sleeved dark-green shirt. Then she looked at him with a quiet, defeated glance of defiance and despair.

Man, she'd missed her calling in not becoming an actress! In deep, reluctant admiration, he nodded. Apart from her eye color, she barely looked different from the women here—dirty, neglected, defeated. Most of the militia wouldn't give her a second glance with all that lovely hair hidden. "Good idea."

She just grinned at him and held out the makeup. He rubbed some dark stuff on his face, grateful for whatever ancestry gave him bronzed skin, dark hair and eyes.

He turned to find Lissa on the bike, Hana on her lap. Mitch used a long strip of twine to tie the child to her, handed Hana a Snickers to keep her quiet. He handed Lissa an assault rifle. "Keep it visible to scare the looters. If they come at us, point but don't shoot. I'll give you lessons on how to shoot before we head out of town. This town's safe enough for the next few days. The rebels are still about twenty-five miles to the west."

Wide-eyed but obedient, she nodded.

He hitched his weapon over his shoulder, got on the bike in front of Hana, and they looked just like any family: any family escaping the horror of a guerrilla war zone.

As he started the bike, he told her, "If we get stopped, let me talk. I've been learning Tagalog the past few weeks. Enough to get by, anyway."

She clicked her tongue. "I should have thought of that."

He yelled over the engine's roar, "I've had months to think of it, and I only started a few weeks ago. You've had twenty-four hours. You're doing well."

She held on to him as he roared out of the hangar.

Apart from what she'd seen in news reports, Lissa had few preconceived ideas of what a town on the edge of a war zone would look like. Keeping her telltale eyes beneath the shade of the old cap, she watched a whole new world flash past her.

Though the scent of drenched mud and decaying leaves and steaming jungle proclaimed this as a tropical area in the throes of wet season, somehow it reminded her of one of Clint Eastwood's old Westerns. Something didn't seem quite right—didn't seem quite *real*. It felt like it was a set: it had the dirt roads, rough wooden houses and newspapers drifting in the wind. She half waited for the stroke of noon and the gunfire to begin.

Men lounged against walls, watching them pass. Checking them out for...what? To rob them, kidnap them, kill them? There was the strangest sense of normality as women crossed the roads with their children to visit smiling friends, kids played with rocks or balls in the street and Gaelic music drifted from the pub at the end of the road.

*Let us eat and drink, for tomorrow we die.*

That was it: the tense, brooding expectation; the sense of...waiting. *It's coming. We just don't know when.* Marking time. Apprehension filled the air, air superheated and drenched in humidity, adding a pulsing underscore to a jarring symphony that remained unspoken, unwanted, inescapable. A desperate people grasping at a precious last few hours of normality before the rebel militia came to destroy their world.

Men ready to protect their families with what few weapons they had. Children having fun out of school. Hedonists in the bars, in the brothels, in the street. Old and young, praying in the church. Opportunists waiting for their chance to smash and grab. All living a strange, unquiet coexistence, waiting for the end...or the beginning.

Why didn't they cut and run?

Mitch turned the bike in at the pub, a half-brick wooden building not unlike a man with messy hair and a three-day growth, seeming sexy in its unfinished, unpolished state. Shouting silently, *come here and try me, baby.*

"We'll stay here tonight. We're best off heading out to Hana's grandparents' village in the morning." He twisted around, untied Hana and gestured to them to dismount. Then he held out a simple gold band to her. "From here on in, you're Sarah Sinclair, my wife, and I'm Alan, your husband."

She looked down at the ring, then at him, in his face paint and cap. A sense of inevitability—of undone déjà vu—overwhelmed her, and instead of taking the ring, she held out her left hand.

His eyes never leaving hers, he slipped the ring over her third finger. *This is the rehearsal, Lissa,* his gaze seemed to say. *Next time it will be real. And forever.*

"I'm your husband," he said quietly. Then like lightning, before she knew his intention, he'd slipped another ring on top of it. A pretty star sapphire twinkled serenely at her from its bed of tiny diamonds. "I bought this for you thirteen years ago, with my first month's pay after I joined the Air Force. I think it's past time I gave it to you."

Too choked up to speak, she just stared. Somehow the ring, in all its gentle, just-out-of-date loveliness, made everything so *real.* Made his proposal real. Made his wanting her real. "Thir-thirteen years?"

He nodded with a twisted, self-mocking smile. "I'd finally worked up the guts to speak. I knew if I didn't I'd lose you for good. I was going to ask you to marry me. I was going to beg if I had to, beg you to leave Tim and come with me." He shrugged. "The day after I bought it, I heard about your engagement."

She closed her eyes. "I wish you'd spoken, Mitch. I wish…"

He shrugged. "I lost hope. What did I have to offer you against what Tim had? I looked honestly at myself, and I had to stay away. If you went with me, you lost it all. With him, you had it all—stability, a life in Breckerville. A name. A family."

*A family.* She dipped her head in despair. Oh, the *fool* she'd been not to see it sooner, not to know the heart of all his reasons for silence! He couldn't see what he had, the courage and generous, giving heart; he only saw what he didn't have—a name and a family. If only she'd overcome her own fears all those years ago, to *see* what he needed so much—her own words of love.

To belong somewhere.

Was it too late now? Was she too damaged to trust, as

she'd always thought? Had he been alone too long? Was his love truly based in the past, for the girl she'd been?

Two days, Lissa.

All she knew was she wanted that same chance—a chance to make up for the past. She could give him what she had to give, here in this place where life could be snuffed out in an instant's deadly hail of gunfire. "It's beautiful, Mitch. Can I keep it?"

His deep, dark eyes came to life. "Always. It's yours, Lissa. No matter what."

She tilted her head, as the unmistakable strains of lilting violin and mandolin floated out to them in wild harmony. "Why are they playing Irish music?"

Obviously willing to be diverted, he grinned. "The owner's an expat Irish-Australian with a stubborn streak a mile wide and a thirst for trouble. Paul O'Donnell built this place after the oil explorations started last year. He said he'd make a mint with the war sure to follow. Wait till you meet him—probably at dinner, since he sleeps all day. He's the craziest guy I ever met." He used a small towel from his backpack to wipe the makeup off his face, then handed it to her, waiting until she'd finished before opening the doors. "We have to be respectable now."

She blinked when he pulled the bike up the steps and inside. Mitch raised his brows and tilted his head.

At least four people were following them, their eyes fixed with unabashed greed on the bike; but they stopped outside the pub, then slunk off when two enormous, rifle-toting men guarding the doors stepped forward, with menacing looks on their faces.

"Most of these people don't have any form of motorized transport to get 'em out when the crap hits the fan," Mitch murmured as they walked with Hana toward the makeshift reception area. "Push bikes are the traditional form of getting around in Tumah-ra. This bike, rough as it looks, is worth gold to families on the run…and those looters outside will do what they have to, to get this bike, to sell to someone or to escape on. Keep your rifle in sight at all times outside this pub. Those security guards could be militia sympathizers, and no matter who or what they are, they'll grab the bike when it all starts, for an easy escape if nothing else.''

She felt sad, sick wanting to help but not knowing how. ''Why don't the people here get out while they can?''

''Where do you suggest they go?''

She looked at him, helpless and half pleading. ''Surely there's somewhere—''

''This is the last bastion. If the rebels grab it before the UN troops arrive—and that's still not guaranteed until the next sitting—they'll offer a deal for control of the oil that would make the West think twice about interfering in the war.''

It made appalling sense. She shuddered but remained quiet as Mitch signed them into the pub and lifted the bike up to their second-floor set of rooms.

Hana, worn out with the day's excitement, fell asleep as soon as she'd eaten, had a bath and lain down on her bed. Freshly showered from her makeup and mud, Lissa watched her, aching.

She'd seen all this as a wonderful adventure only yesterday, a way to prove her courage to Mitch. Now she just wanted to see Jenny, Matt and Luke. To hold her little girl, to hug her boys. To be safe at home, where, if she didn't want to know the realities of life for people living only a few hundred miles from Australian borders, she just switched off the TV. Where newscasts of war and destruction and rape still had the sense of Hollywood unreality and she could give comfortable donations to appeals and feel better about her own cozy existence.

Dear God, what did that make her?

''It's okay, Lissa. We all go through this first time out.''

She turned to Mitch, just out of his own shower, not bothering to ask the obvious question.

He made a helpless gesture with his hands. ''The grief.

The self-hate for having in abundance what these people don't—what so many people in the world will never have, simple peace and security. Hating yourself for all your petty fears and doubts, while these people struggle just to survive, to save their kids from rape, torture and gunfire. Hating that you've ever whined over not being able to afford a big-screen TV, while others dream of clean water and a bowl of rice, or for their families to come out of that shallow grave. It's all too real here. You want to save the world—or at least this part of it—and suddenly you know you can't. And you feel so damn inadequate.''

A single tear streaked down her face. "Does it go away?''

"It's unpredictable. For some it gets less. They become angry or anesthetized—either works to help them do what they have to do to stop the war or get people out. It's not much, but for that one person you've saved, that one family you've reunited, it means the world. And that's the only world we can save.''

Hana stirred in her sleep, sighing softly. "Did it work for you?'' Lissa whispered.

His eyes met hers. "Would you like a nice lie here? If I give you a catalog of my dreams and nightmares, will you accuse me of trying to push you out of the Nighthawks so you'll live a nice, safe life in Breckerville with me?''

She sighed. "I don't think I need a word picture.''

"No. Trust me, you don't.'' He drew her out of the bedroom into the sitting area. "Hana's safe enough here. Let's go down and eat—Sarah.''

"Are you sure Hana's safe?''

"The maid on this floor's coming to sit with her. She'll get more food if she asks for it or bring her down to us if she gets distressed.'' He held out a hand to her, his gaze questioning.

*You're on your honeymoon. You can't keep your hands off each other.* After a moment she put her hand in his. "Okay, Alan.''

The back of the pub looked like an ordinary Australian beer garden, a small wilderness with a long open deck and wooden trestles set up in rough table-and-chair mock-ups. The place was all but full, with people of almost all nations laughing, smoking, eating and drinking, clapping along with the sweet wildness of the violins, piano and percussion being played just off center of the deck on a ministage. A few children danced with each other, or were swung by their smiling fathers. Wildflowers grew all around, adding a gentle scent to the steamy jungle town.

Just like any ordinary Sunday afternoon at the pub—except for the dull booming sounds and guns clattering. Far enough to be safe for now…but not for long.

The hidden desperation reflected beneath the laughter in everyone's eyes.

Mitch sat at a spare table as if nothing was abnormal—but then, war zones were almost an everyday occurrence for him. "I can recommend the steak and Guinness pie. It's an Irish specialty I can never resist. You want a beer, Sarah?"

She thought quickly, then clucked at him. "You know I don't like beer, Alan."

"When in Rome, sweetheart. Come on, you wanted an adventurous honeymoon—and trust me, there's no wine here you'd care to drink. It's beer or cola, basically."

"Okay," she sighed. "Let the adventure begin. Beer it is."

With a smile he chucked her under the chin. "Good girl." Gently, oh, so soft, he claimed her lips.

Mindful of their mission, "Sarah" snuggled into his lap and kissed him back…but Lissa was the one who gloried in the feel of his swift, hard reaction to her touch, Lissa who wriggled against him to take in more.

"Baby, we're in public. There's kids watching us," he whispered into her mouth.

Panting a little she nodded. "Tonight?"

"What'll you folks have—besides each other, that is?"

Mitch grinned up at the laughing publican, a tall, lanky man who reminded her of a big, red-haired, brown-eyed, cheerful dog. "G'day, Paul. Besides my wife, I'll have a heavy-duty beer and the Guinness pie special."

Lissa smiled up at the cheerful man in his early forties. "Light beer and the pie, please."

"Righty-ho, Missus Sinclair."

The pie was as delicious as Mitch claimed, and the strange combination of dark-beer gravy and melt-in-the-mouth steak with chips seemed to fit the pub, the people, the life they were living, holed up in a little town awaiting devastation.

Paul returned after a waiter took their plates away, handing Mitch a beer and a cola to replace Lissa's almost untouched drink. "So, you up for a game of pool anytime soon, Al?"

Mitch gave him a withering look. "I'm on my honeymoon. What do you reckon?"

Paul laughed. "Ah, but I have a few tricks you don't know—new tricks for the game of the century."

"Right-oh," Mitch grumbled. "Later. Now can I get back to kissing my wife?"

"Not yet, matey. You've got to sing for that supper. Hey, everyone, look who's back for a song!"

Mitch groaned as the raucous clapping chant for a song began. "You love to do this to me, don't you?"

Paul grinned, unrepentant, just like a big, loping dog with a Frisbee imploring its master for a game. "Bet your lovely wife doesn't even know your talents, does she?"

"I'd like her to know *some* of my talents, if you get my meaning. And trust me, we don't need an audience."

Paul spluttered with laughter, then turned to Lissa. "Did you know your husband has the voice of an angel?"

Lissa turned to Mitch. "And you hid this from me for seventeen years, for what reason?" Correctly interpreting his red-faced silence, she joined the clapping. "Song. Song. Song!"

"No way. Not in front of you. I can't!"

Sensing he was about to bolt, she kissed him, gentle and sweet. "Sing for me?" she whispered. "For *me*. Don't sing in front of me. Sing *to* me."

He groaned. "Baby, don't do this to me!"

She held his face in her hands. "My restless warrior and wandering prince, who flies into war zones and risks his life to save people, is afraid to sing a little song?"

"Song! Song! Song!" The chant went on, as a hundred wretched souls sought entertainment before they became living targets. Distant gunfire accompanied the lilting violins, adding a touch of wild despair every person wanted to hide. "Song, song, song!"

His eyes glittered. "I'll get you for this, Mrs. Sinclair." Aloud he yelled, "What about a dance first? My wife does a mean Irish jig and riverdance."

It was her turn to panic as the enthusiastic chant changed to "Dance, dance, dance!"

"No! Mi—Alan, how could you? We're in a war zone, and you want me to do a *jig?* I can't do it. I can't!"

He laughed and nuzzled her lips. "Hmmm. Courage deserts when you're the one under fire, huh? So my brave Countrygirl who could kick my arse black-and-blue can't do one little dance? I haven't seen you dance since your parents took me to that Eisteddfod in Bathurst when you were fifteen."

"I can't! I haven't danced in fifteen years. I'll fall on my face."

"Dance! Dance! Dance!"

The band struck up a classic jig.

Mitch pushed her toward the empty dance area. "Forget your fears, darlin'. Remember, these people could die tomorrow," he murmured, pushing her along. "Dance for them. Let them enjoy it. Help them *live* what time they have left."

Again he made terrible, appalling sense. She looked around, to the bright, laughing masks covering the hopeless despair, and found a courage she'd thought long dead. She pulled off her sandals and, barefoot and wearing a simple sundress, she walked to the makeshift stage.

Crazy. Surreal. Pitifully inadequate. But she did it. Fifteen years out of practice, she performed an awkward, half-forgotten jig for the audience as they stamped and cheered and laughed, and kids ran around her, trying to imitate her steps. Mitch watched her, his eyes warm and soft with affection and approval and faith. The faith that told her he'd known all along she'd overcome her insecurity over making a fool of herself and help these people forget the storm inching closer by the hour.

Like lightning in the distance, gunfire crackled.

So she danced again, a riverdance-style line dance. And one by one, kids came up to learn from her. Then the women. Even a few men.

Then Mitch got up to join her, still smiling—and his feet followed the steps she'd taught him long ago on a golden summer afternoon, in a foolish, half-embarrassed attempt to make him dance with her, if only once. Even if they didn't touch. Making a memory to hold inside her when he was gone, long after he'd forgotten the steps.

But he hadn't forgotten.

Sweetness shattered inside her, telling her lonely, stubborn heart how stupid it had been, holding on to the hurt of what had gone before. The past was there. It would always be there between them...and the beauty easily bore the pain on its shoulders. Their past held so much more of joy than rejection. Oh, how could she have forgotten the cherished memories of childhood love—the love that would always belong only to Mitch?

Dancing yet not touching, amid a crowd of desperate strangers in the last oasis inside a war zone, surely was the strangest time she would ever know for a personal revelation. But life was like that, strange and unexpected and horrific and lovely, comedy amid tragedy, laughter and tears intermingling.

And love.

She belonged to Mitch. It was as simple, as beautiful and as scary as that. That was why she clung to the idea of becoming a Nighthawk. She wanted to share every part of his life, his pain and sorrow and the memories he couldn't outrun as much as his passion and joy. She wanted to be his woman, in every sense of the word. To be not just his haven or the mother of his children, or even his lover. Mitch and Lissa, Skydancer and Countrygirl. A partnership based in reality, in sharing all of their life—not the kind she'd had last time or the kind her parents had, even now.

If only in the next two days she could convince him of that—to make him *want* her to be a Nighthawk. Beside him at all times. Trusting her to be a true partner.

The music came to an end. ''More! More!''

Needing to think, she laughingly rejected the attempt and sat at their table, sipping her cola.

''Try a sailor's hornpipe,'' Paul yelled, carrying out another round of drinks.

''That's Highland, not Irish,'' she called back, laughing.

''Okay, then, Al's turn. Get back up there, mate, and sing to your lady.''

Mitch smiled down at her where she sat and, with a silent nod, took the stage.

# *Chapter 11*

"For my lady."

He had the voice of a dark angel, and he sang just for her. Looking to her alone. And the words, oh, the words of haunting beauty moved her soul, John Denver's song of timeless love that he still remembered had been precious to her romantic girl's heart. Annie's Song—but his voice of purest dark crystal made it hers alone, wanting to drown only in Lissa's laughter, to die in her arms...

Lissa shivered and trembled on her rough bench seat, couldn't tear her gaze away and didn't want to. Glory had always come to her life in snatched moments, and this time she wouldn't hide in fear. *Oh, God, please let him mean it.*

*Take the risk, Lissa,* he seemed to whisper to her heart.

He tipped up her face and kissed her when he finished. Then the calls for an encore came and the band started the funky, funny tune of the Proclaimers' famous song. He grinned, mock-growled at Paul and stepped back and declared how far he'd walk just to fall down at her door in the most pathetic Scottish accent she'd ever heard.

She choked on the bubbling joy, the sweetest laughter she'd felt in too many years to count. Oh, that was Mitch! He could haunt her, rip her heart from her chest and make her laugh as he did it. He knew how to *live* his life, and he'd taught her to step outside her old restrictive, crippling shyness and just *be*.

She clapped as hard as everyone else when he finished with a big, goofy grin on her face, but Mitch hadn't finished just yet.

"I'm sure Sarah will understand, and not be in the least jealous, if I dedicate this last song to another very special lady in my life, since she knows how much I love her." He looked deep in her eyes and said softly, "This is for Lissa."

And he sang a sweet, wistful song of a man so much in love he'd do anything, give anything, be anything for the woman he loved—anything. *If I Could.*

She gulped again as the tears rushed back to her eyes. How did he know? How could he know, to see straight into her innermost heart, with all its fears and hopes, and give them to her? And to do so in a room of strangers somehow made it so *real*—like a public declaration of love. He was seducing her with song, the words flying like tiny darts with unerring accuracy to her heart.

The final lovely strains of the ballad ended, and without conscious decision, she got to her feet and walked to him. She took his face in her hands and kissed him, long, slow and oh, so tender, while the little crowd roared raucous appreciation.

The sudden boom of a shell dropping quieted everyone for a moment. Heavy silence filled the air. Tense fear, expectation—

"Free beers for everyone!"

With a distinct feeling of "The Band Played On," everyone cheered Paul's offer and crowded at the open-air bar, laughing and joking.

Lissa stared deep into Mitch's eyes, with the sudden and

haunting knowledge that they could both be dead tomorrow. "Let's go to bed."

He buried his face in her hair, inhaling deeply, as if he'd find hidden strength there. "I promised myself you'd have these two days—that I'd prove you can trust me."

She crowded in closer. "And I promised myself just now, when you sang to me—*for me*—that I'd give you what we both need. That I'd throw out my stupid fears and insecurity over the past and have the man I want—the only man I've always wanted. You."

He whispered raggedly, "My self-control's almost gone. If you change your mind—"

"I'm aching, Mitch," she whispered back. "For you. I've been aching for seventeen years, wanting you, thinking I could never have you. Please don't make me wait anymore."

His gaze searched hers, looking deep inside her, but she had no doubts, no fears worth holding on to—not tonight. "I've heard life's said to be held cheap in these places. But I know now that's not true. I know, like everyone here knows, that living this moment in time, right here and now, is the most precious gift of all—to truly *live* what time we have left."

One click of the lock and her ghosts were gone, her shadows fled. And whether they disappeared forever or were just gone for now didn't matter. She smiled at him. "I've wasted half my life in fears and doubts, gathering regrets like flowers, treasuring them instead of throwing them away. But I know that, whatever comes after this, I won't regret making love with you. I could die tonight or tomorrow. If that happens I want to be with you, Mitch. Let me be your woman tonight."

His eyes on fire, he held out a hand to her, and without a second's hesitation she put hers in it. They walked through the pub and up the creaking stairs to their room. The remains of a child's meal and a curled-up Hana snoring softly on the sofa told them they were free to be together.

In the bedroom Mitch turned to her one final time. "Are you sure? It's your final chance, Lissa. This is about the last second of nobility I'll ever rake up."

With utter certainty she smiled at him and had her reward in a slow, sexy return smile—the unique, just-for-her Mitch look that turned her legs to rubber and her belly into a mass of hot yearning. She wanted him, oh, how she wanted him to touch her, put his hands on her sweetest, most feminine places, kiss her all over…lay her down, move inside her, make her his. The need was a blistering fire scorching her from within. He had to be able to read the look in her eyes….

He had—he must—for his whole face came alive with need. "Me, too, baby," he whispered, drawing her close. "Oh, me, too. When you look at me like that—like I always dreamed you would—I feel as if I could conquer the world. I'd do anything for you, Lissa. Anything."

"Mitch…" Her voice cracked. She wrapped her arms around his neck. Her eyes drifted shut as his mouth touched hers.

Touching, tasting, drinking each other in. Pulling clothes off in sudden, frantic need. Feeling hearts pounding, bodies swelling and heating with arousal. Lissa threaded her fingers through his hair, loving its soft curl, loving that he'd given her the right to touch him, hold him against her. Oh, fantasies come to life were beautiful, oh, so beautiful…with Mitch. Only with Mitch.

Suddenly, she had to tell him. "Mitch— Aah, yes, that's…oh, so good…. Mitch, Mitch—"

"I want you so bad…so bad," he mumbled, nuzzling her breast.

She shivered as his tongue touched her nipple. "Mitch…"

Mitch stilled, hearing the sexual tone change. She was trying to say something. "No?" he asked hoarsely.

She smiled at him, shakily, yet blinding in its beauty. "Yes. Anywhere. Anytime. Don't you know that yet? I don't have the strength to fight it anymore. I don't want to.'' She buried her face in his shoulder. ''Only you, Mitch,'' she whispered. ''I never felt this *alive* until you touched me. I…I never…'' She looked up. The heat of her face flowed down her throat, but her gaze held his, so enchantingly shy and earnest. ''Not until that day with you. I had no idea what it was. I never felt anything much, thought sex was all right at best, overrated. Then you came home, and with one touch, you brought me to life. You kissed me—held me, touched me…there…and it was like my body couldn't do anything else *but* feel. I had no control, and oh, it was the most beautiful thing to ever happen to me. Until that night in Canberra,'' she confessed, the fiery heat all the way down to her breasts now. ''Making you lose control in the spa— Oh, Mitch, I can't even describe how it made me feel. Like I could fly…''

Humbled, amazed, stunned—he was way beyond awed. He'd always wanted to be her first lover, her only lover, resenting life and the world because it wasn't to be. Now he knew there was something far, far better. To be her last lover. To be the first, the only man who brought her to life and feeling and loss of control. To be the one she loved to give pleasure to in return. To know no other man had done that to her and hopefully never would. Just him. Only him. Always him.

It was almost worth losing all those years together, just to know that. Almost.

He caressed the skin of her waist and hip, so gently rounded, soft and golden and silky, feeling her tremble as he moved, oh, so slowly toward her aching hot center. ''As amazing as that was—for me as well as you—there is something better.'' His voice came out in a half-strangled croak. ''Flying together, Lissa-My-Lissa. Being inside you, moving inside of you. Finishing inside you, and lying together after, still a part of you.''

She bit her lip, her eyes uncertain instead of thrilled. ''I guess you'd know more about that than me.''

Tenderness welled up in his heart, for her pain had a depth beyond simple jealousy. "No, baby," he said quietly, caressing her heated cheek, trying hard to ignore her nakedness—for she needed to know this, and what Lissa needed he had to give her. "Would you believe me if I told you I'm working on 99 percent fantasy here? What if I said there's only been one woman since Kerin, and that was before she gave me the boys?"

Her luscious mouth fell open; her soft dove's eyes were sweet and stunned and anxious, too frightened to hope. "Were…did you get together again with Kerin after she gave you the boys?"

He shook his head. "No." He chuckled at the glazed look on her sweet face. "That's right. It's been nine years since I was with a woman in any way. Now you know why I've been a bit, um, out of control with you."

She frowned. "But…but you're so *beautiful.* Why?"

His heart flipped over with the power of her words, like a kid in the throes of first love. But then, he was. He was in the throes of first, last and only love. At thirty-two he was listening to the girl of his dreams say the words he'd thought would be confined to those damn dreams, forever unfulfilled. "I hurt Kerin…bad," he admitted, caressing her shoulders and back, because he had to touch her somehow.

"She hated that it was only a casual thing for me, until she got pregnant. When she came back with Matt and Luke, I was with Shea, a woman in the Air Force. She couldn't handle me wanting to take on four-month-old twins fulltime, taking a desk job so I'd be home for the boys. She walked, and I didn't care enough to stop her." He shrugged again.

"It didn't seem worth it to try after that, not with the kids to bring up. Then when they were gone, I joined the Nighthawks and had more than enough to do. I never met a woman who interested me enough to start a relationship. After Kerin, I never liked or wanted casual sex. It leads to hurt feelings, foster kids like me or unhappy families. So I didn't bother until I came back to you and couldn't keep my hands off you for more than thirty seconds. Then I blurted out my stupid proposal within five minutes of knowing you were free." He grinned self-mockingly. "You might have noticed my self-control's a bit limited when it comes to you."

That was when he saw it, the subtle, radiant, feminine glow no man could mistake. "Kiss me, Mitch," she breathed, standing on tiptoe to reach his mouth. "Make love to me. Now."

Her bare breasts brushed against his chest.

He groaned, crushed her to him and gave the kiss all he had.

In all his wildest dreams—and they'd been pretty untamed—he'd never hoped for such sweet fire, such luminous bliss in simple human touch. Like a miracle long prayed for and suddenly given, Lissa couldn't keep her hands off him. His body gave her so much joy, such wonder. She kept mumbling, through kisses to his skin, "You're so beautiful, Mitch, so beautiful!"

"No. You are," he groaned. "You take my breath away."

"Shh." She touched a finger to his mouth, smiling up at him, with a little cheeky twinkle. "Much as I love some of the things you say to me—especially lately—sometimes the foot goes in. I have better uses for your mouth right now."

He chuckled and touched his lips to the place where her neck and shoulder met, a sensitive, erotic spot for him. "Like this?"

"Mmmm. Aaaah…" She writhed against him.

Taking that as affirmative, he nibbled and sucked on her soft skin and tender muscle beneath, the pad of his thumbs brushing over her breasts, her nipples.

She gave a tiny cry and collapsed against him. He lifted her in his arms and carried her three steps to the bed…and lost his breath again, just looking at her. Lissa lying nude on the bed, her golden-brown skin flushed and radiant, those lovely gray eyes filled with all the desire, all the need he'd ever dreamed of.

"Let's live tonight." She held out her arms to him.

Slowly he lay beside her. He took her face in his hands and kissed her to the slow pounding of the heated night, the beat of waiting, waiting. And Lissa kissed him back, her tongue moving with his in an unconscious beat, the pulsing of the rebels moving closer and a slow fire burning to conflagration. Seventeen years of waiting, all leading to this moment, this steaming, breathless night. Here and now.

Then there was nothing but Lissa and Mitch and a storm of need hitting them like the hail of bullets from enemy fire. Her hands clawed at him, learning his most intimate secrets as he found hers. Her mouth more than fulfilled its promise of forbidden pleasures unbounded. She rolled onto him, dragging her fingers and palms over his fevered skin, hot, hard and hungry. Her tongue followed the path, taking the beads of his sweat inside her mouth, moaning in hunger. Needing more, oh, so much more. She whispered things to him, all the things she wanted to do to him…and then she did them, every single touch, kiss or slide of her tongue. Moving over him, inch by slow, hot, gorgeous inch, making him crazy. Telling him what she wanted him to do, crying aloud in heated pleasure when he did them or whispered erotic words in return. Driving him to the brink, and beyond—a level of sexual frenzy he'd never known.

"Lis…sa," he groaned, hoping like hell she understood his plea, because speech was beyond him.

A low, rippling laugh, and his eyes lifted in a hunger matching hers, drinking in her flushed, naked, sweat-sheened body. She was sitting on him, legs spread over him, fingers splayed on his skin. She was literally glowing, incandescent with radiant desire. "I know." She wriggled back, moving her soft wet heat against his hardness, slow and seductive, in the sweetest drenching any man could want to know. "Mmmm, my strongest sexual fantasy. Me sitting on you, you on your back, begging me to end the torture."

"You want it, you got it," he ground out, sweat pouring down his face and the exquisite pain killing him. "Baby, please, I have to be inside you. Now." He reached into the drawer beside the bed, handing her a packet. "Use…this," he muttered through gritted teeth as she moved on him again, feeling as if he could die of this anguished bliss.

"I've never done this before, either." Her face filled with new wonder, she opened it and rolled the condom over his length, hand over hand, sweet and tight—almost causing him to lose it then and there. "Thank you," she said softly, and eased him inside her.

But he couldn't wait; he was dying by slow degrees. He thrust up, hard and fast, desperate to be inside her sweet warmth, and she gasped and bucked instinctively, in the most glorious friction ever known to man and woman.

He couldn't be slow. Control had deserted him with her whispered fantasies of him, with her hands and perfect mouth fulfilling each one. He was gone, beyond thought of anything but the pleasure gripping him. Lissa, his beautiful, beloved Lissa was riding him, flying on him, her face filled with that same burning ecstasy searing him alive. Her hands braced on his chest, she bucked and rocked with his every thrust, meeting him, flying with him all the way, crying out with each new sensation, moving faster, higher, harder, hotter. Moaning his name, making the guttural sounds of a woman in the grip of the pleasure-pain just before climaxing.

He was gonna lose it now— He thrust up into her again, lifted her and brought her down in a fast hard jolting hit of white-hot—the rush roared through him like a midnight express and, oh, man, his heart was gonna explode, he couldn't stop it—

Lissa cried out his name and fell onto him, her soft wetness clenching all around him.

"I love you, Lissa. I love you," he gasped and poured himself into her, in the sweetest relief and most joyous giving he'd ever known.

Silence—broken only by quiet gasps of breath and muted rat-tat-tats in the distance.

Eventually he found the strength to kiss her hair softly. "You all right?"

She buried her face against his chest. "I'm fine. Wonderful."

But she wasn't. Though she stroked and caressed him, she'd withdrawn somehow. She'd been with him all the way—beyond any imaginings of her he'd ever had, until—

Oh, no. He'd told her he loved her. She knew now—and she wasn't talking.

"It doesn't matter," he said quietly, knowing his voice sounded strangled. *Liar,* he mocked himself. "It doesn't have to change things for us."

"Okay," she said, just as quietly.

*Liar.*

*No! No!* his mind screamed. *Not now.* To have come so far with her and lose her—

But no matter how he tried, he couldn't retract the words. She wouldn't believe him, anyway. She knew he couldn't lie to her, never had lied. "Lissa, I don't want anything back."

Damn it, I am lying to her! I do want something back. I want everything, I want it all—and if she doesn't love me, and one day she finds another man—

This was insane. He was still inside her and thinking of her finding someone else?

As if she read his mind, she gently rolled off him. "It's so hot tonight."

"We just made love and you want to talk about the weather? Don't be so bloody inane," he growled. "Okay, so you don't want me to love you. Forget I said it!"

She didn't flinch as he'd half expected. "I think that's the best thing to do for now." Her eyes met his. For once he couldn't read her expression. "Let's do what we came here for—"

"And be lovers," he finished, the anguish filling his voice with savage mockery. "Constant lovers. I get it. So we take these few days and see. Then we take six months and see, a year and see—if I'm lucky. Excuse me a minute." He stalked to the bathroom with dark thunder filling him, heart and soul.

In a minute he was back, and finding her covered with the sheet infuriated him. "What's the point of modesty now? I've touched and kissed every inch of you, and you've crawled over every inch of me. Don't worry, I'm not exactly in the mood for a bit more of the horizontal tango right now." He snatched the sheet off her. She gasped and jerked up to a sitting position, her hands out as if to ward him off—but he didn't touch her, barely even looked at her as he tossed off words at her like scraps of unimportant information, instead of their being the hardest words he'd ever had to say.

"So let me get this straight. Your idea of living was confined to this. Your big risk taking was having sex with me. You used me to get past what happened in your marriage with Tim—to feel like a woman again, but only for tonight. After being my friend for seventeen years, making me think you were one of the few people on earth who cared about me, you've turned me into a cheap one-night stand. You still want to become a Nighthawk and live the excitement you need to make your life complete, while Matt, Luke, Jenny and I stay home, wondering when we'll ever become a family, while you wander the world!"

She didn't answer; she didn't have to. Her dark, resentful eyes, thinned mouth and flared nostrils spoke for her.

"And I'm supposed to just handle the long separations and become the full-time child carer, am I?"

"Like I did the past five months while you wandered the world and became a hero, you mean?" she flipped at him casually.

"I told you I was giving it up—for you. But that's not enough for you, is it? It will never be enough, because you don't want it to be. What *do* you want? Are you going to keep punishing me for Tim's sins the rest of our lives?"

"Punishing you for Tim's sins? Isn't that what *you* did to *me?*" Her eyes flashed; her whole body quivered. "You left me because Tim told you to. You never came back because of Tim. You never called, never wrote—you didn't even keep up a simple appearance of friendship, no 'thanks, Lissa, for all those years of love you gave me.' You think *I* cheapened *you?* You used me, took my love and then disappeared! You went off and wandered the world and had your action and excitement in the Air Force and the Nighthawks—things I wanted. But did you ever ask me to come? I would have loved to fly, to learn combat training, but I just got left at home to work in a grocery store! I wanted to get out of Breckerville for a while, but no, Tim had his gym, so of course I worked a menial job for six years so *he* could have *his* dream! Even after he left me, I got the child and the mortgage while he got his dreams again! And now you're doing the same to me!"

"Me?" he asked quietly. He had to hear this. She'd reached her limits and was finally going to tell him the real truth.

"Yes, you!" she snapped. "Did you ever *think* about me while I was wondering what I'd done for you to hate me so badly you left me all alone for twelve miserable years? I was so blind in love with you I'd have done anything to be with you—*anything*—but you just walked away. You didn't care enough to even call and see how I was. You didn't think I'd be the one person who cared enough about you to share your burdens and your life when Kerin took off with the boys? No—but you can turn to me for free mothering while you wander the world, using me because I was in safe little Breckerville, just where you want me to be!"

She came to a halt, panting with fury, but he found noth-

ing to say. "You've *had* enough action and excitement.
You're *ready* to come home after a dozen years of wandering, so I'm supposed to go home, stay down on the
family farm, dying on the porch rockers my grandparents
sat on. Nice fantasy, Mitch, but *I don't want it!* Did you
bother to think of that, or am I just the convenient woman
to fulfil your final dreams for you and your kids? Do you
honestly think after twelve years of neglecting me, I can
smile and say, yes, please, Mitch, I still love you? It doesn't
work that way! I *won't* take another chance on a man using
me for his convenience while he forgets I have wants and
needs of my own!"

He opened his mouth, then closed it. Put that way, it
appalled him—his total blindness and selfishness where she
was concerned. Damn it, she was right. Because it was his
dream, he'd never thought she'd want a life beyond Breckerville, him and the kids. He'd never thought about it at
all, never considered her needs or hopes or dreams. He'd
taken for granted his plans for them would make her
happy—and he'd never been more wrong.

"So don't tell me you love me. I don't believe it." Her
voice was quieter now, but no less deadly. "Don't give me
pretty words; I had that with Tim. He told me he loved me
every day, and it didn't mean a damn thing, beyond a way
to keep me at home growing vegetables and working at the
convenience store to pay the bills while he poured all our
money into his dream of running a gym. Pretty words are
cheap, sweet nothings a man says to keep a woman where
he wants her. Dad kept Mum on the farm forty years until
*he* was ready to retire, then he took her somewhere he could
fish and enjoy himself, and she goes along with it because
he *loves* her! 'No, Margaret, you can't have a new dress'
or 'We can't go to the wedding' but he took her to the
Formula One in Europe, because he loves her. Yeah, right.
Tim did the same to me, all the time. 'Sorry, Lissa, I can't
do anything or take you anywhere because all our money
goes into my gym…but I love you.' I won't settle for that

again! So if you love me, *prove it!* I won't feed your down-home-on-the-farm-girl fantasy while you fly off into the sunrise, sunset or the next war zone. I won't have a marriage based on the past or even on great sex. I won't marry another friend who *says* he loves me but refuses to let me into his life!''

Panting, they sat naked on the bed in the aftermath of the loving of his life, facing each other like enemies in a combat zone—a battlefield he hadn't realized existed until this moment.

Unnerved by the force of truth in her words, he took a few moments to think, to turn his brain back around. ''All right,'' was all he could think to say.

It was her turn to look wary, but she nodded. ''Two days,'' she said quietly.

Taken aback, he swore under his breath. Two days? What insanity ever made him think he could prove *anything* to her in two days? He had twelve years of unintentional neglect to make up for. Two days to change everything he'd ever thought or known about her. Two days to change his intensely private, protective nature. Two days to prove that his love for her was not Tim's asexual, brotherly love, not like her father's love—true and lasting love, yes, but un-thinking and selfish, expecting her to sacrifice her dreams for their needs.

Making love had barely scraped at the dents of the depth of unconscious damage Tim's sexuality and choices in their marriage had done to her battered self-esteem, barely lit the darkness of her dad's loving blindness. As his had been until now.

She wanted it all or he'd get nothing.

''Okay. No words. No promises. You want to be a Night-hawk?'' he snapped, more furious with himself than with her. ''Fine. You got it. And I won't protect you any more than I would Songbird or Heidi, the two female operatives I've worked with. But it's not going to be pretty—far from it—and the memories will be bloody ugly. They could take years to go away, if ever. Are you prepared for that? Do you have any idea what you'll have to face?''

''Of course not. I've only ever lived in Breckerville.'' Her chin lifted in bravado. ''But I've seen current affairs shows, and I've been beaten up and kicked by a punk on ecstasy. I've lived through those nightmares. Does that count for anything?''

He laughed with less humor than he'd ever felt, thinking this had to be the strangest after-sex talk any man had been through. ''Baby, I doubt anything in your life will count for what you'll see out there. But just remember, you wanted this.''

She shrugged. ''No blame, is that it? I can handle that.''

''Not from what I've seen so far,'' he shot back dryly, knowing he was blowing any chance of further loving tonight. But he was fighting for forever here, and he had to take the risk.

Her sudden gurgle of laughter took him by surprise. ''You're right. I don't let go easily, do I? And as for blame—'' she smiled at him, her eyes twinkling ''—blame Tim again. He's taken my crap ever since he left me. I guess he figures he deserves it.''

''For what? Staying faithful until he left? For telling you the truth about himself?'' His eyes held hers. ''Did you ever think how hard that must have been for Tim? To admit he asked you out, even married you, because he was in denial of his sexuality? To admit he wanted me instead of you? To say he'd been selfish enough to ruin our lives for years? To love you like he does but leave? You called it the marriage from hell, so why are you blaming him for what he did? Liss, he never left you. He's still a big part of your life. What he did was set you free to find real happiness. Don't you think it's time you thanked him for that?''

All her pretty color drained; her eyes turned dark. ''You don't get it. You'll never get it. I was always glad he left me. It was living with me at all I can't forgive!''

"Who can't you forgive for that?" he asked in soft meaning. "You seem fine with Tim. It's me, isn't it? You blame me for your marriage. I didn't tell you I loved you when you needed it. I didn't stop the wedding. I didn't take you away from Breckerville and fly you into the sunset. He'd never have touched you at all if I'd asked you to the formal first. You think I should have known how you felt. I should have fought for you. That's why you don't want my love now. You think it's too late."

Her eyes darkened even more, like storm clouds at night—dark with fury and loss and devastation so complete it shattered his argument. "Yes." She turned away, taking the sheet with her. "I can't sleep with you tonight. I'll be out with Hana."

He'd pushed her as far as he dared. "No, let me. I've slept in worse places."

She turned on him. "So have I! I've slept for six long, cold years with a man who got it up with almost every girl—and presumably could have with almost every guy—in town, except me. Don't you think I'd *rather* have slept where you've been? Now just shut up and let me go for once without mollycoddling me!"

He let her go. She walked on unsteady feet to the outer room, picking up her bag on the way, trailing the sheet with her; and with sudden and chilling clarity he knew that traveling through a war zone the next two days would be the least of his worries.

# Chapter 12

A dull booming thunder filled her ears.

Lissa jerked to a sitting position as she heard Hana scream in the sweltering darkness of predawn. She rushed over to the child, petting and soothing her as she'd had to do several times through the night, with every round of bullets, with every shell thrown. Her terror went way beyond anything Lissa had ever experienced, even with Luke—memories that might never heal, visions a four-year-old couldn't begin to understand.

Why her mummy and daddy had fallen into a big hole and not gotten up. Why she'd been jerked into the arms of a stranger and taken to a strange land, with no family or familiar people to cuddle her and kiss her and tell her everything was all right.

Why men in funny uniforms came and made little holes in the people of her village or hung them up on ropes until she had been the only one left, crying at the hole for Ima and Tatay to wake up, wake up!

Lissa continued caressing Hana, reassuring her she was

alive and safe as she screamed uncontrollably, tears in her own eyes and an aching lump in her throat, rocking Hana, knowing this was all she could do. Feeling helpless, useless, made stupid by her inexperience in war and horror and hatred and greed. Unable to understand because of her sheltered existence in Australia.

Knowing that if Luke were here he could do a better job of helping Hana than she was at this moment.

Mitch strode into the room, fully dressed, his face grim and cold. He held out his arms, and she put Hana into them. He handed her his cell phone. "Anson wants to talk to you."

As she took the phone, he started dancing around the room with the sobbing child, humming a silly ditty, dipping her, swinging around in crazy arcs, bumping into furniture and yelling "Ow!" between dance steps.

Hana giggled, distracted.

Feeling even worse, she spoke into the phone. "Hello?"

"Do you want to work with us after this assignment?" Anson asked with what she realized was his usual bluntness.

She watched, aching, as Mitch continued to play with Hana, succeeding where she'd failed. "I don't know. I want to think about it for a few days."

"I didn't ask if you'd do it. I asked if you wanted to. I realize Skydancer's not exactly thrilled with this turn of events, but frankly, Lissa, we could use you."

"This has nothing to do with Skydancer. It's my decision, and since I have three children, I have a lot to think about before I make up my mind about whether I'd like to be used by you or not. Do you have anything to tell me about this assignment or can I hang up now?"

A short, startled silence followed. Then Anson chuckled, a rich, full sound. "Lady, you don't pull your punches, do you?"

She laughed. "A few people have mentioned that. Have you found out who our watcher is?"

"Skydancer will fill you in on what we have. As to instructions, take your cue from him. He's our expert in getting in and out of combat zones—which is another reason why I want you in the Nighthawks. He'll stay on if you sign on with us, no matter what he's saying now—and we need him. The kids he saves need him. And, like I said, we could use you, too."

He hung up.

"Feeling guilty yet?" She turned to Mitch, to find him watching her with little expression. He nodded. "Thought he'd get to you. His idea is, the world is more important than one family. But he's not a father. He's never met our kids, so they're unimportant to him. The idea of saving people in crisis is his big thing. Our kids are safe in Australia, so they don't need us like the people here do." He made a fatalistic gesture. "Like so many nonparenting adults, he thinks bringing kids up is no hassle. Make sure they have food, clothing and shelter, throw 'em some money, give 'em rules to follow, a few hugs now and then and everything's all right."

She nodded. She'd gotten that distinct impression.

He turned aside, playing "boo" with Hana's bear, making the little girl laugh.

He was giving her space. He'd told her what she needed to know and held back all he wanted to say.

"Better get dressed. We have to go soon. The rebel lines are closer now than last night. We'll run out of options— or get mobbed for our bike—if we don't take off before sunrise. Make yourself up again as a Tumah-ran woman. The rebels will take Westerners for hostage money if they can."

She nodded and ran for the bedroom without a word, wondering how long she'd keep feeling awkward with him. This situation was too weird. How long it would be before she could look at him without visualizing last night, how he'd looked as she brought her most vivid fantasies to life?

She could barely look at herself in the mirror as she made

up her face to Asiatic-islander darkness. Who was that woman last night that took over her body, reveling in such wild wantonness, crawling over every inch of his body in such untamed sexuality?

Whoever that woman who'd been living for the moment was—so free of fears and restraint and convention—Lissa wished with a sudden, aching fierceness she'd come back, but that woman had disappeared the moment Mitch said three fatal words.

*I love you.*

The words her father had always used on her mother to get what he wanted. The words Tim used every day in their marriage; words he still used now. Words that meant nothing in the end.

Oh, she knew they both meant the words. Tim had loved her as much as he could any woman. Her father, too, adored her mother—but it didn't stop him stomping on her mother's dreams to have the life he wanted, to feed his insecurity and keep his wife to himself. Mum's little dreams withered and died every time Dad heard about them. *Margaret, we can't afford a trip to Queensland; we need the money for the farm. I'd love to get you a dress for the wedding, but I can't afford to; I just bought the tractor. I'd love to take you to see your old friends in Sydney, but it's harvest time.*

Always, always *No,* but accompanied by three words that made every negative all right. *I love you.*

Just like Tim. Their money restrictions never stopped him traveling the country for his weight-lifting contests. It just stopped her going anywhere. But he loved her, so that made it all right. Even sex had the same theme. Every night, Tim would hold her in his arms and tell her he loved her with such helpless fatalism, when he couldn't perform. Couldn't be turned on by her. Couldn't give her a baby.

She'd grown to hate those three words. Hated the power it gave a man over a woman, until she would beg and plead for something she wanted or needed, or for him to say those

words that would miraculously make everything fine
again—

"We have to go," Mitch said quietly, and she jumped
around. He was watching her, still with that curious lack
of expression. "We have to head out before the rebels start
heading this way."

*This is as real as it gets. I won't protect you.* She nodded,
shoved her hair under her cap, her clothes into the backpack.

He handed her a banana, a small sweet roll and a cup of
coffee. "Eat it all. We may not have anything else for
hours."

A slow dread settled in her stomach as she looked at his
grim face, and she ached for the night in his arms she might
never have again. Hating the memories that came without
warning, crippling her spirit. Wanting to take a chance with
her heart as well as her body, but not knowing how.

Five minutes later she carried Hana down the stairs while
he half lifted, half rolled the bike down, keeping a wary
eye out for looters.

And keeping an assault rifle out and ready to shoot.

They walked behind the pub to a creek trickling by the
outer fringes of town. They kept on in silence until they
entered the jungle, walking the bike, not daring to use the
engine. Finding tiny paths among the trees, pushing through
the overhanging thick masses of snarled shrubs and vines
winding from tree to tree. All was still and silent, the pulsing *boom* around them, inside them, a quiet scream splin-
tering false security.

Then, as the first fingers of light filtered through the tangled undergrowth, Mitch turned to her, his face tense, and
mouthed, *Get on the bike.*

Quickly, silently, she hopped on the rear of the seat,
tying Hana in front of her and herself to the back handle,
blessing the fact that Hana was as quiet as Jenny was noisy.

Rustling sounds came to them on soft feet. Someone was
there. Watching them. Getting ready for their move.

He hopped on in front of them. "I'm gonna floor it. Don't yell if we bounce—yelling in English will ensure the rebels will chase us. Move what plants you can for me as I ride. Be careful if we fall off. There's no antivenom for the snakes and spiders here. They're not lethal, but you'd get bloody sick. Hold this while I start up." Mitch tossed her the rifle, threw his leg over the bike and turned the key.

The engine spluttered like a lawn mower…and died.

"No. No," he murmured grimly, and tried again.

*Splutter, splutter,* silence.

A sudden yell, and a bunch of about ten young men— most of them no older than sixteen—emerged from the bushes surrounding them, brandishing knives.

"Shoot up!"

Lissa lifted the rifle and pulled, slamming her spine into the back handle with the ricocheting force as the rifle exploded into sound. Mitch, using the other rifle, shot at the leader's feet, making the boy yelp in terror and scream an order; the kids scattered.

"They'll be back with guns in a minute." Mitch turned the key again, swearing as the engine refused to kick in. "I'll flood the engine if I keep doing this—but engines aren't my thing."

"Pull the choke out," she suggested, pointing to the small pull-out button on the left.

"Mmmm. A practical suggestion. Thanks." He twisted around to grin at her, pulled the button and tried again.

The engine roared.

More yelling indicated the ragged bunch of kids were on their way back.

Mitch revved up and let the bike fly.

"This is going to get rough," he yelled as he twisted the bike around rocks and vines.

Glad they'd tied Hana to her, she used both hands to move what vines and brush she could as they sped along the thick jungle path. But more than once she had to cover her mouth as startled screams emerged. The bike literally

flew as they bounced up over rocks and tree roots and
Mitch wrestled with their balance and the handlebars to
bring them down safely, crashing back on both wheels, time
after time.

Hana cried out in terror, snuggling her face into Mitch's
back, and Lissa smothered more than one cry of pain as
her back, bruised from the handle, jolted up, down and
against the steel behind her.

Just when she was considering begging him to stop, he
spoke.

"We're far enough from those kids now—but we're
close to where I got my last report on where the rebels
are." Mitch stopped the engine. "We'll have to walk from
here."

Lissa, stiff and awkward, climbed off the bike and
stretched before giving another little smothered cry of anguish.

Mitch took a step, reaching out to her; then he stopped,
his face wearing that mask of impassivity once again. "I'll
take Hana for the first shift until you work out the kinks—
but we can't slow down. You can push the bike, lean on it
while we go uphill and stretch your back to work out the
kinks. I bought a light-frame bike—the lightest off-road I
could get. Unfortunately I don't think we can risk using it
again until we skirt the rebels."

With a little stab of regret for the tender concern she'd
always known from him, she nodded. "I just bumped my
back when I shot the rifle. It'll be fine soon. Especially
since I can leave my backpack on the bike." She hesitated.
"I think we should leave the keys in the engine in case we
need to ride quickly. What do you think?"

"Good idea." He reinserted the keys; then he swung
Hana onto his hip, his backpack over his shoulder, and
started walking. He didn't look back as she trudged up the
muddy, slimy hill, pushing the bike beside her.

Determined not to slow him down, she pushed herself,
performing kickboxing stretch exercises for her back over

the bike, using it as leverage and for balance when she slipped. The pain soon dwindled.

The heat of the day was relentless. Her scalp itched under the cap she dared not take off, as sweat trickled all around. Her face felt as if hot rain lashed it. Her bra was wet, her breasts drenched; her feet swam in the running shoes. Several times when she'd slip inside her own shoes and on the slimy ground, she'd watch Mitch stiffen, and knew he was forcing himself not to look back, not to offer help. She felt the corresponding desire inside herself to ask, but she stiffened herself, gritted her teeth and trudged on. She needed to do this, both for him and herself. She would earn his respect or live the rest of her life without him. As she'd seen with her parents' marriage and discovered during her time with Tim, there were worse forms of loneliness than being on your own: loving too much; being married to a man who loved you with a passion that was totally asexual, holding you night after night without being turned on, until you felt you never had what it takes as a woman; falling in love all over again with a man who wanted you, all right, but who loved what you represented, not what you really were.

That one just might be the worst of all those causes of loneliness, but even harder to deal with than that was the knowledge that she had no control over it. It was happening. Loving his body was unimaginably beautiful. Having him want her so badly he broke out in sweat when she touched him was pure night magic, heat and fire and moonlight and starlight, almost every wish come true. His constant cherishing was as precious as it was infuriating. Even his fury touched her heart. Could it mean he was stepping outside his fantasies of her to find love for the real woman beneath the dreams? If he could—

A soft touch on her shoulder made her head jerk up.

He had a finger to his lips. He tilted his head to the left. *Over there.*

The sounds of talk and laughter came to her; the smell of cooking food made her stomach growl.

*Move very quietly and watch for sentries. I don't think they've heard us yet.*

She nodded and took Hana from him. He hoisted the bike up in his arms in grim-faced silence. Without conscious decision they skirted around the rebel camp to the right, watching for every leaf and rock on the jungle floor, every sense on the alert.

Somewhere in the middle of the clearing a girl screamed, made pleading noises. Then she screamed again, and there was scattered laughter and yells of encouragement.

Hana looked up at Lissa with a look no little girl should ever have to wear on her face. Helpless acceptance. She might not know the word, but she knew the lady in that camp was being hurt—and there wasn't a single damn thing they could do about it.

Lissa gagged.

Mitch put down the bike and turned to her. *Give me one of the bundles of money.*

She didn't need to ask what he planned to do. She knew, as surely as the sun would rise tomorrow, that he was about to risk his life for that unknown girl.

She reached into her backpack and handed a bundle to him while he grabbed something from his own bag.

He smiled briefly and touched her face. *Wait,* he mouthed.

She held her breath as he turned, vanishing slowly into the rebel camp.

The volume increased to shouting levels within seconds, the rebels all jabbering together as the sudden infiltration of their hiding place. The tension reached out to her with coiled fingers, the insecurity of scared and violent men, and she shivered. Please, God, don't let them kill him, please…

Silence. Then Mitch spoke in Tagalog. *"Ako na ang magdadala sa bata."* And he pointed to the girl cowering from the boy intent on raping her.

Lissa finally released her aching lungs. He was all right—

A cacophony of laughter hit her like a slap, then one voice rose above the rest, tense, hard, authoritative. Barking orders.

Mitch spoke again, his voice tight and cold.

The voice in control spoke again, high-pitched and shrill.

"No." The hard, chilling sound in Mitch's voice terrified her. Hana whimpered and clung to her.

Was Mitch warning her? Asking for her help?

Gently, she put Hana down on the bike, motioning to the child to sit still. She tied up all their gear to the back, then she crept toward the tangled growth surrounding the clearing, her rifle loaded and aimed, ready to shoot.

Mitch stood in the center of a ring of grim, angry young men and a few women, facing their leader. All of them had a weapon trained on him.

Her heart leaped into her throat; her tongue dried and she couldn't swallow. She had to help, had to save him, but she didn't even know if she'd be able to shoot this thing at all, let alone make her target. One two-hour lesson at a rifle range in Darwin hadn't prepared her for this reality. She'd have to kill someone if this turned ugly—put a bullet in one of those furiously earnest boys or girls, none of them older than twenty, fighting for a cause they probably didn't even know was corrupt.

All her life she'd been a nurturer. A true earth mother. What the *hell* made her think she could become a Nighthawk? She didn't have the guts for this....

Then Mitch opened his fist to reveal a wad of notes. U.S. currency. At least twenty thousand dollars.

A slow gasp went up; and she could see the quick tallying in the leader's mind. Tumah-ran currency wasn't worth the paper it was printed on. If Mitch had offered Aussie dollars, worth about six times theirs, it would have been stunning enough. But U.S. currency, worth twice that again, was gold to these kids. Guns, bullets, food—holding out for another few weeks when the international soldiers came in to restore peace.

With shaking hands and glistening eyes the leader reached out for the notes.

Mitch shook his head and pointed at the corner of the camp, where the girl in a torn dress stood struggling in the grip of a half-naked young man. He spoke again, shaking the money as if to say, There's more where this came from.

Lissa closed her eyes and prayed he hadn't said that to this bunch of greedy, angry kids…

The leader, his gaze still fixed on the money, barked out a quick order. The boy, looking sulky, released the girl.

The leader yelled something and waved his hand to Mitch. The girl, looking no older than fourteen, stumbled over and fell to her knees before Mitch, tears pouring down her face, and her hands raised in pleading.

With a sharp motion Mitch waved his hand to where Lissa waited near the bike and snapped out an order.

The girl ran.

The rebel leader said something, very softly. Mitch nodded, cocked his rifle and handed over the wad of notes.

With a small, evil grin, the leader took the money and snapped out another order.

Mitch threw something onto the ground, and the clearing filled with smoke—thick, choking stuff that made her eyes water and her throat gag. From its dark cloud Mitch appeared, wearing a small apparatus over his face, which he thrust at her. "Put this on, take a clean breath and get on the bike. We've got to get out fast before they come looking for more money." He got on the bike and spoke quickly to the girl, who hopped on his lap, her feet over the handlebars.

Lissa climbed on behind Hana, and they took off with a roar—four people cramped together on one small motorbike, barely outrunning the hail of bullets from behind.

## Chapter 13

Finally, after winding around on half-forgotten, rock-strewn paths, they reentered the jungle road. The fading sound of gunfire told them they were safe for the moment. Lissa gave a sigh of relief. If she'd had to shoot someone just then—

"Close your eyes, Lissa!" Mitch yelled suddenly.

"What?"

"Please, just close your eyes!"

She blinked—then gave a stifled, high-pitched scream as they passed a pile of bodies slumped against a massive tree. Men and women, young and old, shot, stabbed, hanged—hacked to pieces.

She shut her eyes a moment too late, knowing the vision would be forever seared into her soul, burning in her memory whenever she closed her eyes.

The girl perched awkwardly between the handlebars and Mitch's lap sobbed; Hana's tiny body shook all over.

All Lissa could do was hang on to Mitch's body, using her own as some sort of comforting shield for the child, and pray that this madness would end as Mitch drove them away from the grim reality of life—and death—in a war zone.

*"Maraming salamat. Ah, maraming salamat!"*

The elderly couple kept bowing to him, their sweet, honest, wrinkled faces beaming as they held Hana like a treasure of gold and silver against their hearts. *"Wala pong anuman,"* he replied sincerely. Moments like this almost made sense of the atrocities he put himself through for the job.

The girl he'd saved—probably too late for her innocence, but at least she was alive—was standing behind the couple, taken in as a temporary member of the family until they knew whether any of her real family still lived. She gave him a sad, watery smile, too old for her young years. *"Maraming salamat din,"* she said softly in Tagalog. "I, too, thank you."

*"Mabuti naman at nakatulong ako."* He smiled gently. "I was glad to help you."

The girl turned away, eyes red-rimmed and swollen, and ran into the hut behind her.

He wondered if Lissa realized yet that the bodies she'd seen belonged to the girl's village—family and friends gone forever. Well, by now she understood exactly what it was he'd wanted to protect her from and why he'd hidden parts of his world from her. But would she ever forgive him for exposing her to his life for the sake of winning her trust, her body…and her love?

Selfish bastard—when it came to Lissa, at least.

All his young life he'd settled for close to nothing, grateful for scraps thrown at him by his latest foster family or orphanage, until he came to Breckerville. Until one blisteringly hot summer afternoon, when every other kid on summer vacation swam or played, and he was working Old Man Taggart's field under threat of being sent back to the orphanage. He mopped the sweat from his face, wondering if the old man would bother to take him inside if he passed out.

Then he saw a dainty, honey-skinned girl crossing the field to where he worked. She wore shorts, a tank top and a simple, battered straw hat; she was carrying a glass of ice-cold water, a sandwich and another hat. "It's so hot. I thought you might want something to drink. And…and I noticed you didn't stop for lunch today. Mr. Taggart isn't very nice to keep you out here so long," the girl had said softly, a hint of sweet blush staining her cheek, her soft gray eyes looking at him in shy admiration. Her incredible, oh-so-kissable mouth smiling at him alone, awakening things he hadn't known his fifteen-year-old body was capable of wanting. "My name's Melissa Miller and I live next door. What's your name?"

"M-Mitch," he'd stuttered, feeling like a total dork. "M-Mitch McCluskey."

"Hi, M-Mitch," she'd replied, her smile warmer, friendlier for his stammer, as if she liked it. She placed the old straw hat on his head, a matching one for her own. "Maybe you should call me Lissa, like my mum and dad do. My name's long enough without adding another syllable to it."

He'd fallen then and there. Taking her hat and sandwich and water, giving his heart and soul in return.

Seventeen years, wanting her, loving her, aching for her—always wanting more. Wanting it all, with a raw intensity he'd never come close to feeling with any other girl or woman.

Now he was about to face the music over bringing her to Tumah-ra—and see the damage he'd done to her in trying to win her, in trying to make her see the man he really was. He'd brought her to Tumah-ra to show her he was nothing like Tim. That he wanted to be her husband in truth, not hiding inside a lie; that he loved her with all his heart, body and soul, not as a sister, friend or refuge from prejudice.

Damn it, he should have known the price she paid would be too high. He still paid it in regular nightmares.

But he'd made love to her once…and she'd loved him. A memory to carry with him when she kicked him out of her life.

"What do we do now?" she asked softly, making him start.

Everyone was gone, disappeared into their huts with a sudden explosion of gunfire not far off.

He turned to her. "I make a report to Anson, then we head out of here." He spoke to his boss via the contraption that looked like a cell phone but wasn't, sketching the situation he anticipated and requesting backup, and lots of it—fast. Then he closed it and hid it back inside his belt. "There's a beach two miles north, with a shallow cave inside a hidden cove. We'll sleep there tonight. If the rebels find us here—and they'll be out in force tonight, looking for more easy cash or a ransom—they'll destroy the whole village and kill everyone. It's best if the villagers can honestly tell them we left before sunset."

"We'll have to walk," she said, still soft. "They'll follow the tire tracks to us." Her eyes searched his, looking for signs of approval.

What the hell was going on? Why was she seeking his respect, instead of hating his guts for what he'd put her through?

"Mitch, we don't have time to muck around here. Do we ride or walk to this beach?"

He started. "We'll have to ride for a couple of miles. They're getting too close. If they hear us getting out of here on the bike, they'll know we're not hiding here. That'll save the villagers some grief. If we're lucky we might have backup when we get to the beach. But just in case, we'll go with your idea. We'll ride three miles east and go uphill to wear out the rebels if we can, then we'll cross back northwest a few miles before heading north to the beach."

She nodded and hopped onto the bike. "Let's go."

She was right. The rebels were getting closer. He got on, roared the bike to life and took off, Lissa holding tight to his body, as if for comfort.

She probably needed it, even if she acted as if nothing out of the ordinary had happened. As if she hadn't seen a pile of dead bodies or gruesome, twisted things that were once people, hanging from trees like grim signposts all the way to Ka-Nin-Put. He was the only familiar thing in a time of unending shocks, and she needed the warmth and comfort of human touch. He wasn't fool enough to take it personally.

After the three miles, mostly roaring loudly uphill to fool the rebels into following them, he stopped the bike. Lissa climbed straight off and pulled at her running shoes. "I've got to change my socks before we go any further. My feet feel like they're in a sauna."

"I wish I could say to wear sandals, but the snakes here are venomous," he sighed. "I'm sorry."

She glanced up at him, then returned to changing her socks. "You didn't make the snakes, Mitch. Why are you apologizing? You're not responsible for their being here."

She really meant it. He gazed at her in wonder. "I'm responsible for *your* being here."

She gave him a wry grin. "And who died and made you God over my life and conscience? And how do you think you'd have stopped me coming? I have no one but myself to blame for being here."

"That's not true. You wouldn't be here at all if I hadn't contacted you about the boys. If I hadn't proposed to you and stayed in your life long enough for that jerk to threaten you."

"No," she agreed quietly. "I wouldn't. I'd still be in Breckerville, where I was safe—safe from wars at least. But I'd still have been robbed and mugged. I'd still have been alone with Jenny in a security-rigged house, watching life through a TV set, scared to death of taking a risk, wishing to see the world but too afraid to leave home. Wondering if any man would ever want me. Hating you for never coming home to me.'' She got to her feet and reached out with a gentle hand to touch his face. ''If you think I blame you for today you're nuts, McCluskey. I don't even blame myself. I'm glad. Glad I had the guts to come—glad to know what I'm capable of. Glad you took up my challenge and didn't try to protect me from all this. I think I'll be a better and less selfish person when I get home.''

''*If* you get home,'' he muttered. ''God, baby, how can you be so positive about what I've put you through?''

''Because I trust you to help me get out of this,'' she said simply. ''Because you're trusting me to help you get out, too.''

Her artless words, like a beam of sweet sunlight, warmed his dark and chilled heart. ''Lissa,'' he uttered raggedly, reaching for her.

She wrapped her arms around him, holding him close. ''Don't give up on me yet.''

''I thought you'd given up on me,'' he confessed, trying to bury his face in her hair, feeling only her damp cap. He kissed her cheek. ''I don't know what I've done to deserve your trust.''

She smiled up at him. ''You brought me here,'' she said softly. ''You took me into your world and made me part of it.'' She nuzzled his cheek. ''We don't have much time, so I'll say this fast. *Stop blaming yourself.* I knew what I was getting into. I've seen enough stories on war zones to know what I might see. But you've seen it all and brought me anyway, trusting me to handle it—and I'm doing my best.'' She shuddered. ''I don't think the memories will ever go away. I don't think I'll become anesthetized, either. Thank you for your honesty, Mitch. It can't have been easy to say to me, knowing I'd probably put the worst possible slant on whatever you said.''

He felt dizzy. She hadn't just forgiven him, she'd set him free. She believed there was nothing to forgive him for. "You don't hate me for this," he said slowly, unable to take it in.

She put a finger to his lips. "I think we'll have to ride to the beach and hope they don't find us before the cavalry arrives. The rebels are too close."

He heard the crashing sound at the base of the hill they stood on, and wanted to kick his own butt for allowing himself to be sidetracked so long. "Damn it," he growled. If they hurt Lissa—

She hopped on the bike and started it. "Just ride, Mitch!"

He threw himself on the bike and took off fast. "Hold on tight!" he yelled, feeling Lissa's arms grip him, her thighs straddling his from behind, her sweet breasts tight against his back through his thin shirt.

Damned if he wasn't as horny as a kid again. He'd thought the action-filled life he led as a Nighthawk was best experienced alone. But sharing the adrenaline rush with Lissa, trusting her to work with him, depending on her as much as she was depending on him, knowing they'd probably make love again tonight in celebration—if they lived that long—was as exhilarating as it was terrifying.

He now blessed Anson for forcing him to familiarize himself with the island before the hot spot upgraded to full war. He knew this terrain well enough to head further east, soaring down the hill like the man from Snowy River on his horse, confident he'd find a fork in the path in another couple of miles. He knew the bike would make it, even if they flew down the hill like a wild roller coaster.

He felt Lissa leaning right back, pulling him with her. The compensation in the lean helped, if only psychologically—it slowed that terrified, *I'm gonna die* free-falling attitude. He began a mantra, chanting on and on in his head. *We'll make it. We'll make it….*

For Lissa. Because of Lissa. He hadn't come this far with her to die now. And he sure as hell hadn't found his family only for the kids to lose both their parents—or to go through this time after time, whenever Anson called with another job for them.

*God, let this be enough for her. Let her not want to be a Nighthawk after this mission!*

He lifted the front wheel and jerked up the handlebars as they neared the gully at the base of the long-dormant volcano, and the bike flew up and over, landing with a double thump on the ground as a high-pitched whining noise sounded in his ears.

Lissa jerked and screamed. The bike veered over, careening to one side—

He twisted, taking the burning impact of the bike's landing on his leg and hip, but his arm and shoulder landed heavily on her. He rolled off fast, breathing raggedly with the thump his butt had taken—but Lissa cried out again, with a pain far beyond his fall on her. He switched off the ignition, stopped the wheels' useless spinning and pushed the bike away, flipped it over and turned to her. "Liss, are you all right?"

"My...back," she whispered.

Shouts came from the top of the hill. Another shot came.

Nothing showed at the front of her shirt. Filled with sick dread, he turned her over. She moaned deep in her throat, a low animal keen of anguish.

A small hole burned through her shirt into her body between her spine and shoulder blade. A small hole coated in blood. A bullet was lodged inside her. Sickness shot through him. Oh, God, Lissa was hurt because of him—

"Get me on the bike," she whispered, and slumped against him.

The yelling came closer. He picked the bike up, flicked open the stand, then lifted her in his arms like a baby. He put her on the bike, careful not to jar her, and climbed on in front. "Hold on to me, sweetheart," he said quietly, loathing himself with all his being—but he did the only thing he could to slow the filthy, money-grubbing little bastards who'd shot her. He pulled the rest of the money from his pocket and threw it backward into the swirling wind, hearing their joyful yells in disgust—but he'd bought some time. It was all he could do for now.

He roared off as fast as he could for the beach, hoping like hell Irish was waiting with the boat.

He swiveled down the left-hand path, thanking God for the relatively bump-free ride, and only a mile and a half to go—

"Mitch…dizzy…"

He had to strain to catch the words, and he knew she couldn't last, not even that short mile and a half. He stopped the bike. "It's okay, baby. I'll fix it." He reached into his backpack and got the coil of rope she'd used to hold Hana to her. "I'll tie you to me, Lissa. Hold on as long as you can, sweetheart. Fall over if you have to, but fall on me—and try not to fall asleep. Once we're on the beach I can do something to ease the pain."

As soon as they were tied together, she fell against him, her breathing rapid and shallow. And in the grip of a terror he'd never known—terror of losing the one person he loved beyond life—he took off for the cove where he begged God the boat would be. "Just keep breathing, sweetheart. Don't give up now, do you hear me?" He kept talking, babbling constantly he didn't know what, until he reached the cliff above the cove, harsh, stark, inaccessible to any form of transport but human feet.

He'd have to carry her from here. Jolting her every damn step of the way down a small, winding step-path while the late-afternoon monsoonal wind clawed at them with heated paws—and, judging by the heavy, swirling clouds fast closing in, the rains that pelted the coast every afternoon in what was classically called in ironic understatement "the wet."

With shaking fingers he untied the ropes binding them. Then he pulled out a thermal blanket Anson issued as standard on every job, and threw it on the grassy verge. Tenderly he lifted Lissa off the bike and onto the blanket facedown. Quickly he did what he could, cleaning the wound with antiseptic wipes and squirting antibiotic lotion into the hole. Then he pulled his T-shirt over his head and bound it with the rope over her back, arm and shoulder to stop the sluggish flow of blood.

Then he took everything they'd need from the bike, hoisted the backpacks over his shoulders, lifted the bike up, walked to the cliff's edge and tossed it over.

"Salvage *that,* you miserable bastards," he muttered when it crashed onto the rocks and broke apart in a quick burst of fire.

He checked over the little harbor. No sign of the boat.

*Damn* Anson and his sacrifice-of-one-to-save-many ideals. If it cost Lissa her life—

With exquisite tenderness he cradled her in his arms, the thermal blanket wrapped around her, and started down the tortuous path to the beach below. Stepping over every rock with care, watching for every knot of grass, every lump of dirt.

Talking to her constantly.

"Almost there now, baby. We're gonna make it. *You're* gonna make it! Just hang on, okay?" Yet with every bend in the path, her breathing grew just a touch more rapid, a bit more shallow. But she had no fever, and he hung onto that single hope like a beacon shining in the night. Sweat mingling with tears down his face, he knew he would give *anything* if she lived through this. He'd give his job, his every ambition, sell all his planes—he'd give his life to see her safe.

His hope of gaining her love in return. Marrying her, making them all a family, baggage and all.

"Just stay alive, Lissa, you hear me? Even if you never love me back, you have to live!" he cried, unable to hold his fear inside. "I love you too much. I can't lose you now—not like this. I'll walk away again if I have to, but you're not gonna die, baby. I can't let you!"

Her lashes fluttered. "Mitch…" A threadbare sound. "Cold."

*No.* The fever had begun. He tried to move a little faster, but the sun was sinking low in the sky, and one jolting step, one trip over a rock could drive the bullet in deeper and touch a vital point. "Hang in there, sweetheart. I'll build a fire when we're down on the beach."

"Can't," she whispered, coughing. "They'll see it."

"I don't give a damn. I'll shoot the lot of 'em for hurting you," he growled, half to himself.

"No," she murmured, her voice fading. "Not for me."

His eyes swimming in tears, he looked down at her. "Yes, for you," he murmured back, his voice filled with tender love. "I'd kill them all to save you, Lissa. I'd die for you. Only for you. Don't you know that yet?"

But her eyes had closed again, and he didn't know if she'd heard him or not. Or if she wanted to hear.

One of his tears fell on her face and gently rolled away.

Grimly he trudged on down the path as day became night, looking for a flicker of light, a movement, any sign that Anson had kept his word and the Nighthawks were here.

Nothing.

"Hang on, Liss," he urged her, trying to infuse his warmth and strength into her, holding her as close as he dared.

She moaned. "So tired…" Her head lolled onto his bare chest. She was giving up.

"Hold on, Lissa! Do it for the kids. They love you, baby. They need you. Hang on for me, Liss," he groaned in anguish. "I'd want to die if you die. Oh, God, baby, I love you so much. I need you so bad. I don't care if you don't love me right now—I'll make you love me. Or I'll leave if you don't want me. Anything, Liss, anything—just don't let go. You have to live!"

Finally, just as he reached the final stair, a late rain started falling in heavy, fat plops, following the fickle winds. He turned to the left toward the overhanging wall. "There's a cave in the cliff face here, Liss. They won't look for us now. They'll go back to camp until the rain passes—which could be all night. Then Irish will be here with the boat, okay? I'm gonna build us a fire, baby. I'll get you warm."

She didn't answer. Her face glowed pale and serene in the rising moonlight, dull and cold behind the clouds. She looked like an angel...or like an angel had just touched her.

An angel of death.

He swore softly and settled her on the blanket, tummy down, pulling off her wet cap to let her hair dry. He built a fire with the fuel bricks and waterproof matches that were part of Anson's usual survival kit, and set water to boil in the tiny billy.

Lissa moaned as she turned instinctively to the warmth.

He removed his crude bandage from her back with barely any difficulty and cut her shirt in a swift rip of scissors but didn't take it off. She needed all the warmth she could get right now. Using a flashlight, he checked the wound for the dreaded red line his medic course in the RAAF told him to watch out for. Surely there hadn't been time for systemic infection—

No line, thank God—but the wound was puckered and dark, and his makeshift pressure bandage hadn't stopped the bleeding; and though the ooze was slow, it was constant. It had soaked through his shirt, and was still seeping.

And he'd been relieved when the shirt came off so easily.

"Idiot," he muttered beneath his breath. "I should have known it meant it was still bleeding. Please, God, don't let the bullet have touched anything vital! Lissa." He touched her face, soft but urgent. "Lissa, wake up, sweetheart."

No response. She didn't even move.

He didn't dare shake her, and he couldn't give her a shot of painkiller. If that bullet was lodged in her lung, he—

He frowned. *Idiot!* If he dressed the wound properly

now, she'd barely feel it—or it would wake her up. Either way, he'd have a head start on the infection.

He grabbed the sterile kit from his backpack, washed his hands in antiseptic solution in the rain, heated his hands as long as he dared over the fire and started washing out her wound with saline solution and iodine. She shuddered a little and moaned again, but that was all the intense sting did for her.

He watched in dread as the strong antiseptic did almost nothing for her wound. It continued to swell in a slow, relentless red march across her skin.

He had to probe the wound, see how far in the bullet went—and how close it lay to what he dreaded most. Thank God, her aorta was safe on the other side; but that was cold comfort if another artery or major vein was nicked or, worse, severed, and bleeding internally. If she bled into her lungs—

Stop it. She's still breathing. You'd have known about any pneumothorax by now, or big internal bleed. She'd be—

He shuddered, unable to even contemplate the word.

He poured more iodine and some local anesthetic gel into the wound, pulled on one of the sterile latex gloves and inserted his little finger into the hole.

Lissa cried out in anguish.

"Don't move, baby." Relief clenched his gut. She wouldn't have woken from a coma that easily, even under such painful stimulus. "I need to see how far the bullet's gone in, all right?"

"Mitch—"

"Let me help you, Lissa. Let me do what I can for you."

"Can't...take it out," she moaned. "Lodge it—more deeply."

"No, I swear I won't. I—"

"It's...near...pulmonary artery," she whispered. "Third...intercostal...muscle hurts like hell. If you move it—"

He got the picture and broke out in a cold sweat. "How do you know?"

"Part-time…paramedic. Football season. St John's Ambulance. Did…course…two years ago." A wistful smile crossed her pale, perfect lips. "Good way…to meet…nice guys, Mum said."

He almost laughed at that. "What do I do?"

"Take…your finger out," she uttered through gritted teeth. "Slow. Gentle."

He did as he was told. "I was so scared you'd gone into a coma. I didn't know what to do."

"Have to sleep. Didn't…get much…last night. Kept hoping you'd come to me…seduce me." Another sweet, ghost-like smile flitted over her pale, sweating face. "Sleep…best thing now. Pack wound with something to stop bleeding. Need…antiseptic."

"I have iodine, and antibiotic cream in my first-aid kit."

"Weak stuff," she scoffed. "Need…big guns. Got… garlic?"

"I don't want to roast you over the fire, babe," he joked back. "I'm trying to keep you alive. I'll think about eating you at a later date—but it won't be with garlic."

Another tiny smile. "Idiot. Powerful…antibiotic, anti-fungal—anti-everything. Have you got…any?"

He sighed. "Sorry." Then he clicked his fingers. "But when I toured the island earlier this year, the villagers said something about a plant with medicinal properties growing wild on the hillside above this beach—all over the north of the island. I can't remember what it was they said it did, but you have to use the root. It's got a purple flower. Does that help?"

"Stop blabbing," she whispered. "It's all we have. So go and get it."

He poured more iodine into the wound, making her swear, then covered it with a gauze square. "I'll be back as fast as I can, sweetheart, okay?"

"I'm not…going anywhere." Her lashes fluttered down.

In the light of the fire her face looked pale and spiritual, with a peace that terrified him.

He slung the rifle over his shoulder and bolted out into the teeming rain.

And he thanked God for Lissa's ridiculous antibiotic, antifungal, anti-everything speech, for, sneaking down the path, led by torchlight, were at least half a dozen rebels.

# Chapter 14

He had no time for strategy. Lissa's life lay in his hands. He took aim and fired just in front of the lead torch, then ran forward ten yards and fired another half dozen shots. Before their startled yelps became shots, he rolled to the ground and sent off another round.

A sudden scream told him he'd got in a lucky shot. Unable to afford an international incident, he'd fired merely to hurt, not to kill, and the frightened yammers told him they thought he wasn't alone.

Good. From what he'd seen of these so-called rebels...

Oh, yeah. Just as he'd thought. One more shot, and they turned tail and bolted up the path, falling all over each other on the slimy rock stairs to escape. Another shot, and they were screaming. The torches flailed comically in the air as they pushed past each other to get off the stairs first.

Whew. He wiped streaming rain from his face, immediately replaced by more. He needed to get up those stairs and fast. He had to scare 'em right out of the area, so he could find this healing plant for Lissa without worrying they'd sneak back and get to her first. And what they'd do to her, a helpless, injured woman, before they sent out a ransom note—if she made it that far—

He trudged up the stairs more quietly but just as grimly as he'd come down, firing into the air in case the cowards waited at the top.

The clearing was empty. He flashed his light on the path and saw the fast-filling divots in the mud going in the opposite direction, proof of their hasty exit.

But they'd be back soon enough, with reinforcements.

He had enough worries on his mind right now. Drawing in a harsh breath, he turned and searched the hillside for the telltale purple flower. *Dear God, let it be a late bloomer....*

A few withered purple flowers told him where the plants grew—but they were long past their prime. He gathered what he could, hoping the root was still strong and fresh enough to help Lissa. As quickly as he dared he descended the rugged path down the cliff face, praying for a long-overdue miracle.

For Lissa's sake.


The pain was searing, burning her from the inside. She could feel her own blood, as hot as the fever within, trickling out from the gauze square Mitch had put on it, itching her. And she was thirsty, so thirsty. Her stomach grumbled from lack of food, but she'd only throw up if she ate.

Mitch had been gone too long.

The shots were long over. What if…what if he was lying facedown like her, lying in the rain with a bullet in his back or his chest? What if he were lying out there dying, and she was helpless to go to him?

A chill hit her, and despite the heat of the night, her growing fever and the blazing little fire, she shivered. "Mitch," she moaned. She couldn't afford to move; she could feel the heavy pulse of her blood pumping through the artery right beside the bullet. Any sudden movement could push the bullet right in, or into her upper lung. She had the children to think of. They couldn't afford to lose both parents—

*I'd want to die if you die.*

"Mitch!" Without conscious decision she tried to struggle to her feet, but only flopped back down after two inches.

"Baby, what are you doing? You could move the bullet!"

"Mitch," she whispered on a sob, thankfulness flooding her at even the terror in his voice—she'd take him any way he came right now. "You're alive."

"Of course I am." His voice was soothing. "With your anti-everything plants. A whole handful of 'em."

"There...there were those shots...and you didn't come back. I...was so scared...." Her whisper was disgustingly weak and broke on a small sob.

"Oh, baby, I'm sorry." He lay down beside her, looking at her in solemn tenderness, caressing her hair. "The rebels were on their way down the cliff. I scared 'em off. I should have come back after the shots, told you I was all right. I'm just so used to working alone."

"That...that's not how it works, you dork!" She sniffed back tears. "You *tell* me what...what you're do-doing. You *stay* with me. W-we're...together, Mitch McCluskey, you hear me? You don't just...just—" Her fear wouldn't be denied any longer. The tears spilled over. "I can't lose you, Mitch!"

"You won't, sweetheart. Ever."

"Hold me," she whispered. "I need you."

He carefully laid his arm around her, avoiding her wound. "I wish I could, Liss, but I'm too scared of what I'll do to you."

"You could kiss me." She heard her own voice, weak and soft and shaking. "Please. That couldn't hurt."

"No," he agreed, his eyes full of agony. "No, baby, that couldn't hurt." He closed his eyes then, and gently, tenderly kissed her, bumping noses because of the awkward facedown position.

Overwhelming beauty. Blinding gentleness. He kissed her as if she were a rare, priceless antique that might shatter with a strong touch. And, oh, this was what she needed, his tenderness amid a world that made no sense, spinning out of control into pain and degradation and bullets in her back.

A world where she'd give almost anything to hear those words she'd so despised—no, the words she'd been so damn *afraid* of—only last night.

"Thank you," she whispered, when he finally broke the kiss.

"You're welcome." He touched her face, and a frown of concern replaced the melting sweetness in his eyes. "You're sweating. You've got a fever."

Without warning the darkness began taking over; she felt her mind being sucked down into blankness. *No. Just a few more moments. He has to know how I feel!* "You're everything to me. Best friend, lover…my only love. Stay with me…grow…old. Drown…in laughter…die…in—" She sighed as the relentless hands pulled her under, and her eyes closed.

Mitch shook his head. A tender, wry smile twisted his lips. "Ah, Lissa, why is the timing always wrong for us, huh?" He sat up and looked at the tubal roots in his fist. "Now what do I do with these things?" He blew out a tired sigh, rubbing his forehead. "Pack the wound, I guess."

He walked back out into the rain and washed the dirt off the plants, cleaned his hands with antiseptic, cut the stems from the roots and dipped them into the slow-boiling water to sterilize them as much as possible.

He frowned after that. "Liss, I need you now. What do I do with this to help you?" Feeling helpless, he squirted more antibiotic gel into the wound, but it came back up with the slow-pulsing blood flow.

Pulsing. Oh, God, no. No! She'd tried to get up to find him because he'd been so damn long. If the bullet had nicked the artery— The tiny hospital here had been shelled two weeks ago, the only doctor and two nurses taken at gunpoint. The nearest hospital now was in Papua, New Guinea, or Darwin, two hours' flight away. She'd never make it in time.

He closed his eyes, fighting panic. "Damn it, McCluskey, fight this. Fight for her!" His eyes snapped open. Getting out his knife, he sterilized it and cut the ends of the roots open, then stuffed the dripping open ends down the wound, one after the other, sandwiched with the antibiotic and anesthetic gel, bound it hard with iodine-packed gauze, taped it down, then put his stiff, blood-soaked shirt over it and tied it to her, making sure no part of the rope touched her skin. He opened his emergency flask of water, dropped soluble paracetamol into it, opened two capsules of antibiotics and shook the damn thing to Kingdom come.

Then with exquisite care he turned her over, laying her across his lap. "Lissa, sweetheart, you have to have some fluids. Wake up, Lissa. Come on, help me now."

Her head flopped back; she groaned his name. Whether in need or protest he didn't know, and he had no time to sort it out. He lifted her head into the crook of his arm, kissing her cheeks, her eyes, her soft, unresponsive mouth. "Wake up, Liss. Come on, baby, come back to me."

She stirred. "Sleep," she mumbled.

"In a minute, sweetheart. Just have a drink first."

Her lashes fluttered. "Thirsty…"

"Good girl. Open your mouth."

Her lips parted, and before she could speak, he dribbled some liquid down. With the first touch of water on her tongue, she moaned and made gulping motions. He poured it down as slowly as he could, as long as he dared, until she fell asleep in his arms.

He watched her dreaming face in dancing firelight and a thin slant of moonlight coming in from the cave mouth:

pale, carved marble and warm, living flesh. A face to launch a million ships: she was love and laughter and tender memory from child to woman, with a heart so rare and beautiful he'd never even tried to replace it. He belonged to her. Totally. Completely. Always.

"I love you," he whispered, knowing the words so were so pitifully inadequate for the bursting tide of emotion inside him. A tide of love so long held back in fear it would not be denied now—when it could all be too late.

It couldn't be too late. She had to live!

He buried his face in her hair, its usual sweet sunshine scent replaced with mud and blood and sweat and pain. Suffering.

Lissa was unconscious, in danger of losing her life. Because of him. No matter how she exonerated him for it, he alone was responsible for where they were right now.

He didn't deserve her. What the hell had ever made him think he had a hope of making her love him? It was always going to end like this—in mud and blood and death. A place where he fit in, where he'd always belonged, but she didn't. She deserved a long, happy life, a husband who adored her and whom she would love in return, children, safety. Not this. Not hiding out in a dank cave on a bloody, war-torn island, slowly bleeding to death while he sat holding her in helpless anguish and his boss made up his mind about whether to save unknown people somewhere else in the world or just a couple of unimportant operatives.

"Damn you, Anson," he growled, looking out the cave mouth for impossible salvation. And somewhere in the silver-black lapping waves, a light flickered once. And again.

"Thank God!" He laid her with slow, gentle care back on the blanket and bolted out into the pounding rain with his flare.

Moments after the red smoke faded, white smoke joined it.

He frowned and returned to the cave to get everything ready.

Within five minutes two strangers walked up to him. Familiar strangers somehow…they even looked alike.

They looked like—

One grinned and nudged the other. "I think it's coming back."

The other nodded, unsmiling. "He never saw me much, and you were a bit young when he saw you last." He watched Mitch with unnerving intensity. "Mother's Day ten years ago. Before you dumped our sister while she was pregnant and left her so depressed she got onto crack."

Mitch gasped as the final pieces of the strange puzzle of who'd threatened Lissa fell into place. "Darren. Will?"

"Bingo." The unsmiling one, Darren, lifted his hand. The cold barrel of his gun gleamed dully in the moonlight. "Get that pretty woman of yours, McCluskey. You're both coming for a ride on our boat."


Lissa woke to a strange sensation—little jolting movements and dripping water on her skin.

Groggy, yet her mind clear, she opened her eyes. Two strangers carried her on a makeshift stretcher toward the water.

So the cavalry had come! "Mitch?"

"Sorry, pretty Lissa. Your boyfriend's, um, a bit tied up right now."

She turned her face. The man she'd last seen in a gray suit in Canberra smiled at her as he carried his end of the stretcher. "I don't think you can see him right now. Oops…he fell down again. Shame about that."

The man carrying the other end said, "Don't bother hoping he's gonna try anything, Lissa. He knows if he gets up to any tricks, we'll just drop you." The swishing sounds told her they were crossing the water now, probably to a dinghy. "See, Lissa, there's a bit you don't know about your boy here. You swallowed his story about bringing the kid home—about the footage he took—but he lied to impress you. He's not a big-time spy. He's nobody's hero.

He's just an unwanted foster kid with a chip on his shoulder and a million lies to look respectable."

"Cut the crap, Will. You're not her type. Did McCluskey tell you he got custody of our nephews from our sister?" the intense one demanded of her. "That when she wanted them back, he used the fact that she'd been on crack in the courts, publicly humiliating her to keep sole custody? That the shame sent her back down the spiral into using crack, just as she'd got clean?"

He jerked his arm, and Lissa heard Mitch make a muffled sound.

"Oh, dear, he fell down again," Will remarked with a laugh. "And in the water, too."

Feeling like the silent viewer of a crazy good-cop, bad-cop routine, she decided to up the ante, inch by cautious inch. "So which of you is the cop?"

Darren, the one who'd touched and mauled her, was the one who stumbled, with a vicious curse.

She smiled at him. "So you're the screenwriter of this bad *Dragnet* rerun, huh?" she asked, coining Anson's term for it. "Is Will obsessed with getting revenge for Kerin, too, or did you force him into it?"

"If I let go of my end of the blanket you're dead—and don't think I won't just because I happen to be hot for you," Darren growled. "Then who's gonna take those precious kids of yours—two of whom belong to us?"

"I see," she said quietly, fighting for breath. "How many…people have you killed to get to Mitch? How many…courts allow convicted murderers to have custody of kids? And, Will, that's what you'll…be if he drops the blanket—if you haven't killed other people already. Even if you haven't…and he has, you're an accessory. I hear that's about…ten years inside."

She heard Will drag in a quick breath, and wanted to do the same; her small store of strength was fading with each word. But she made herself speak to Darren. "If I've worked out that you're a cop—and a Federal one, I'd guess, by the way you tried to lead me away from the Feds by making me believe ASIO did immigration stings—what's the bet everyone else who needs to know already knows by now? How long do you think it'll be before they check into McCluskey's past to see who could possibly have a grudge against him? How long until they check your computer to see if you've dug into his files, or they talk to your boss to see if you've been asking about him?''

Darren whitened so fast she knew she'd scored a direct hit.

''Maybe all you can be accused of now is playing a malicious prank,'' she said quietly. ''Isn't it time you thought about the rest of your life and where it'll head if you go any further?''

''At least I'll have a life,'' he snarled. ''Kerin doesn't have that luxury. You have the only things that mattered to her in the end—her kids and McCluskey.''

''And how would Kerin feel if she knew you killed the father of her children and left them alone?''

''Shut up!'' Darren screamed. ''I swear I'll drop this—or I'll shoot McCluskey this minute!''

Will said softly, ''Daz, think about it. She's right. Kerin loved the guy, loved her kids. She wouldn't want this.''

''I know she loved her kids. That's why I snatched them for her back in Bondi. That's why I'll get them away from this creep now. Kerin was delusional about McCluskey. She *loved* him,'' he sneered, ''and look where it got her. Where did it get her, McCluskey?'' he yelled. ''You refused to marry her when she got pregnant. You threw her out like trash. What the hell's wrong with you, to treat our sister that way? Answer me!''

''Uh, Darren? He can't,'' Will said, still quiet, a strange note lacing his voice. ''You taped his mouth when you tied him to the blanket.''

''He can answer when he's on the boat then.''

Within seconds they'd reached a small rubber dinghy.

"Lay her down carefully," Darren ordered, sharp and terse. "I don't want her hurt."

"You've been saying that from the time you started watching her," Will remarked, "and every time you listen to her talk, or watch the videotapes you made in Canberra."

"She had nothing to do with Kerin," Darren retorted. "It's only McCluskey we want."

"I don't want either of them—well, maybe I want her, but I don't want revenge at all. I swear to God, Daz, this is getting downright loopy. If you weren't my brother..."

"Well, I am," Darren snapped, "and I'm the one who lost my twin! So pull the creep in and start the bloody motor before his mate fixes the hole in his boat and gets here!"

Lissa, lying on the floor of the dinghy in helpless anguish, watched as Mitch, hands bound and mouth taped, was pulled in by the hair and shoulders, landing headfirst. Darren ripped the duct tape from Mitch's mouth and yelled obscenities in between demands for him to answer his questions about his relationship with Kerin.

"How did you know where we were?" she asked Will quietly.

Will sighed and placed the edges of the blanket over her to keep out the worst of the rain, then started the dinghy's motor, heading for the boat. "I was the one who followed you in Canberra, but Daz took my place to meet you and planted the bug down your top. He hoped McCluskey would find it. That was the point of the cheap bugs in the first place, in case you blabbed—to make us look like amateurs. When he groped you, he slipped a state-of-the-art heat detector in your jeans pocket, a tiny, flat one he knew couldn't be found on a quick sweep. We counted on your not having time to wash your jeans—and being a single mum, you wouldn't just chuck them out. You'd pack them and take them with you," he murmured wryly. "So we headed north when you did and saw you get the kid. We flew here on a charter plane ahead of you, and hired a boat when we knew we couldn't get through the rebel-held areas like you had. We waited for you to head for the coast, and we got there before your cavalry, whoever they are.''

''Shut up!'' Darren screamed. ''For Pete's sake, Will, can't you keep anything to yourself?''

''I'm a medical student, not a Fed,'' Will shot back. ''I'm distracting Lissa from her pain, keeping her mind on other things. That's what *I've* been trained to do!''

''Can you help Lissa, Will?'' Mitch asked, low. ''She needs help now. There's medical stuff in my backpack—''

Darren's arm shot out, connecting with the side of Mitch's face. ''She's not your concern, get it? You've lost her. For once you're gonna learn how it feels to lose the other bloody half of your heart!'' With savage ferocity he slammed his elbow into Mitch's temple.

Mitch slumped at the side of the dinghy while Lissa watched, unable to move, her mind spinning. But she had to help him somehow. ''If you think you're going to punish him...by taking me away, you're way...off base,'' she said quietly, struggling with the words. ''He doesn't...love me like that. We're old friends.''

''Old friends who have a great ol' time in bed,'' Darren shot back. ''If that's the sort of friendship you give out, babe, you must have a line of blokes at your door every day.''

She dragged in a breath, feeling the air go out less than usual, trapped in the aching lung, twisting in sharp-edged points. ''We did nothing until I...told him about the surveillance, and your threats. And even then it was all...an act. Everything you heard...an act.''

Darren told her what he thought of that, succinct and crude.

She sighed. ''You heard what I said...about my ex-husband...about his not wanting me? That there'd been... no man since? Do you think I have the sexual self-esteem to make this up? Mitch...doesn't love me.'' Every breath was agony, but she kept forcing the words to save

Mitch's life. "He needs…a mother…for the boys. A family. I'm…just an…ideal…to him. That's all."

Will took her pulse. "She's not good, Daz," he reported quietly. "I think she's telling the truth here."

Darren looked at her and nodded. "You're right. She's really got no idea." He chuckled a little. "Since it makes no difference to him, but it might help you feel better about yourself, I'll show you something." He lifted her left hand in his. "See that ring? Kerin found it in his drawer. She thought it was for her. She got so excited. But when she told him she'd found it, he said if he ever married her—*if*—he'd buy her another ring. That this one belonged to the girl he loved." Then he reached into Mitch's pants and retrieved his wallet. "Then he showed her this."

He flipped open the wallet—and in the money fold lay photos. Picture after picture, memory after memory, faded, folded, well viewed, well loved.

All of her, from girl to woman.

A stupid photo-booth shot of the three of them: Tim, Mitch and Lissa, all pulling goofy faces. A shot her mother had taken of her at an Irish Eisteddfod. Another one of the day she'd taught him a riverdance. All dressed up for Tim's formal night and her own special night.

Her engagement night. Her wedding.

But not with Tim. Photos of her with Mitch.

Darren stuffed them back in the wallet and into Mitch's backpack. "I'm telling you, no man carries around a bunch of photos of his childhood mate or any bloody ideal. With a guy it's always sex. *I* think of sex when I think of you. So does Will. At least seventy percent of the male population thinks of sex when they look at you. You're a bloody gorgeous woman, and probably the only person who doesn't know it is you." He chuckled. "It tickles me that he never got any after all the years of waiting. All those years obsessing over you, keeping away from women because of you, and when he finally comes home he gets nothing!" He laughed. "Oh, yeah, if I never got revenge for Kerin, you already did it for me. Poor jerk, I almost feel sorry for him.''

Lissa closed her eyes, wondering how on earth she'd ever been so stupid, so blind that a stranger could see so clearly at a glance what she never had. For in every photo—photos she had copies of at home—the look in his eyes said it all.

Mitch loved her. No idealized woman, no Madonna fantasy, no home-and-hearth girl. He *loved* her, boy to girl, man to woman. Then and now. And always. Maybe it had been faulty at times. Maybe he didn't know everything about her, didn't understand what she needed. But he still loved her. Just as she loved him.

The dinghy rocked as it approached the boat. A fresh wave of pain seized her and she cried out, choked off as her right lung suddenly became gripped in an unseen fist, unable to push the air out, locked hard and choking.

''Darren, we got a real problem here! Her breathing and pulse is way too fast—and I can't hear any lung sounds. I think she's got a pneumothorax from a broken rib,'' she heard Will say tersely as she slipped into unconsciousness again. ''We have to get her onboard bloody fast or she'll die!''

# Chapter 15

"I think she's got a pneumothorax. We have to get her on the boat fast or she'll die—but move her carefully. I need the floor beneath her to get the air out."

Will's words hit Mitch with the force of a jackhammer to the brain. He'd long since come to, and though his head pounded and he was pretty sure his left wrist was broken, he knew his only chance had come—a chance to save Lissa at least. He had to get her to a hospital—fast.

He had to get her away from Darren, who'd obviously inherited the same unstable emotional state Kerin had. He'd formed a passion for Lissa, that much was obvious. If he got Lissa alone and helpless, he'd lock her away, like Kerin tried to do with him—like that movie that still made him sick, *The Butterfly Collector*. He had to destroy Darren's plans for her and make the most of what weapons he had to get her free.

He just hoped to God Liss was playing chicken with them to give him time—or that Will could save her.

He'd almost worked his hands free. They'd barely notice him while they got Lissa onboard.

He didn't move a muscle when Darren snapped, "Check him. I'll carry her, but I won't leave him unless I know he can't move."

"Jeez, Daz, just get her up there!" Will released the rope binding him to Lissa's blanket-stretcher and checked one of his eyes, flashing a light.

Mitch flinched involuntarily despite his best effort not to.

"He's out," Will yelled.

"Tie the dinghy to the boat, bring his bags and lift the gangplank up with you when you come. He can stay there until I want him—if he doesn't fall off first. What a shame that'd be," Darren said, with a hard laugh.

Will flipped him over, using a knife to cut his bonds, then placed the backpacks into his right hand. "He's still tied up tight, and by the looks of his left wrist he won't be trying any Houdini stuff for a few weeks. Now get the poor woman onboard so I can help her...and don't hitch her around. Keep her as still as possible, or I swear she'll be dead in minutes!"

With a swift mental resolve to make sure Anson went easy on Will, Mitch crept out of the boat, carrying his and Lissa's backpacks, with the fast-dwindling but precious bags of tricks. Tricks even Darren, an obvious Fed, wouldn't know about.

Darren Burstall was a Federal cop, and a renegade one. Damn if Lissa hadn't worked that out before him—and her logic had been irrefutable. Smart, fast, fit and willing to learn, selfless and incredibly brave, trying to save him while in excruciating pain. Anson was right—she'd make a first-class Nighthawk. He had no right to stop her, even to think about stopping her. He knew that now. She didn't belong to him, never had belonged to him, much as he wanted her to. It was her life.

If he could save her first.

He used a rope hanging on the side of the boat to swarm up to the deck, finally grateful for all that ridiculous rope climbing in his combat training with the RAAF. His cranky old sergeant's bluster had ensured he could climb quick and quiet, even with a broken wrist—and any noises of pain he made were masked by the ocean's lapping and the rain.

When he reached the top, he peered over, trying to make out where they'd taken her.

They must be inside the cabin. *Whew.* He carefully laid the backpacks down and tumbled onto the deck, holding the rope still and landing curled on his back to minimize the thump. He snatched up the bags and crept toward the light inside the large cabin.

Tense words drifted to him before he reached the door. "Will you get out of my face? I need the light!"

"Can you help her?" Darren asked, sounding frantic.

"Not until you move!"

"I'm gonna kill McCluskey with my bare hands if she dies. What sort of weirdo is he, to get his kicks killing innocent women who love him? First he leaves Kerin to die, now Lissa! How is she?"

"I need a bloody Angiocath—but a wide-gauge needle and syringe'll do for now, to get the air out that's trapped in her lung," Will growled. "If you want to help her, stop pacing the floor and look in the first-aid kit."

Mitch pushed back into the wall as the door flew open and Darren stalked out, muttering to himself about taking Lissa away where no one would hurt her again.

Mitch bolted into the cabin, holding out another sterile kit and a whole set of syringes to Will, who merely smiled at his frantic entrance. "Bullet's lodged near the third intercostal."

"Thank God." Will started swabbing the site an inch above the bullet hole. "If it had been the second we'd be up the creek. If I can pierce through the second intercostal without moving her broken rib we have a good chance to get her breathing again."

"Thank you, Will," he said quietly, then he slipped back out.

He was risking his life, but he didn't care. Darren might be crazy, but he had one thing right. He'd left Kerin to die by neglect—by saving himself from her jealousy and overwhelming obsession with him—and now Lissa was dying because of him.

He would let the truth impale him with its anguish later. He'd punish himself for the sin of loving too much. He had to stop Darren from taking Lissa now. He had to help Will save her.

But a sudden yell told him Darren had gone to check on his prisoner and found the cage empty.

He stepped out of hiding and shoved the cabin door shut with his hip and faced Darren, who was standing in front of him with a savage grin, pointing his own assault rifle at him.

Darren grinned. "This is for Kerin," he cried over the noise of the storm, and Mitch faced him squarely. It didn't matter. Lissa, Matt and Luke and Jenny had to stay safe—and if Darren's revenge died with him, it was no more than he deserved.

The sudden loud whirring of helicopter blades created a wet, blasting wind on them before the blinding light fell right where they stood. "Drop your weapon!" came the disembodied voice of Anson himself.

From there everything passed in a blur. Darren was there one moment, the next he wasn't, just as operatives came swarming down ropes suspended from the chopper. "Get down, Skydancer!" Braveheart yelled, firing over the side of the boat.

A roar, and the dinghy was off into the night.

Mitch grabbed a walkie-talkie from Irish and yelled into it, "Countrygirl's down. Needs immediate medical assistance."

"We'll lower a stretcher," Anson replied curtly.

He flung open the door. Lissa looked pale and tired, but she was breathing again; that pallid gray shade was gone. Will, drenched in sweat, nodded. "The needle did the trick for now. She's breathing normally, but I don't know for how long."

"Thank God…and you," Mitch said, with a heartfelt

sigh of relief. "The chopper has a stretcher to take her to Darwin."

"Where's my brother?"

"On the dinghy—with operatives not far behind."

Will sighed. "I thought of this as a game," he said quietly. "A bit of stupid dress-up fun, playing Spy versus Spy. A way to pass summer break until I started my internship. Daz was obsessed with this, so I offered to do the legwork for him, be visible for him—he's traceable through the Feds, and I'm totally clean. I knew they wouldn't know who I was. And, yeah, I wanted to make life uncomfortable for you, see Matt and Luke—I don't know. I never realized how unstable Darren is—or how dangerous—until we got here." His eyes were haunted. "I never wanted it to go this far. I thought I could stop him from hurting you, and others—but I had no control at all." He sighed. "He told me he killed some hacker in Sydney."

Mitch nodded; he'd tell Anson. He wanted nothing to do with running Kerin's brother down or with the Nighthawks at all right now. "Let's get Lissa on the chopper."

"I should go with her, in case. I know I'm not qualified—"

"You saved her life," Mitch replied simply, and swept his hand to the door. "Let's get the stretcher."

Minutes later, with tender care, inch by inch, a carefully tied Lissa was lifted onto the chopper by pulley rope.

Mitch and Will swarmed up the ropes moments after, both immediately looking to Lissa, to be sure the needle and syringe hadn't moved in her transportation.

"Who's this?" Anson demanded, his face immediately filled with suspicion.

"This is Will. A medical student who happened to be in Tumah-ra at the time," he reported briefly, checking Lissa's pulse while Will worked on her chest. "He saved Lissa's life. We need him for the flight to Darwin."

"He's the rogue we couldn't trace," Anson growled. "I saw his picture. What the hell's going on here, Mc-Cluskey?"

Mitch met his boss's eyes. "He just saved Lissa's life—and mine. He had almost no part in this, except for following us in Canberra. Darren Burstall's the one you want—he's a rogue Fed, and my ex's twin brother. Will was just trying to stop him from getting in trouble. As far as anyone needs to know, Will's just a medical student on holiday." He caressed Lissa's face, so pure and cold in the darkness of the chopper.

"I don't like it," Anson growled.

"I don't like the fact that you're worrying over Will while Lissa's lying here half-dead!" he returned, low-voiced for her sake. "For God's sake, Anson, this was personal, aimed at me, and nothing to do with your precious bloody Nighthawks—so tell Wildman to head for Darwin now!"

"One of us has to get off," the pilot, code name Wildman, called in over the walkie-talkie. "We need two chopper pilots—"

He snatched the walkie-talkie from Anson. "There are two, Wildman—you and me," he snapped. "And one man with medical qualifications to help Countrygirl. So either Anson goes or Linebacker, because it sure as hell won't be me." He met his boss's eyes in grim challenge. "We did what you asked, and she's almost dead. I'm a civilian from now on—and so is my fiancée, until she tells you otherwise or signs a contract. Your first duty is to get us out of here. We're both injured."

Anson nodded curtly. "I'll go. Linebacker can come with me. I'll steer the boat into harbor, Irish can take the other, and we'll try to get the people of Ka-Nin-Put out. The rebels have started torching one side of the village. The people are heading for the beach, so it'll make our job easier. Take these three civilians to Darwin," Anson called to Wildman.

"Roger that, sir," Wildman called back.

Without another word Anson and Linebacker, their newest operative, slithered down the rope to the boat. They heard Anson yelling instructions as he landed on deck.

Wildman turned the chopper in the direction of Darwin, the northernmost city in Australia. The last Mitch saw of Tumah-ra was a blazing fire in the jungle, the blasting of mortar bombs and the streaking silver fire of bullets in the night.

Somehow it felt like a classic script. Lissa felt light shoot pain into her eyes, even beneath her heavy eyelids. She stirred and moaned. *Heroine comes to slowly, to the gentle touch of the man she loves holding her hand....*

"Hey, sweet thing. About time you came back to us."

She stirred again and lifted her lids, feeling something akin to mild shock. "Tim?"

Her ex-husband, holding her hand, grinned at her. He looked pale, strained, completely exhausted, his face stark against the plain antiseptic white of the room. "Yeah, Liss, it's me, since I'm definitely no angel. How are you feeling now?"

She looked around at the hospital room, realizing she was sitting up, not lying down. Chest injury, then. "W-why...are you...? Where's...kids?"

"They're here, too. You might call this our first joint family holiday—thanks to you. We're all in the great never-never to see you." He caressed her hand. "Ron's here, too. We closed the gym for a few weeks until you're better."

Her mind felt clogged. Her last memory was something about a plant. "Never-never?"

Tim laughed. "Yeah, you know, the Northern Territory ads— 'You'll never-never know if you never-never go.' We're all up here in Darwin—and spending all our time in the hospital."

"Darwin," she whispered. "Wasn't I here the other day?"

Tim lost his smile. "Yeah, darlin', and in Tumah-ra after that. You were shot, Liss. Mitch called me from the chopper to say a plane would bring us all here. Your parents are arriving tonight from Monte Carlo. Alice should be here tomorrow from Sydney." He kissed her lips gently.

"Thank God you're okay, Liss. You had us all bloody scared."

She smiled at him, feeling an overwhelming rush of love. "I guess I'm useful for something, if only emotional shocks to my family."

The hand holding hers shook. "For a hell of a lot more than that. Don't you know you mean the world to us all? I adore you, Lissa. I always have. I always will. The flight here was the most terrifying time of my life. Don't do that to me again, you hear? You're not just the mother of my daughter, you're my best friend. I couldn't stand to lose you."

The tears in his eyes splashed over onto their linked hands.

A quiet realization came to her in that moment. He might have made a terrible husband, but Tim was a wonderful friend, the best she could hope to have or ask for. He always had been. And she'd lost sight of that for so many years. "I love you, too—but I'd love you more if you got me some water," she croaked.

He tilted a glass to her lips. "Do you know that's the first time you've said that to me since I left you?"

She gulped down the water, seeing the pain in his eyes and feeling a twinge of conscience. She realized how right Mitch had been about punishing Tim instead of thanking him for setting her free. Free to find real love. "Yeah, well, all good things come to those who wait," she joked, to lighten the mood. "Where's…everyone else?"

"If you mean Mitch, I pushed him out of here about two hours ago," Tim replied, getting to the heart of her question with his usual accuracy. He knew her too well. "He hadn't slept in two days. He'll be back any minute, probably. What the hell have you been doing to the poor guy, Liss?"

"Is he all right?" She heard the frantic note in her voice. "He…he isn't hurt, is he? That man—" Patchy memory assailed her—the stumbling run to the boat. She gasped, "He wanted to kill him. Mitch! Is he—"

"Apart from a broken wrist, he's fine…physically. But

he hates himself for what happened to you. If you ask me, he's gonna walk as soon as he knows you're okay.''

"No," she whispered.

"Yes," Tim retorted gently yet with grim strength. "Lissa-girl, it's time we had a talk. I've put off telling you this for ten years, because I was too weak. But you'll hear it now because if you don't, you're gonna lose him. And it'll be my fault.''

"No, Tim," she said sadly. "Not your fault. Mine."

"Yeah, well, that, too." He grinned to soften his blunt words. "Baby doll, you became a woman before your time. You've worked at jobs you hate and sacrificed your wants for your parents and me, especially after Alice married Brad and left for Sydney, then for Jenny and the boys. You gave up your life for all of us, but when it comes to Mitch you're acting like a kid. You won't look at the truth." He drew a deep breath. "Lissa, he loves you like no man has or will, even me. He worships the ground you walk on."

"I'm his ideal woman," she finished, in soft bitterness.

"And what the hell's so wrong about that?" Tim demanded. "Didn't we both idealize Mitch? Didn't we worship him? Should he resent us for that? Did it stop us from loving the person he is?''

The absolute truth of that stunned her. She opened her mouth, but no words came out.

"I don't get you, Liss. You've spent seventeen years of your life in love with him, so why are you pushing happiness away? Why are you punishing him for what he can't help? Who taught him to love? Wasn't it us? A pair of dumb kids who didn't know who they were? People who are as much dreamers as he is? So why should it surprise you that he wove a few ideals and dreams around you? You can't honestly think he'll stop loving you if you fall off the pedestal. Liss, you fell off it years ago when you went for safety and married me, and he still loves you. You've been apart twelve years and he still loves you so much he's gonna walk away because he thinks it's what you want. What the hell else do you need? How much more real does it get for a man than that?''

''I…don't know,'' she croaked. ''You're the man. You tell me how real love gets, because I don't have any experience at it.''

''Damn it, Liss, cut it out,'' Tim suddenly snarled. ''Stop torturing yourself over us! So I couldn't make love to you. If I felt wrong touching you, it wasn't because you're not pretty, or that I didn't want you. You want to know why I couldn't touch you? It was guilt! I knew you and Mitch belonged together and I destroyed it. I broke the hearts of the two people I loved best in the world and didn't have the guts to change it, because it meant accepting myself for what I was, which was too bloody scary. I took the coward's way out and left you feeling like crap, and it *kills* me to see you still feeling like crap, twelve years later! But I won't stand by and watch you push Mitch away, from fear. It wasn't him that hurt you, it was a dumb bloke called Tim Carroll. Mitch isn't me, and he's not your dad, getting everything he wants at your expense. He *loves* you, Liss. So don't ruin your life—and Mitch's life—because of me.''

She flinched with Tim's spot-on assessment of what she'd been through the past twelve years…and what she was doing now. ''It's not your fault,'' she said quietly.

Tim waved it aside impatiently. ''In a world that's treated him like a bloody chocolate wrapper to use and throw away, you and I loved him for what he is inside. Do you realize how bloody hard it must have been for him to love you the way he does and not say anything? *We* have families, people who taught us acceptance and security, who'll always be there for us. What did Mitch ever have but us? How could he come between us? How could he tell you he loved you? If you loved him, he lost me. If you didn't love him he lost us both. All the love he'd ever known, gone in a second. Would you have risked it, Liss? *Did* you ever risk it?''

Lissa bit her lip, feeling tears of exhaustion and shame rising up. ''Tim—''

"But *he* did, didn't he? He told you he loves you, I know he did. With everything to lose—again—Mitch had the guts to risk it all. You and I never did, unless we were safe. And I'd say you shoved it back in his face, by the look of him, just like I did at our wedding. He's hurting so bad, and you—"

Defeated, she snuffled back tears. "Tim...don't..."

Tim's rant came to a screaming halt. He kissed her hand linked in his. "I'm a bloody idiot, lecturing you when you're sick. What a jerk. I've just been holding this in for so long, figuring you'd work it out yourself one day."

She gave him a weak smile. "What, me? The original Blind Freddy? I didn't even believe him when he said he loved me. What ever made you think I'd stop playing the martyr long enough to try a bit of self-examination? I was too busy blaming the world for my awful life. I needed you to put me over your knee and spank me for this years ago, Mr. Carroll."

He kissed her forehead. "Good girl."

She swiped at her tears. "Now, can you go get Mitch for me and take the kids for something disgusting for an hour or so? I think I have a bit of groveling to do—" her eyes twinkled "—and a reluctant fiancé to propose to."

Tim caressed her cheek. "It's a tough job, but I think I can handle it, with Ron's help." He got to his feet.

"Say hi to Ron for me...and...and thank him for coming."

He smiled at her. "Just another in your legion of fans, my sweet thing."

Then he left the room, and Lissa, fretting over what she would say to Mitch, fell asleep.

## Chapter 16

"You said she was awake, Tim. What is this, a stupid joke? She's still out, still sick because of me!"

Mitch's low, strained voice stirred Lissa from her light doze. She opened her eyes and saw him, one wrist encased in plaster, healing bruises all over his face. "It's no joke...and I've told you more than once to stop blaming yourself, McCluskey. Don't you ever listen to me?" She stretched and yawned, feeling the painful twinge in her back. "Ow. I think I should leave the aerobics until the hole closes over completely. You know, dear, not listening to your wife is a lousy way to start any marriage."

Tim snorted, but the frenzied worry in Mitch's eyes flattened with her gentle teasing. "We're not getting married."

She lifted a brow. "Wanna bet?"

Tim grinned. "I think this is my cue to, um, take the kids for ice cream." He opened the door to the private room. "Mitch, my old mate, may as well give in now. Never argue with a woman who's finally decided what she wants—especially not this woman. You don't have the guns for it. I know Liss from way back.''

"Get out of here, will you?'' Lissa demanded, her gaze fixed on Mitch. "No offence, Tim, but you've interrupted our love life a few dozen times too many.''

Tim gave his rich, full-bodied chuckle. "You're right. I'm outta here.'' The door swished as it closed behind him.

Mitch stood tense near the door, looking as if he wanted to bolt but his legs wouldn't cooperate. "How are you feeling?''

"Like a woman who's been given a second chance at life,'' she replied softly. "A woman who's not giving up on the man she wants without a fight.''

"I can't take it, Liss.'' His undamaged hand, curled in a balled fist, shoved into his pocket so hard he ripped the lining. "When you were shot—'' His face twisted in anguish.

"I love you,'' she said quietly.

He jerked back as if she'd stabbed him to the heart; his eyes were dark, tormented. "Baby, I'm no good for you. I don't deserve you. You weren't in any danger until I came home. You've been threatened, attacked, separated from the kids, had to bolt the country—you were shot far from help. You almost died, and none of it would have happened if I hadn't been near you!''

"I wanted to be there, Mitch. I wanted to share your life.''

"Yeah, well, welcome to it,'' he muttered savagely. "Welcome to the life of Mitch McCluskey, the kid who doesn't even know his real name. Welcome to the mess and blood and mud and the worst forms of hatred and abuse in the human race. It's where I came from, where I'll always be...where I belong. You deserve so much better— the best life can offer. So run, baby. Run as far and as fast as you can. Keep yourself safe—keep Jenny safe—keep Matt and Luke safe. Keep away from me, all of you, even the boys. They deserve better than the freakin' mess I put them in all these years, just by being their father!''

She felt his agony—the self-hate clawing at his very soul. Denial was his only lifeline. He had to reject her, or face the fact that he couldn't save her from hurt. He couldn't protect his family from the worst that life could throw at them. One day he might even have to watch helplessly as the people he loved beyond life died. The only people he had in the world.

What could she do?

*Take the risk. Step outside your safety zone for once and give him what he needs!*

She gulped. ''All my life, I've tried to make sure I was safe, Mitch—safe in Breckerville, safe with Tim, safe from the pain of loving you. Protected from the world. It hasn't made me feel any better about myself. I've never felt happy from the day you left me until you came back. Until you kissed me. Until you opened your world to me. Don't you understand?'' she cried as he shook his head, his eyes hollow, so haunted with guilt. ''I'm not Sleeping Beauty. I'm an ordinary woman with needs—and I need you. I *love* you, Mitch! I want to be in your world and you in mine. Being safe doesn't guarantee my happiness. Being with you does! It's the closest I'll be to Heaven in this world, having you love me—sharing a life with you and our kids!''

He pulled his hand from his jeans pocket and tugged at his uncollared T-shirt as though it strangled him. ''I'm...sorry,'' he said awkwardly, and turned to the door. ''You'll find someone else.'' The words were halting, choked, as though everything inside him rose up in rebellion against the words he spoke.

He opened the door.

''No! Mitch!'' In blind panic, she scrambled off the bed and tried to chase him, stumbling as a shot of intense pain hit her back, chest and arm. She cried aloud and fell to her knees, her IV trolley crashing on top of her.

He flew back to her, his face etched in terror. ''Lissa!

Oh, God, baby, don't. You'll rip open your wound or hurt your lung!'' Despite his plastered wrist, he swept her into his arms, untangled the IV line and carried her back to bed, laying her down with exquisite tenderness. "Does it hurt?''

Tears pouring down her face, she whispered, "My heart hurts, Mitch. Fix it for me. Tell me you're not leaving me. Please.''

His face twisted; he stepped back. "I'm not leaving you. I can't bring myself to leave this time—not when I know how it feels to be with you. I'll be at Old Man Taggart's place, where I belong. Lissa's ghost,'' he jeered himself bitterly, "watching from the window of a fallen-down rat trap while you find life and love and everything you're entitled to. It's a fitting end for ever believing I had the right to make you love me.''

She ached and hurt for him, her gallant, limping hero. She ached with love and fierce protectiveness. "You didn't make me love you,'' she said softly, once the pain subsided. "I fell in love with you of my own free will. Why don't you deserve that, Mitch? What separates you from the rest of the human race, that you can't be loved like any other man?''

"I'm nothing,'' he grated harshly. "Just a hooker's unwanted bastard pushed around from place to place, good only for unpaid labor. I don't give a damn about the title I've got or the work I do—I'm still the baby on the church steps, the kid who latched on to you and wouldn't let go. I took you, ate and drank up your love, treated you like you were mine. You deserve so much more than that.'' His eyes met hers, hard, hurting. "You deserve more than I can give you. When you were shot, I realized what the hell I'd done to you by bringing you into my sordid life. The princess and the pauper.'' His face filled with self-loathing. "Go find your prince, baby. He sure as hell ain't me.''

"I'm not a princess, Mitch, even though that's how I've always felt around you,'' she said quietly. "I'm just an ordinary woman who wants to be loved by the man she loves. I love our kids dearly, but I need you. You're the most beautiful thing to ever come into my life. I don't give a damn if you're a prince in disguise or a hooker's child—you're the man I love. I loved you at fifteen, and I love you now. And you have rights, because I give them to you—the right to love me back, the right to marry me, live with me until we're old and share a life with our children and our children's children.''

He was shaking now. ''Damn it, Lissa, I can't. I—'' He wheeled around, ready to bolt.

''Don't make me hurt myself again to follow you, Mitch,'' she said quietly. ''And you know I will.''

With a strangled curse he fell into the chair beside her, burying his face in his plastered arm. ''What do you *want* from me, Lissa? Tell me something I *can* give you.''

''All right.'' She laid a tender hand on his mess of curls. ''You told me, when you sang to me, you'd do anything for me.''

He lifted his face to hers, ragged and raw. ''Do you doubt it? But I can't marry you, Liss. I'm not good enough for you.''

She ached so bad, trying not to show it. ''There's something else I need. Something only you can give me. Then, if you want to leave me, I'll let you go.''

''*Want* to leave you? I—'' He raked a hand through his hair. ''What is it you need?''

She could feel the tears shimmering in her eyes, the old terror of rejection welling in her heart; but still she said it. ''Your child, growing inside me,'' she said softly.

His head snapped up, but he didn't speak. He didn't look capable of words.

''It might take a while, though. I'd like two babies, maybe three. We might have to get a lot of practice in. You'll have to make love to me an awful lot.'' The hovering tears finally spilled onto her cheeks, but she smiled. ''I know we already have three kids. But I've been so jealous of Kerin for having what I wanted. Your love. Making love to you. Your children inside her.''

"I always loved you, Liss. Always," he said hoarsely. "Kerin knew that, which is why she never told anyone I married her—she was too bitter." When she gasped he nodded, pulling out his wallet. "I told you I wouldn't let my kids have the same sort of life I did. I married her as soon as she told me she was pregnant. But because I didn't love her, she ran off a couple of months later, telling me it wasn't my baby, anyway, and she'd send divorce papers. Then when she came back later with the boys, hoping for a reconciliation, she was furious that Shea was there. She was always unstable, on the obsessive side. She hated playing second fiddle to you. It drove her crazy." He shrugged, and handed over a folded piece of paper. "I kept this for the boys. I wanted them to know they were wanted, loved—by me, at least."

She looked at the paper in her hand. "Certificate of Marriage for Mitchell John McCluskey and Kerin Ann Burstall."

Her eyes swimming in tears, she handed it back. "I should have known—I should have always known you married her. A pilot, an officer and a gentleman. My honorable Mitch," she whispered.

He shrugged, clearly uncomfortable, and stuffed the paper back in his wallet. "Not enough to stick with her, to get her off the drugs. I should have helped her more, seen what was coming."

"She was a drug addict. She stole from you and kidnapped her own children. She'd have ruined the boys' lives as well as yours. You didn't kill her. She chose to do what she did, and would probably have done it if you *had* loved her. With some people, more is never enough." She gave him a lopsided smile. "Like me. I know you love me, but it's not enough to have your love from a distance. I want to marry you, grow old with you, have more babies with you. Make love with you for the rest of my life."

"Baby, I'm not good enough for you! Don't you get it? I've already let you down, more than once. I'll do it again."

"As I'll let you down. As I already have let you down. I've tested you and hurt you and thrown your love back in your face. I didn't believe you'd married Kerin even though I knew you better than that. Did that stop you loving me, needing me?"

"Never," he uttered hoarsely.

"Then why should the fact that you saved my life when a bunch of greedy kids shot me in a place I went to of my own free will change how much I love you, how much I need you to be with me? Why should it stop us making a life together?"

Slowly, a soft, needing light came to life in his eyes, and she prayed he was starting to believe. "You said you didn't want a life with me in Breckerville."

She gave him a wry smile. "I know. And part of me meant it. Then. Before I knew what danger I'd put myself in by being so stubborn about your protecting me, being so romantic about the Nighthawks and wanting to be a hero— like you were with Hana." She sighed. "But at the moment life in Breckerville with you and the kids, and maybe a few more babies, sounds perfect."

"And the Nighthawks?" He watched her closely. "Do you still want that?"

She shrugged, embarrassed. "What can I say? Something about it calls me…I never knew myself until this case came up. Maybe I'm a danger addict. Maybe I want to make a difference. And we did, Mitch. We made a difference to Hana's family, to that girl. Your photos might get the world involved, and the war will end. I want to be part of that work in other areas. I'd like a limited, non-life-threatening role, since we have the kids to think of. But if it comes to making a choice between you and the Nighthawks, I take you."

"Lissa, I can't make guarantees. I've made other enemies in my line of work. What if some other jerk decides to get revenge on me through you or the kids?''

"What if we get run down by a bus tomorrow? What if I get leukemia or cancer? Or one of the kids? There *are* no guarantees in life, Mitch. We take what we can get, and thank God for what we have—family, love, a partner for life. We can have all that, but only if you trust me to keep loving you. As I'll have to trust you to keep wanting me, loving me through the good times and the bad. And with four, five or six kids, there's going to be loads of ups and downs for us." She smiled again, so sure she was winning. "Baby, you may think you don't deserve me, but *I* think I deserve to finally have what I want, and what I want is you, the man I love. The man I'll always love." She drew another breath. "Marry me, Mitchell John McCluskey. Marry me and share my life, my bed, the good times and the bad."

"Liss, I don't want you to be a Nighthawk," he said raggedly. "I hate the thought of you being in danger."

Sadness shafted through her, but she didn't hesitate. She'd never be happy being a Nighthawk if he weren't a part of her life. "All right."

He held up a hand. "I hate it. I don't want it—but I'll live with it. If it's what you want. We'll do it together." He smiled slowly. "But I have one stipulation—we do backups, pickups or info gathering only—social stuff at embassies, etcetera—and turn down everything when you're pregnant with those babies you want, or when they're too little. We wait until they're weaned, and never take any missions longer than a week. Our kids need us."

"Done." She bit her lip as joy bubbled up inside her heart. "So it's yes? You'll marry me?"

He grinned, the shadows gone, his eyes mirroring the sweet wonder she knew inside herself. "Tim was right. I haven't got the artillery to fight you, despite knowing I ought to. Yes, Melissa Jane Miller, I'll marry you, father your babies, share your life and bed, the good times and bad—and a few Nighthawk missions to fulfil your craving for excitement or making a difference to the world. I may not deserve your love, sweetheart, but I'll sure try to have earned it by the end of the next fifty years or so.''

She held out her arms to him. ''So why aren't you kissing me already, Skydancer?''

''Hmm. No idea, Countrygirl.'' He moved into her arms. Their lips met in a kiss saturated in love, a love with foundations in the past, strengthened by the love of the present, painted in bright colors with anticipation of the future. A lifetime of loving together.

Then he crawled beside her on the bed, caressing her face. ''Do you have any idea how much I love you?''

''Tim made me aware of it today, when he told me off.'' Her eyes crinkled with her cheeky grin. ''And he made me aware of what I was throwing away if I didn't take the chance now.''

''Best friends have their uses,'' he growled, nuzzling her lips. ''It's about time he threw something positive our way.''

She flushed. ''Um, actually, he's been trying for years. He told me to call you the day he left. He told me you loved me then. He said you'd bolt back home to me. He's been nagging me to tell you I was free every time he's seen me since then.''

His brows lifted. ''And your reason for not doing this was…?''

''Um, you want another recital of all your supposed sins, or the one about my imaginary fears?''

He groaned. ''I think I know them all off by heart by now, my prove-it-to-me woman.''

''What happened to Darren and Will?'' she asked suddenly.

''Darren got away somewhere on the island. We think he might have joined the rebel army. Oh, by the way, the UN has decided to get involved. They're sending in a peacekeeping force from the South Pacific region. With the lack of resources and numbers, the rebels won't last longer than a month.''

"Good," she muttered viciously. "And Tumah-ra can get back to normal. I hate to think of such a beautiful place destroyed."

"We let Will go back to his teaching hospital in Sydney to finish his internship. Along with that plant, which apparently stopped any infection setting in, he saved your life, Liss. He got you breathing again and kept you alive until we got here."

"We should invite him home one day, to see the boys. He's their uncle."

He kissed her. "I adore you, you know that?"

"Oh, I know." Her eyes twinkled. "An appropriate emotion for my husband to express on regular occasions."

"Um, I'm happy to volunteer for wedding-dress collection and organizing a wedding here—provided I'm best man, of course," Tim said, standing in the doorway with Ron and the kids.

Grinning, Mitch cradled Liss in his arms. "This is a really weird sort of déjà vu, don't you think?"

Tim laughed. "I was sort of heading in the direction of poetic irony or delayed justice, but hey, I'm easy."

"Mummy!" Jenny tiptoed over to them, her eyes bright. "Are you all better now?"

"Much better, darling." Lissa cuddled into Mitch, and held out a hand to her daughter. "You want to be my bridesmaid?"

Jenny turned to Tim, but when his smiling face reassured her, she nodded. "Can I wear my pretty dress?"

"That's what your daddy bought it for."

"What about you guys?" Mitch grinned at his sons, hovering uncertainly in the doorway. "I'm looking for a couple of guys to make sure Uncle Tim doesn't botch it for me. He hasn't got a great track record with weddings."

Tim choked on laughter, and patted Mitch's shoulder.

"Only when I'm the groom, mate. Best man I can handle...and I promise I won't get drunk this time."

"Don't I get a hug, boys?" Lissa asked. "I've missed you so much." She held out her other hand to them, but still they hovered, identical in their terror-filled memories.

Lissa's face gentled. "I'm fine, guys. I'll be out of here in a few days, and we'll head to a resort for our honeymoon. After all, we're all getting married here. Becoming a family. Always together." She turned to Mitch, her eyes glowing with love, with tender understanding of his sons' fears. "Isn't that right, Dad?"

"Dead right. We're a family, guys." He gestured to the boys, and smiling in identical joy, they bolted into their parents' waiting arms. "And that includes your aunty Alice and uncle Brad, your cousins and Nanna and Pop. They'll all be here to see us get married, and Nanna and Pop will be staying with you guys in a resort next door to ours, while Mum and I do a few, um, honeymoon things. The nights will be ours," he added softly, for Lissa alone to hear.

"Good," she whispered back, her eyes shining.

Tim choked again. "Uh, Ron, I think this is our cue to fly back to Breckerville and get Lissa's dress and the paperwork." Smiling, the two men headed for the door, while Lissa and Mitch kissed their children again, then each other.

Love had finally proven to be its own miracle.

# Epilogue

Ten days later Mitch heard the words he'd been dreaming of for seventeen long years. "Squadron Leader McCluskey, you may kiss your bride." The local RAAF chaplain smiled and winked.

Mitch, standing proudly in his RAAF uniform, bent to kiss his new wife, dainty and unspeakably lovely in her soft ivory lace, wearing her star sapphire, her wedding band and a certain old, slightly faded and rusted, still-cherished pink locket she'd made Tim bring up from her jewelry case back home.

Lissa. Lissa McCluskey. Finally his bride. His woman, his brave, beautiful Nighthawk woman, to stand beside him and share his life forever.

As he'd share hers.

"My husband," she whispered, her eyes filled with love.

He kissed her again, then wheeled her in the hospital-issued wheelchair to sign their marriage papers. Then he'd sign his wife out of the hospital to start their life together.

After a quiet champagne dinner at a local seafood restaurant, Lissa linked her hand in his and gave him that look—the look of yearning and love he would cherish for the rest of his life. He smiled and kissed her softly, in loving prelude; then he cleared his throat. "I think everyone will forgive us if we disappear now." He grinned and ruffled his sons' heads and blew a kiss at Jenny. "We'll see you guys tomorrow."

Lissa, glowing incandescent, kissed their children, her joyful parents and sister, Tim and Ron, hugged them all, then put her hand in his. "Let's go."

About to walk out the door, Lissa turned back, and the three kids ran into her arms, hugging her with tender care for her recently healed wound. But she called softly, "Tim."

Her ex-husband looked at her, brows raised.

"Thank you, fairy godmother." She smiled, wrinkling her nose in gentle teasing. "Best friend. Father of my daughter. Family forever." Her arms full of Mitch and the children, overflowing with love, she beckoned.

Mitch grinned and nodded. "Get over here, you geek. You, too, Ron and Will and Marie and Stan," he added to his new parents-in-law. "Everybody, in fact. Can't you tell the appropriate moment for group hugs?"

Tim came to them, followed by his smiling partner, Lissa's joyous parents and sister, Alice, with her family, and finally Kerin's hesitant brother, unable to believe he'd been so forgiven. "Now *this* is the weird déjà vu, if you ask me," Tim remarked, laughing. "The two best friends I have in the world, finally together. The universe getting appropriate revenge on my selfish, immature and indeed dastardly manipulation of events—"

Mitch met his wife's gaze over the heads and bodies snuggling into them, saw Lissa as brimful of joy and laughter as he was. "Shut *up,* Tim," they chorused together, as they'd done so often as kids. Then their lips met again, holding all the people they loved best in the world—her family, now his family, too. His own family at last.

Finally all he'd ever dreamed of was his...because of Lissa. Always Lissa. Forever Lissa.

Nighthawk's woman.

\* \* \* \* \*

Coming in March 2003 from

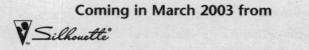

# INTIMATE MOMENTS™

# KAREN TEMPLETON
## Saving Dr. Ryan
### (IM #1207)

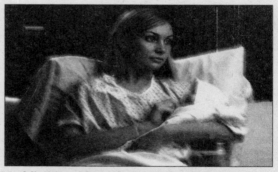

Maddie Kincaid needed a doctor, stat, for a very
special delivery! And the only M.D. in this part of
Mayes County, Ryan Logan, was happy to do the job.
But could she heal *his* broken heart?

**THE MEN OF MAYES COUNTY:**
**Three brothers whose adventures led them far afield—**
**and whose hearts brought them home.**

And look for Hank and Cal's stories, coming in fall 2003,
only from Silhouette Intimate Moments.

*Available at your favorite retail outlet.*

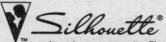
*Where love comes alive™*